DEFENDING HOPE

DEFENDING Hope

DEFENDING HOPE

Half Moon Bay
Book 2

ERIN BROCKUS

GREEN SAGE
PRESS

Edited by Misha Carlstedt

Cover design by GetCovers

Ebook ISBN: 978-1-7358127-6-2

Paperback ISBN: 978-1-7358127-5-5

Hardcover ISBN: 978-1-7358127-8-6

Chapter One

AUGUST . . .

HOPE COLLINS SAT in her home office, staring out the window with a dreamy smile. Her email tone sounded, snapping her attention back to the matter at hand. All morning she had been trying to keep her mind on business.

And failing.

Her computer screen displayed the website for Half Moon Bay Resort in St. Croix. Hope had owned the resort for five months, though it could have been a lifetime ago that she'd lived in Chicago. As she tried to prepare for a staff meeting that afternoon, her mind was repeatedly diverted by thoughts of a certain dive guide who worked at the resort.

Of course, dive guide didn't exactly describe Alex Monroe, any more than what a person saw of an iceberg described its entirety. Besides leading dives, Alex was the dive operations manager of the resort. And as Hope had discovered recently, he used to be a Navy SEAL before being terribly injured in an ambush that had ended his career.

And there was one other position he'd recently added to his resume. Hope closed her eyes and took a deep breath as the dreamy smile returned. But instead of inhaling Alex's intoxicating scent, her nose wrinkled at the stuffy air of her home office.

Frowning, she rose, crossing over to the window and opening it to admit the fragrant tropical breeze. It was time for the meeting, so she left through the back sliding glass door, pulling her shoulder-length chestnut hair into a ponytail as she walked up the beach. The resort was on the western edge of the island, making for stunning sunsets but sultry afternoons.

As she passed four guest bungalows, she waved at a couple relaxing on their porch, enjoying the afternoon with a beer. Soon, Hope approached the heart of the resort. A restaurant and a brick patio next to an infinity pool were on her right. On her left was a long wooden pier with a complex of rooms halfway down and a thatch palapa at the end. The resort boat, *Surface Interval*, was tied at the end, ready for the next day's dive trip.

As Hope climbed the stairs onto the pier, she checked to make sure her white tank top and skinny capris were in order, then wrinkled her brow. *Should I have changed into a staff shirt?* Since she'd been working from home, she hadn't worried about her appearance. With a shrug, she continued. *Too late now—and it's not like anyone at the meeting cares.*

Thunder rumbled over the mountains to the east, and a threatening roil of clouds crowned the jagged peaks. But the last thing Hope wanted to be reminded of was storms. The resort had weathered a major one when their boat sank. She'd recently bought its replacement, the boat tied at the end of the pier.

As Hope strode toward the dive classroom, the boards under her sandals were still wet from the afternoon rain, and the air smelled delicious, a mixture of fresh rain and damp wood. She'd called an informal meeting amongst herself, Alex, her star chef Gerold Harrigan, and Patti Thomas, the general manager of the resort.

The dive classroom was the best place to hold it, private and blessedly air-conditioned. It was a simple affair, a wooden box twenty feet square with three rectangular tables lined up behind one another. Two long whiteboards hung side by side in the front, and a tall bookcase stood in one corner.

She was the last to arrive. Patti sat at the back table, her blue staff shirt hugging her ample frame. Alex and Gerold bantered back and forth at the middle one. Gerold still wore his white chef's coat, his dark skin a pleasing contrast.

Hope sat on the table facing them before placing her feet on the seat of the chair in front of her. Slapping her thighs lightly, she said, "Thanks for coming."

Alex smiled widely and winked one vivid blue eye at her. As usual, she feasted on him with her own eyes. His short, sandy hair was still damp from a recent shower—he lived in an apartment above their current location. His good looks and warm smile never failed to get a reaction from her. Hope pulled herself back together. She had unconsciously mirrored Alex's position when teaching her scuba class. "How does it feel to be on that side of the classroom, Alex?"

Gerold and Patti both grinned as he leaned back in his chair, saying, "Well, I seem to have gotten used to taking orders from you, so I guess we're just taking things to the next level."

Hope didn't miss the gleam in his eye but ignored it. "I wanted to give you all an update on some plans I have for the resort and get your input. One of the major projects I wanted to tackle this summer was a total revamp of our website and the creation of a cohesive brand for the resort. But that's going to cost some serious money, and with the new boat, I've had to modify my plans a bit."

Alex's teasing smile disappeared. The previous resort owner, Steve Jackson, hadn't wanted to spend the money necessary to complete extensive repairs to their venerable boat, so Alex and the boat's captain Tommy Williams had nursed it along with the plan of dry-docking it in the fall for an extensive overhaul. Unfortunately, a series of minor issues had snowballed into the boat-sinking disaster. They had lucked into an even better replacement boat, but Alex blamed himself for the accident.

She continued, leaning forward. "The one part of the project I am definitely going ahead with is adding an online booking portal to the website, and I'm increasing our advertising budget with the PR company.

"I've looked at a lot of other resorts' websites, and I plan to offer *only* four- and seven-day packages on the portal. One package of accommodations plus meals, and another with that plus a two-tank dive trip each morning. We'll still have our Miami travel agency for phone bookings, of course, but guests would have to call to book anything but the four- or seven-day packages.

"Most people prefer to book online since they hate calling. And if their only choices are four or seven days, hopefully they'll pick seven and we'll get more revenue. What do you guys think?"

"A lot of dive resorts run on a standard seven-day schedule, usually Saturday to Saturday," Alex said. "We're small enough that I don't think we need to mandate a specific day of the week, but it's a great idea. It will give the divers a better chance to know us, and for us to know them."

Hope nodded. "The main reason I wanted to bring this up is that I think it will make us busier, and we're going to need more staff. Patti already has a new housekeeper working, but Gerold, we need to get you a sous chef. Somebody who can fill in when you're off. I'll admit I had fantasies about applying for the job, but I don't think that would work well for either of us." She laughed.

"I told you, there's always a job for you in my kitchen."

Hope enjoyed helping when Gerold was shorthanded, but she was no substitute for a real sous chef. "You can definitely do better than me."

Hope's attention drifted to Alex, whose gaze was locked on her chest as he eyed it intensely. She disregarded it as she addressed her next statement to him. "You've been able to get fill-in divemasters when you've needed them, but I'm wondering if we need to put Robert on the payroll permanently."

He widened his eyes, snapping out of his trance. *What has gotten into him?* "I don't think so. When he's not available, I can use his friend April. But the day may come."

Hope nodded, glad he was paying attention again.

Patti cleared her throat. "While we're together, I wanted to make sure Charles is workin' out. I've had no issues with him, but I hired him mostly because his father was desperate for him to get a decent job and start on a new path. And his dad has always been my favorite cousin." Patti was a St. Croix native with an extensive local family.

Alex's and Gerold's faces went blank. "He seems fine to me," Gerold said.

Alex nodded, shrugging. "We work in different parts of the resort. I've hardly had any interaction with him. He's a big guy —he should get a job as a bouncer."

Hope held her tongue regarding their new landscaper. Patti had told her Charles had completed several stints in jail. It was mostly for petty crimes, but he made Hope uneasy. He was a hulking man, though that was advantageous for a landscaper.

But working here had done wonders for Clark, their

bartender. After a minor scrape with the law, he was now a model citizen, so Hope wanted to give Charles a chance. Patti would never hire him if she thought he was dangerous.

"Good," Patti said. "I told him he's on a tight leash, so hopefully this will be the change he needs."

Hope turned to Alex and Gerold again. "I'd like to start a regular schedule of days off for you guys. Patti and I already have something worked out for her to have two days off each week, but both of you work way too hard." They opened their mouths to speak, but Hope held up a hand. "We'll have to wait until we have extra staff in place, but I'm serious. I want each of you to work toward *at least* one regular day off each week, ok?" Gerold nodded, and Alex stared at her levelly.

Oh, you stubborn man.

Patti spoke up. "What about you, Hope?"

"What do you mean?"

"When was the last day you took off completely?"

Hope thought for a moment. "The day we got the new boat." She slid her gaze to Alex, who slowly smiled, again devouring her with his eyes. That had been a big day for them. The memory brought a pleasant jolt through Hope's body. She and Alex had spent an incredible day on deserted Horseshoe Key.

A day that had also brought revelations.

The same ambush that had nearly killed Alex had also proved fatal to eight members of his platoon, which he'd revealed when they'd first made love. There was no hiding the wound covering his right hip. For years, he'd been so traumatized by the experience that he'd buried it deep and had refused to discuss personal matters, let alone get involved in an intimate relationship.

Alex was a complicated man—charming and affable unless matters turned to uncomfortable subjects. Then he shut down.

"That was weeks ago, child." Patti glared at the back of Alex's head. "You have to start takin' better care of yourself. Let me know what I can do to help. *Someone* needs to look out for you."

Alex pressed his lips together and gave an exasperated grunt. He was turning around when Hope intervened. "Patti! I'm ok. It's fine. Answering guest surveys from my laptop while sitting on the porch is hardly working, and I've had plenty of days like that. Besides, this meeting isn't about me."

She and Alex hadn't been open about their new relationship, but they hadn't hidden it either, so it was no surprise the staff had figured it out.

"How can you say that?" Alex asked. "We wouldn't be sitting here if it weren't for you. Patti's right—if we're taking a day off, you are too. Though I'd like to see her try to get you to do something you don't want to."

"Ok, fine. I surrender. Happy now?"

He gave her a private smile. "Yes, very happy."

Chapter Two

AFTER THE MEETING, Hope ambled to the end of the deserted pier, enjoying the cool shade under the palapa while she peeked over the edge. Colorful fish darted below. She was leaning forward and examining a bright blue fish when someone clasped her hips, steadying her.

She yelped.

"Careful. Don't want to fall in the drink."

After her heart started beating again, Hope turned around to face Alex, who was dressed in his work uniform of a staff T-shirt and board shorts. Instead of reprimanding him for sneaking up on her, she stood on her tiptoes and kissed him. "I think the meeting went well. Patti and Gerold are on board, and I'm excited about longer bookings."

Alex returned his lips to hers, speaking against her mouth. "I don't care."

Hope pulled away. "What?"

"You show up to a staff meeting looking like that, and you think I can pay attention?"

She looked down and lowered a corner of her mouth. "I'm wearing a tank top and capris."

"Believe me, I know." He cracked a small smile and brushed the hair away from her forehead. "That outfit brings back a memory for me. You've affected me since you first arrived on St. Croix, Ms. Collins. I've been attracted to you since the second time I saw you. Though I fought like hell against it."

"Really? That long ago? Wait—why the second time?"

Alex's smile widened. "The first time, I wasn't sure I liked you. You were distant when we met on the dock, but then I learned why. Steve sure didn't do you any favors. But the second time—that was a different story. It was early evening, and I was sitting on my deck when you walked below me and stood right here. You wore tight jeans and a white tank top." He ran his gaze down her body, then back up. "God, you were gorgeous and ready to take on the world. I'll never forget it."

She was all warm and fuzzy inside. "I don't remember that at all. What did we say to each other?"

"Nothing. You didn't even see me. I was pretty stunned at my reaction. I wanted to keep the moment to myself and not let reality screw it up."

"Probably just as well. You weren't the only one fighting your feelings." She squeezed his waist. "I think the reality we have now is pretty good, don't you?"

"Oh, yes."

Hope smirked. "I hate to burst your bubble, but I bought these capris in Frederiksted. There's no way this was what I wore that night." Located a few miles south of the resort, it was one of the two major towns on the island.

"It's close enough. The whole package blew me away. It does even more now."

Hope's eyes were riveted to his as her heart pounded with his admission. "I love you."

"I love you, too." He brushed her lips with a feather-light kiss. "But I have to finish up. Later?"

"You'd better believe it."

*

AFTER FINISHING work in the lobby that afternoon, Hope shut down the front-desk computer. She panned her gaze around the room, making sure everything looked neat. The lobby was a single-story cottage-style building, and she left the ceiling fans spinning to cool the room in her absence. Feet sinking into the sand, she nodded at a guest powering through a beach run as she walked home. After he passed, a small frown crossed her face. She'd been a steady runner while living in Chicago. *Maybe it's time to take it up again.*

Hope's text tone went off the minute she walked into the house. The open-concept living area contained a kitchen near the front and a great room facing the ocean, with the kitchen island between. Sitting at the table, she smiled at the sender's name—her sister, Hurricane Sara.

Hope had kept her updated on the boat sinking, but they hadn't talked since picking up *Surface Interval* and all the changes that had brought between her and Alex. Hope had to admit she'd been enjoying her little secret.

> Sara: Did you ever find a new boat?

> Hope: Yes! It's much better than the last one.

> Sara: How do you get a dive boat, anyway? Do they just drive it to you?

> Hope: No. Alex and I went to St. Thomas, picked it up, and drove it back.

As soon as Hope sent the text, her mistake was clear.

> Sara: WHAT? Only the two of you?

> WHAT? Don't ghost me, Hope.

> Hope: Ok. Alex and I are a thing now.

> Sara: OMG! I need details! Well, not too many details. You know what I mean.

> Hope: We stopped off at a little deserted island for lunch, and one thing led to another.

> Sara: OMG! Sex on the beach? Really?

> Hope: Yes.

> Sara: Hey—no one-word answers from you. You know what I'm waiting for.

> Hope: No, Sara.

> Sara: Come on! Please tell me it was a B! I need to know my sister is happy!

Hope laughed at the reminder of their conversation discussing physical intimacy in letter-grade terms when her sister had visited. Well, mostly Sara's conversation. And despite her exuberance, Sara could be trusted completely. She wasn't asking for intimate details, after all.

> Sara: Hope

> Hope

> Hope

Hope: Stop it! Give me a sec.

Sara: Tapping fingers . . .

Hope: It was an A. No question.

Sara: I'm so happy for you!!

I'm being serious now.

Hope: I know. I'm happy too. So is Alex. :)

HOPE HAD ALWAYS BEEN TOO afraid of getting close to a man to experience a deep relationship. But with Alex, she'd found the courage to jump in with both feet. It had been more than worth it.

A WEEK after the staff meeting, Hope sat on the porch couch as Alex came out from the kitchen with two open beers and handed her one. This was her favorite part of the house. The covered porch extended the full width of the house behind the great room and master bedroom. A cozy sitting area, complete with a couch and a loveseat, was balanced by an outdoor table and chairs on the other side.

They clinked bottles and drank, taking in the 180-degree view of the beach and ocean, though this afternoon only show-cased a steady rain pouring down. Alex enjoyed a beer at the end of the day, so she made sure her fridge was always stocked, which was easy enough when she could take a six-pack from the bar at any time.

Cruz lay nearby with his head on his front paws, ever watchful. He was a medium-sized yellow short-coated dog who was slowly adopting Hope. Or she was adopting him. It was hard to tell—the dog was skittish. Hope smiled at him, and Cruz's tail thumped in response. Then he stilled and looked back at Alex, narrowing his eyes.

"If dogs can glare, that is exactly what he's doing to me right now," Alex said, putting his feet up on the coffee table. "At least he's not barking at me anymore."

"He's warming up to you much faster than he did with me. That must be your magic touch. I've felt the effects of that a time or two myself."

Alex nuzzled her neck, and then Hope straightened up. "I didn't want to say anything during our little meeting last week, but I've been looking over payroll reports. I don't think Steve paid you very well. I don't know the going rate for a dive operations manager/instructor/guide/superhero, but I'd think you've got a good argument for a raise."

Alex laughed. "I'd say I got a spectacular raise recently. I don't need much. I'm not a real big spender, in case you haven't noticed. Steve covered my apartment plus meals, so I get by just fine."

"If you say so."

"I do."

Hope let it go and allowed her mind to wander. The weekly managers' reception was quickly approaching—hopefully without the rain. She'd started it a couple of months ago, and it had been an immediate hit. After some reluctance, Patti was now enthusiastically on board. A smile came over Hope's face at the memory of her conversation with the one person she hadn't been able to get on board.

"Every week? Do I have to?" Alex had grimaced, looking like he'd been in physical pain.

"No, you don't *have* to. You're so friendly—I thought you'd enjoy it."

"No way. Formal receptions like that give me hives—reminds me of junior high school dances." He shuddered.

"Really?"

"I spend several hours every day with the guests, you know. Isn't that enough?"

Hope held up her hands. "Ok! You're excused."

Now Cruz settled near the stairs, happy to stay out of the rain. Smile lingering, Hope gave Alex a sidelong glance. They hadn't been a couple when she'd first asked him, but now he'd agree to go simply because he wanted to make her happy. Besides the daily morning trips, he led afternoon and night dives, so his free time was precious. She didn't want to impose.

"How have things been going with your dive group?"

"Good. Everyone did well on those two days we had the storm so it's been a good week, despite the rough weather."

"I'm glad that storm only skimmed over the island. We're heading into hurricane season."

Alex nodded, gazing at the horizon. "Yeah, this is the time of year the weather can get a little exciting."

"Let's hope it doesn't get too exciting. We've had enough problems."

Hope returned her gaze to the puddles forming on top of the sand. What storms did the future hold?

Chapter Three

AS ALEX WALKED down the pier with a towel around his shoulders, dawn was a palette of pink and red sky to the east, and the air still held the faint scent of frangipani blossoms. He'd tried to interest Hope in joining him for a swim, but she'd groaned and pushed him out of bed. He grinned as he strode to the palapa and drained the rest of his coffee, setting the travel mug on the bench along with his towel.

Alex dove into the water with no goggles, relishing the feel of its warmth enveloping him. He loved swimming in the early mornings when the air was cooler than the water. He'd repeated this morning swim most days for over five years now, but the sensation of saltwater washing over him never failed to induce a sense of renewal—of coming home.

Even more so now.

Alex let the comforting routine allow his mind to wander as the world became light around him. Before Hope, he'd kept a tight rein on his thoughts, preventing him from thinking about his former life too much. But in recent months, he'd learned burying pain didn't cure it. Alex was a long way from being healed from his experience in Syria, but at least he'd opened the door a crack and was willing to peek in.

Lying on that beach with Hope in his arms and telling her about that night in Syria was one of the most difficult conversations he'd ever had. He'd feared telling someone and facing those memories for so long that no one in St. Croix knew the full story of his past.

Alex hadn't been worried she'd react negatively to his scars. He'd only dreaded one outcome from her—pity. Instead, she had accepted him fully and continued to show no signs of feeling sorry for him. He loved her all the more for it.

As an elated surge flowed through him, Alex jackknifed his body and dove. The water was forty feet deep here, and he had no trouble touching his hand to the sandy bottom, even without fins. He lifted a handful and let the silky grains drift through his fingers. Without goggles, he couldn't see anything with clarity, but that didn't matter. He didn't need clear vision to experience the ocean. Alex free dove for several minutes before returning to the surface to turn back and resume his freestyle stroke.

His thoughts soon returned to Hope and the fact she'd had a revelation of her own—that her first serious boyfriend had beaten her so severely she'd ended up in the hospital. She'd pressed charges, resulting in the asshole's conviction, but the event had scarred her deeply, affecting her life for years.

His pace had increased dramatically, and he forced himself to slow. That had been difficult to hear—very difficult. Alex believed in defending what mattered to him. It was why he'd been drawn to the military in the first place. As a SEAL, he'd fought out of duty and honor. It was never something he'd relished.

And Hope brought out those protective instincts in a big way.

She was the most incredible mixture of vulnerability and

fierce steel beneath. He'd never asked her for details of the beating and doubted he ever would, not sure he could stand knowing. He'd suspected a bad relationship in her past, but had been stunned at the depth of it.

Hope wasn't a large woman, maybe five and a half feet, with a beautifully toned and athletic body. But she was no match physically for a grown man, which made Alex despise the asshole even more, if that was possible.

It was a miracle how much she trusted him, given her history. How well did she understand his past, though, and what it had meant to be a SEAL?

After eating breakfast in the main kitchen, Alex passed Charles, who was getting an early start trimming one of the flame trees. The man was several inches taller than his six foot one and bulging with muscles, his hair a mass of dreadlocks contained in a colorful knit cap. Charles cut off a thick branch, tossing it aside like it weighed nothing.

"Morning," Alex said with a friendly smile.

Charles nodded, curling his lip in a look perilously close to derision. "Mornin' it is. You have a nice little swim?"

Alex stopped dead, keeping his face expressionless.

He had no intention of getting into it with Patti's latest project, but he didn't think this guy was another Clark. Alex had spent years honing his ability to spot trouble in a very short amount of time, and he didn't have a great feeling about Charles, despite what he'd said at the staff meeting. "Very nice. Didn't realize you were so concerned about me."

"Nah, it's not that. Just seems like it would be great to spend all day in the water instead of haulin' trees around in the hot sun. Hell of a lot easier."

"Is that right?"

"Oh, yeah. Maybe I'll become a dive tour guide someday."

Alex stepped closer, crossing his arms. "Are we going to have a problem, Charles?"

He burst out laughing. "I don't see how we could. No problem here, man." The smirk lingered on his dark face. "I better get back to work. Gotta long day ahead of me. You enjoy leadin' the tourists around on their water tours, now." With that, Charles turned his back and sawed the next branch, his arm muscles straining his T-shirt.

Alex had uncrossed his arms and was clenching both hands now.

Do not engage this asshole.

He spun around on his heel and marched toward the pier, walking around the corner of the kitchen. Two female guests walked by, and he stopped to make sure Charles acted appropriately. Alex could see him, but not the reverse.

The big man gave them a small smile and an imaginary tip of his cap.

"Hey, Charles!" one woman said. "Starting early today, huh?"

"Yes, ma'am. Gonna be hot today. You two enjoy yourselves, now." Charles smiled and went back to work as the women waved and continued to the restaurant.

Alex chewed on his cheek as he climbed to the pier. *Guess it's just me he can't stand.* As long as Charles did his job and treated everyone else with respect, Alex could handle him. With more important things to think about, he shook off his misgivings. Time for work.

IT WAS A GOOD MORNING, despite a quick moving squall that kicked up the ocean for the first dive. But after so many years, he and Tommy worked together without even thinking about it. They had a full boat today, and their other divemaster was April, who filled in for Alex's friend Robert Davis now and then. They were back at the dock now, the guests on their way back to their bungalows.

April turned to Alex after she dunked a Buoyancy Compensation Device in the tank. "I didn't see that turtle cleaning station at all on the second dive. I feel bad my group didn't get to see it. Maybe you and I can dive it alone sometime so you can show it to me."

April had a fun, upbeat personality but could be very earnest at times. She took her job seriously, which Alex liked, but she always wanted him to show her things.

"Oh, don't worry about it," he said as he hung a wetsuit to dry outside the dive shop. "Next time we dive it, I'll give you the landmarks beforehand. It's easy to find." He was surprised she didn't know about it—there was usually a turtle there getting cleaned.

Besides, he was in a hurry to finish today, and April liked to talk his ear off.

"I must not have eaten enough breakfast," she said. "I'm starved. You want to have lunch with me? You guys have such great food here."

"I can't. I'm having lunch with the boss."

April laughed. "Uh-oh. In trouble?"

"Don't think so. If that were the case, I think she'd want to see me alone in her office." He grinned, loving that idea.

"Well, I work tomorrow. Let's have lunch then, and you can tell me all the good stuff . . ."

April droned on, but Alex wasn't listening anymore. Hope walked with confident grace toward him, dressed in a staff shirt and black skirt. She was a consummate businesswoman and completely stunning.

April smiled as Hope joined them. "Hi! Alex said you wanted to see him for lunch. I was giving him a hard time about being in trouble."

Hope turned those golden eyes to him, and his mouth went dry. "Oh dear. Have you been misbehaving again?"

"No more than usual." He made sure his tone was friendly and professional.

"I'm glad to hear it." Hope's voice was low and throaty, immediately arousing him. Which was certainly her intent, though her managerial, self-assured manner gave no hint to her subtext. "I'd hate to have to put you on a performance-improvement plan. That could be a lot of effort for both of us."

"Oh, I didn't mean to get Alex in trouble!" April tried to cut in, but his blood was so hot he could barely hear her. She wrapped her hand around his bicep as he fought the urge to yank his arm away. April could go overboard on the friendliness sometimes. "Alex and I work so well together—I don't want anything bad to happen to him."

Hope stilled, darting her eyes to April and narrowing them before she straightened and resumed her managerial tone. "Alex and I can discuss any problems over lunch, though I haven't noticed him coming up short so far." She shifted her gaze to his, daring him to react. He crossed his arms and bit the inside of his cheek, determined not to let her see him grin.

She turned back to April with a smile. "Thanks for helping us out. The divers love you."

"Of course. I'll make room whenever you need me—this is my favorite place to work."

Hope nodded and turned back to him. "Are you hungry?"

"Starved." He wanted to jump her right then and there.

"Let me take a quick shower first." He ran up the stairs and unlocked the door as Hope talked to April. "Hope?"

She looked up at him.

"I forgot something. Can you come up here a second?" Without waiting for her answer, he entered his apartment, leaning back against the kitchen counter.

Hope appeared in the doorway and sauntered over to him. "And what did you forget?"

"This."

He jerked her to him, smashing his mouth to hers so hard their teeth scraped as she moaned softly. "If you have any problems with my performance, maybe we need to discuss them. Now."

She reached down and squeezed him. "Definitely no shortcomings here." She backed away with a smile. "We don't have time to take this any further." Her smile faded as she gazed aside with a frown. "Especially with *her* down there. Time to get in the shower, Mr. Monroe. Make it a cold one."

Taking Hope's advice, Alex took an ice-cold shower and was back in control of himself by the time they sat down at their corner table in the restaurant. Thunder rolled overhead, and the air was heavy and thick.

A couple had just finished eating and were leaving when Alex got their attention. "You might want to have another beer and wait a few minutes. It's about to pour buckets. But it won't last long."

He'd just finished his sentence when the sky opened and rain hammered on the roof, pouring in sheets onto the ground. The couple sat back down and ordered another round.

Charlotte, the resort's main server, brought beers for Hope

and Alex before taking their order. "Hoo boy. Look at that. Good thing it'll blow over."

"How do you guys know how long the storms will last?" Hope asked.

"Experience. Especially from being on the water. You should see Tommy—he's a master at it. But this one's easy. You can already see blue sky behind it."

Clark came in with a case of beer to restock the restaurant refrigerator, his raincoat dripping. Hope followed his progress with a small frown. "I hope the weather cooperates for the mixology contest."

Alex grinned. "It is indoors, you know. I think Clark will manage not to drown."

"This is important, to both Clark and the resort. I want it to go well for him, and it would be good advertising for us too."

"Last I heard, he still didn't have his drink worked out. He'll probably finish it five minutes before the competition."

Less than ten minutes later, the rain stopped as suddenly as it had started. The sun returned, warming the drenched earth as tendrils of steam rose skyward, as if eager to return to where they had started.

Chapter Four

THE NEW BRICK patio was lovely. Laid out next to the pool, it overlooked the ocean and took full advantage of the sunset, which was gorgeous tonight. Hope looked over the reception, pride swelling at the turnout.

I did this.

She and Clark had spent hours decorating, placing solar lights in the potted plants and stringing Edison bulbs liberally overhead. The result was classy and romantic. Of course, the open bar was a draw as well. Charlotte circulated with bottles of red and white wine, her dark skin glowing with the humidity as she refilled the guests' glasses without being asked. A steel trough nearby held ice and bottles of beer, water, and soft drinks.

They had a full house with all eight bungalows booked. The new online booking portal had been up for a few weeks and was already producing results. All in all, Hope couldn't be more pleased.

In the shadows, Charles crept by with his rake. He met her eyes and nodded. A shiver ran down Hope's spine, but she met his gaze head-on as he continued out of sight. He'd never acted inappropriately around her—it was probably her overreactive instincts rising up.

With effort, she turned back to the reception. Patti laughed with a couple who were long-returning guests. She made eye contact with Hope and winked. Clark approached, carrying a single glass on his server's tray. Stopping in front of her with one arm tucked behind him, he inclined his head. "Good evenin', Hope. I have a special surprise for you. I present my final recipe—I think this is the one for the competition."

Clark had his sights set on winning the island-wide mixology contest, which was next month. He was a talented bartender, and Hope encouraged him in any way she could. Unfortunately, some of his creations went through less than pleasant iterations like a sulky, gangling teenager. His last cocktail had nearly made her gag, so Hope set her expectations fairly low. "Oh, thank you, Clark. I can't wait to taste it."

The cocktail was a blended pale-green drink, luminous and mysterious, and garnished with a section of banana. The stem end had been split with a maraschino cherry wedged between— like a dolphin with a ball in its mouth. Hope took a deep breath and closed her eyes before taking a large drink.

The taste exploded in her mouth. It was cold and refreshing, sweet and sour with just a hint of bitterness. All her taste buds lit up. There was a circle of sugar around the rim that perfectly balanced the bitter tone. It was spectacular—like drinking a liquid moonbeam.

Hope opened her eyes wide as she swallowed. "Oh my God, Clark. This is incredible! I've never tasted anything like this. What on earth is in it?"

"Oh—that's my secret, isn't it? But I'll tell you the name. I'm callin' it the Half Moon. . . Hope!"

Tears sprang to her eyes. "Clark, I think you've got a real

winner for the competition here! This is the best drink I've ever had. Try prying it out of my hands."

He beamed, puffing his chest out. "Don't need to. That one's just for you. I'm not makin' any more until after the competition."

"It's coming up, isn't it?"

"Yes! Soon, and I can't wait." He bounced on the balls of his feet.

"Well, I plan on being there for sure. I'm really proud of you, Clark." She gave him a quick hug.

"Thank you so much. I'd better get to work." With a bottle of wine in each hand, he began circulating.

Hope sipped her glorious drink as she moved among the guests. She stopped to talk with a couple who were long-time returning guests.

"We're having a great time," the woman said. "I love what you've done with the patio here. It's beautiful, and the sunset doesn't hurt, either."

The man pointed out Alex, holding a glass of red wine and laughing as he talked to two couples. "Alex has been a lot more relaxed this year. He has always been fun to be around, but he and Tommy have been a riot this week."

He came!

Alex wore a blue plaid shirt and gray cargo shorts. Her heart soared as he grinned, talking to the couple before him. And she had to give him credit for dressing himself appropriately—fashion was not his strong suit.

Hope tore her eyes away, focusing on her couple. "I'm glad you're enjoying your stay. This is a special resort, and I plan to keep it that way." She glanced around, working out how she could intercept Alex, when Patti made a mysterious announcement.

Patti clapped her hands to get everyone's attention. "Ladies and Gentlemen, I am pleased and honored to present to you a St. Croix tradition, our very own mocko jumbies. These are spiritual guardians, whose presence here tonight is a special blessin' to all of us."

Hope had no idea what a mocko jumbie was. It sounded like one of Clark's new drinks. There was movement to one side, and her mouth dropped open as two towering figures dressed in costumes and on stilts ambled onto the path, hats and masks covering most of their faces. One of them was at least seven feet tall, and the other over eight.

They were a riot of color. The taller one, dressed in a fluorescent yellow smock and pants, wore a pointed straw hat and a blue mask with eyeholes and a slash for a mouth. The other was in bright green with a pink border around his lower sleeves and wore a bright pink feather headdress—twelve-inch vertical feathers surrounded his head.

The two figures meandered around the patio, walking and weaving and bending down to peer at the guests before capering away. They entranced the children in attendance. The green one shuffled over to a small boy who backed up as the mocko jumbie stepped forward and presented him with a flower. He accepted it, his face shining.

The towering yellow one danced and bobbed over to Hope, bending down to peer into her face as he tilted his masked head from side to side. She couldn't help the huge grin that lit up her face. The figure slowly reached out a white-gloved hand and lifted her hand to his lips, kissing it. Then he staggered back, hands raised as if the kiss had caused an explosion, as the crowd laughed.

The two figures never spoke, and after several minutes of wandering around the patio, bending over people and dancing, they made their way back to the garden path and ambled off to great applause. Hope clapped so hard her hands hurt.

Oh, we have got to get them back!

There was a theatrical sigh behind her.

"Great. I leave you alone for an hour, and you've already got some other guy kissing your hand."

Hope spun around. Alex must have liked what he saw on her face because he started laughing.

"Oh, they were wonderful!"

"I didn't realize you'd never seen them before. They're a staple at any major event or festival here on the island."

"I'm so glad to see you! Thank you for coming. The guests love seeing you here, and I'm a little fond of you myself."

He leaned close. "I can't deny my boss anything. It's a real problem."

"Thank you. I mean it. I don't expect you to be here, but it means a lot to me."

He swirled his wine and turned a mischievous smile to her. "If I'd known I'd have to fight off the competition, I might show up more often."

"I think you know better than that."

He gave her a quick peck, his eyes promising more. "I saw you with Clark. What's up with the drink?"

"Taste it. It's what he plans to enter in the contest."

Alex took a big drink, and his face went blank as he swallowed audibly. "That's amazing! What's in it?"

"He wouldn't tell me. It's his secret. But would you believe he's calling it Half Moon Hope?"

"Yes, I would. You have quite an effect on people, you know?" He gave her an appreciative glance before his face went slack, his eyes widening. "You know, he's not the only one with a great idea. I know exactly what you need. Ms. Collins, what would you say if I asked you out to dinner?"

"What, away from here? Like a date?"

"I know it's a radical concept, but yes, that is exactly what I had in mind."

"Then I accept. But if you're taking me out on an official date, Mr. Monroe, I expect to be picked up at my front door. None of this getting ready together nonsense."

"How about tomorrow at 6 p.m.?"

"I'll be ready."

As he walked away, a lightning bolt went off in her head on *exactly* how to floor him. Then she nearly laughed. She had made one other purchase in Frederiksted sure to be the icing on the proverbial cake.

Chapter Five

ALEX CLIMBED the stairs to Hope's front door, breathing deeply to quell his racing heart. *What are you, sixteen? You do know her rather well. Get a grip, man.*

He reached out to ring the doorbell before hesitating, his finger hovering over the button. Finally, furious at his nervousness, he stabbed the doorbell.

Hope opened the door, and Alex forgot all about his nerves. She was dressed in the white tank top and tight jeans of his favorite early memory of her, their form hugging her every curve. His gaze traveled slowly down her body.

There was a difference, though.

This time, instead of flip-flops, she wore a pair of bright red high heels. His breath caught at the sight of them. As he moved his gaze back up her body, Alex snapped his wide-open mouth shut, his teeth clacking. By the time he met Hope's eyes, he was breathing hard, and his pulse pounded in his head.

"Well, good evening, Mr. Monroe. Do you intend to stand on my doorstep all night?"

"No," he growled and moved forward, pushing her against the wall as he pinned her mouth with his.

She allowed this for a while before pressing him back with a playful squeeze. "I thought you might appreciate this outfit."

Alex leaned his hands against the wall on either side of her head to keep his balance, still breathing hard. "You have no idea." He nuzzled her neck, inhaling deeply before moving up to breathe in her ear. "God, you smell incredible. You look incredible. We could just skip dinner, you know, and head straight to dessert."

Hope ducked under his arm, heading toward the front door. "Oh no. You promised me dinner, and I expect you to deliver on that promise."

"Oh, I plan on delivering."

He opened the passenger-side door and steadied her as she entered his old Land Cruiser, then drove toward Frederiksted.

Alex intentionally parked a few blocks from the restaurant, gesturing Hope ahead of him toward the waterfront. He couldn't stop watching the way her hips swayed in her high heels, making him think about how much he'd like to throw her against the trunk of the banyan tree they passed. *Don't think that would go over well.*

He grinned, catching up to her and taking her hand in his as they walked down the brick-paved boardwalk. A gentle breeze blew as the sun neared the horizon, casting an orange stripe on the ocean to their right.

When they reached the restaurant, he gave the hostess his name. She led them up a flight of stairs to an elevated open-air patio, gesturing to a corner table with a spectacular full vista of the ocean. He smiled at the hostess, pleased they had come through on his request for a private table with a view.

Hope looked around with a smile lighting her face. A short wrought-iron fence surrounded the patio. A wooden arbor soared overhead, with the branches of tropical trees weaving in and out. The trunks of the trees stood at all four corners while rattan lanterns hung from the arbor above, bathing the patio in a soft yellow glow. "This place is beautiful! I love it. Do you come here a lot?"

"Actually, I've never been here before. I've always liked the look of it and thought it would be a good place to take someone special."

Hope stilled, looking at him with full, glittering eyes. Afraid what he'd said sounded stupid, Alex buried his face in the menu. He was saved from further embarrassment when their server, a guy about twenty-five years old, approached and asked where they were from, assuming they were tourists.

"A few miles north of here," Alex said, not looking up from the menu.

Hope laughed. "We both work at Half Moon Bay Resort."

The server looked up, tapping his pencil against the pad as his tousled brown hair ruffled in the breeze. "Oh. Locals, right on. Wait—Half Moon Bay Resort—you guys are the ones who lost the dive boat, right? And had the divemaster who saved everyone?"

Alex tried not to scowl. He couldn't wait for his newfound notoriety to blow over.

Hope grinned. "Well, you're talking to the right man. Hero of the hour, right there—Alex Monroe." He glared at her, making her smile more.

"Really? What can I get you to drink, man?" He turned quickly to Hope. "And you too, of course."

After the server came back with his Leatherback and her glass of white wine, Hope was still smiling at him. "Oh, Alex, I never want to see you uncomfortable, but I do love seeing you flustered."

He couldn't help laughing. "All right. Touché." She had a

way of talking him out of his grumpy moods. And the night was much too wonderful to waste on sulking.

Their eyes met throughout the meal, and his pants became progressively tighter, especially since her *flustered* comment brought back memories of a conversation they'd had on their private-island afternoon and what had occurred there.

He ordered snapper, and she ordered sea bass. As their food arrived, a band started playing—two acoustic guitarists set up in the patio corner with an expanse of bare pavers in front of them. The music complemented the romantic atmosphere well, and several couples were already dancing.

While he wasn't normally self-conscious, the fact his last real date had been in the Stone Age made Alex more quiet than usual. He tried to concentrate on his food, but he couldn't take his eyes off Hope. The candle on the table flickered, causing a similar result in her eyes. One of her bra straps peeked out from under her tank top, and his eyes kept returning to it.

There was a hint of pink in her cheeks. "You keep looking at me," she said.

"Why shouldn't I? You're the most beautiful thing here." She was definitely blushing now, and his heart rate increased further.

"Do you know that shirt matches your eyes exactly?"

He shrugged—he'd picked out a shirt he was sure wouldn't clash. "I just like the color blue."

Hope leaned back, smiling. "The last time I saw you in that shirt was when you first met Sara. She'd been grilling me on the phone about you, so I told her you were a dumpy little guy I hardly noticed. Oh, she saw through me a mile away after she arrived."

They both laughed. "She acted like I was some sort of predator or something."

Hope's eyebrows flew up. "Alex, she's your biggest fan. She gave me hell for trying to resist you."

She reached out her bare foot to stroke his lower leg, and he pressed back.

"If she's a fan of mine, I'd hate to see what she does to her enemies."

"It would be wise to never find that out."

They ordered a slice of cheesecake with two forks, and the manager brought it out to them. "Please enjoy yourselves as long as you'd like. Your dinner is on the house tonight."

Alex started to protest, but the manager wouldn't hear of it, and backed away from their table.

"Well, how about that? It's kind of nice to be dating the local celebrity." Her foot was under the hem of his pant leg now, stroking his shin.

Alex reached out and drew a finger slowly down her hand, his eyes locked on hers. "I'm not interested in any notoriety. The only thing I'm interested in is you."

The band started playing a slow bump-and-grind song—exactly what he'd been waiting for. "You want to dance?"

Hope's eyebrows rose, and she sent him a smile that made his pulse go supersonic. "Yes, I'd love to."

Alex led her to the dance floor and wrapped her in his arms. "Surprised? Didn't think I was the dancing type?"

Hope failed to hide a smile. "No, actually, I didn't."

"Maybe I have other hidden talents you don't know about yet," he breathed in her ear, flames igniting his whole body now. "Those shoes are amazing. You have no idea where my mind is right now."

"Oh, I might have an idea. Why do you think I wore them?" She pressed her hips harder into him, making him groan into her ear. They continued dancing for a few songs, each one now punctuated with several long kisses.

Alex ached and pressed his mouth to her ear. "I need to get you out of here, and I don't think I can wait until we get home."

"What are you going to do, take me here on the dance floor?"

He ran his fingers down her spine, smiling at her shiver. "That's the best idea you've had all night, but I'll try to find something a little more private." He stepped back and took her hand. "Let's go. Now."

THE NIGHT AIR WAS WARM, and a scattering of stars lit the sky as Alex led her down the stairs to Strand Street, then took the first left into a small alley. He continued until they came to a cross street. Alert, he quickly scanned the area, but everything was deserted this late.

This will work.

He turned down the cross street, which was the back-facing entrance of the shops on either side. Kissing her, he walked her backward until she was pressed against the brick wall and brushed his tongue over her upper lip.

"What are you doing?" She peered over his shoulder, her eyes darting about.

He moved her head back to his. "What it looks like." Then he broke off to meet her gaze. "It's ok, baby. We're safe here."

He lifted her arms above her head while lightly tracing down the inside of her arm with his other hand. Gooseflesh appeared on her skin as her breath deepened.

"We can't do this here! What if someone sees?"

"Let 'em." He pulled her shirt out of her jeans, and she sighed as both his hands found what he was looking for. He smiled against her mouth, desire coursing through him. As he started to unbutton her jeans, she grabbed his hand.

"Alex! We could get arrested for this."

He laughed but didn't lift his hand. "This alley is deserted. No one's gonna see us." The smile faded, and he breathed into her ear, then flicked it with his tongue as she shuddered. "Why?" he breathed. "Don't you like what I'm doing to you?"

He had her zipper down now and sent his hand to investigate. "Liar."

She moaned against his neck. He pulled back, watching her face as he stroked her.

"Oh, my." Her eyes were closed, and she was nearly gasping.

He moved to his knees and slowly pulled her jeans down, inhaling deeply. He removed one shoe, then the pant leg, before replacing the shoe. Looking up, he said, "The shoes stay on." Alex repeated the maneuver with her other leg. Her chest heaved, and she pressed both hands against the brick wall.

Then it became very obvious where he was.

Well, I might as well enjoy myself while I'm down here.

He hadn't even gotten started when she hissed down at him, "Alex! Don't you *dare!*"

Alex had to laugh, but obediently returned to his feet.

He kissed her again as he ran his hands down the outsides of her bare hips. She was groaning now, and he was ready to explode. "I don't think I can be gentle with you right now."

Hope broke away and leveled a direct gaze at him. "When a woman wears four-inch red pumps, gentle is the last thing she wants." She gave him a sultry, throaty laugh he'd never heard from her before, and it seared through him.

"Oh God, do that again."

"What? Do what ag—"

He closed her mouth with his.

She opened his pants, and he picked her up in a single movement as her legs wrapped around his waist. Alex entered her and slammed her into the wall, then did it again. He broke the kiss to watch her face carefully, but she was enjoying herself completely, her eyes closed. He continued, every nerve in his body alight.

Some time later, Alex regained enough of his sensibilities to see puffs of dust being expelled from the wall every time Hope's back hit it and became concerned he was hurting her. He gentled his motion, and in response she raked her fingernails down his back under his shirt, saying, "Don't stop. Alex, please don't stop."

"Ok. You asked for it."

THE NEXT THING he was aware of was standing with his hands underneath her, holding her against him as they both shuddered, breathing in gasps. She was kissing his neck, so he angled his head around. Her legs were crossed at the ankles behind him, the red shoes hanging from her heels.

His entire body jolted again, and he turned back. "Are you sure you're ok? That was . . . that was . . . wow."

"Oh, yes." She unwrapped her legs as he set her gently on her feet, kissing her softly. She broke away to gather up her jeans and kicked off her shoes to redress.

"Be careful. There could be glass down there."

"I'm fine." She didn't seem to want to look at him now, and a red flush rose on her face.

"What's the matter? Are you sure you're ok?"

"Yes, honey, I'm fine." Her gaze was firmly turned to the ground.

A smile crept across his face. "Wait a second. Are you getting bashful on me? Now? After *that*?"

She gave him a shaky smile as her face became even more

crimson. "It's just . . . Alex, I've never done anything like that . . . I'm not . . ." Her face became serious. "Only for you."

His heart melted into a puddle, and he took her in his arms, holding her so tightly he was afraid of breaking her. "Oh my God. I know that, baby." He laughed softly. "That was a first for me too."

Chapter Six

SEPTEMBER . . .

HOPE SETTLED in the hollow of Alex's shoulder, his arm draped over her as they watched the dawn break. Drinking coffee together had become one of their favorite rituals. Alex continued to swim every morning, and Hope joined him more often than not. By unspoken agreement, he spent much of his time at the house rather than Hope at his apartment. She had gone so far as to clear a large section of the master closet for his belongings.

"Why don't you join me on the dive this morning? I'm going to give April the group of eight and take the group of six, so I can add you easily. You're supposed to be taking a day off, you know."

Hope considered April for a moment, then gave Alex an appraising glance. "Today sounds like a great day for a dive."

"Just don't wear any staff apparel on the boat. That way, the divers know it's your day off and you're off-limits." He leaned close. "Except to me, of course."

AFTER THEY ATE BREAKFAST, Hope returned home to change as Alex headed toward the boat, where Tommy was already on board loading tanks. She stood in her closet, deciding what to wear. She relaxed against the wall as she thought about April.

And whether Hope had a problem.

This was April's second of three days in a row working with Alex, and she was their go-to when Robert couldn't work. April was a blond thirtysomething with a happy, effervescent personality. Hope had chatted with her on several occasions and couldn't help but like her.

But when she'd had the lunch date with Alex, things had become clear—April was besotted with him. He appeared to be completely unaware of it. Hope had been playing it cool so far, knowing Alex only had eyes for her. The last thing she wanted was to come across to him as clingy. Or worse—jealous and possessive. Still, spending several hours with him in front of April might not be a bad idea.

Apparel decision made, Hope changed and was soon walking toward the boat. An early shower had passed, leaving a bright sunny day as a light mist rose from the wooden planks of the pier. One of the last to arrive, she tried to be nonchalant as she stepped onto the fiberglass deck, dressed in her black string bikini with matching fishnet cover-up.

Alex had most definitely seen the bikini before, but never the cover-up, which didn't really cover much. Fortunately, one of the female guests wore something similar, so Hope didn't feel too out of place as she traded a hello with Tommy. Giving her boat captain a critical eye, she made a mental note to order him an even bigger staff rash guard. The fabric on his current one could have snapped across his stomach at any moment. Tommy was a big man with an even bigger personality and heart.

Proceeding to the dry area, Hope kept a straight face as Alex whipped his head in a double-take when he saw her and froze. She gave him a demure smile, but couldn't deny he also needed a bigger staff rash guard. But for very different reasons than Tommy. The thin material strained over his biceps and was tight over his shoulders and chest. Alex possessed the perfect male V-shape, with his shoulders going on for miles before his torso narrowed to a trim waist. She snapped out of her reverie at his cocky grin. With a regal nod, she turned away, refusing to admit he'd caught her ogling him.

Admittedly, the situation kept Hope occupied as they rode out. She chatted with the guests, keeping one eye on Alex and April. He was his same professional self, but she was something else, practically batting her eyelashes. Hope had to bite back a smile at how oblivious Alex was to her advances—he was indifferent to his effect on women other than her.

As they motored to the dive site, Hope talked with a couple who were new divers and a bit apprehensive. In her mid-thirties, Ginny was a little shy, with light-brown hair braided into a long tail down her back. Her husband Evan was at least six and a half feet tall. Hope had to crane her neck to look at him.

As Alex gave the dive briefing, Ginny raised her hand. "Uh, I still have trouble clearing my ears. The last vacation we were on, I couldn't do some dives because of it."

Alex gave her some tips to help before addressing the rest of the group. "We have about a fifty-foot drop to start the dive. There's no current, so we're not in a rush. Relax and take your time descending."

Hope removed her cover-up and returned to the stern in her bikini, pulling on her wetsuit. Alex had placed Hope's equipment next to April's, and she helped Hope into her BCD. Hope asked her how long she'd been on St. Croix, making an effort to be friendly.

"Almost three years. I like it here a lot. I'd love more hours—Alex and I work great together."

I'm sure you think so.

"We're getting busier all the time, so you might get your wish." Hope determinedly ignored the slithering creature that crawled out of her gut. She didn't want to name it, but its color was definitely green.

As Alex went around the group making sure everyone's tank was turned on, he reached Hope and leaned in, murmuring in her ear, "I saw what you have on under your wetsuit. That brings back some memories. And I absolutely noticed the cover-up."

Alex started to straighten up before, to her astonishment, leaning down and quickly brushing his lips over hers. Then he trotted to the other side of the boat to get into his own gear, darting his eyes back to her with a smile. Hope shot a quick glance at April, who was sitting still as a rock, her face blank.

Well, she certainly saw that.

Hope was one of the last to jump into the water, and when she reached the bottom, she gave Ginny the ok signal. Ginny returned it emphatically with both hands—Hope smiled at her. *Ear problems must be better now.* Then she looked for Alex, not seeing him.

Hope looked up at the splash of one final diver entering the water. Alex entered fins first like everyone else, but instead of popping back up to the surface like she did to make sure all her bits and pieces were together, he continued to descend like a stone. He'd skipped the wetsuit today, wearing the rash guard and board shorts. He sank upright with his legs crossed at the ankles and arms folded above his BCD, completely relaxed as he scanned over his group to make sure everyone was ok.

Hope was so focused on how effortless he was that it took a

moment to register Alex hadn't pinched his nose to equalize a single time in nearly fifty feet.

How can he descend without clearing his ears?

A pneumatic sound echoed through the water as he added several blasts of air to his BCD. Then, just before his fins were about to touch the coral, he bent his knees and tipped down into a horizontal position, knees still bent so his fins stayed away from the coral and perfectly buoyant. He looked around again before applauding Ginny, then beckoned the group to follow.

AFTER THE DIVE, Ginny couldn't suppress her excitement at her newfound ability to equalize. Hope smiled as she stood off to one side, eating one of Gerold's cookies and watching Alex try to work while Ginny yammered in his ear.

As he finished the tanks, a memory about the dive popped into Hope's head. "Ok, I have to ask you something."

"Anything." He brushed his foot over hers.

"It's diving related," she said with mock seriousness, pulling her foot back. "I watched you descend on that last dive, but you never cleared your ears. How did you do that?"

Alex reached up and hooked his hands over the fiberglass canopy, swaying with the motion of the boat. "I cleared my ears. Kind of hard to dive if you don't." The foot was back over hers. "I use a different technique. I learned it in the Navy, and it's also one a lot of free divers use—I don't teach it because it's trickier to master, but it comes in handy on rapid descents."

She pulled her foot back again. "Maybe I'll let you show me sometime."

This time he stepped up to her and rested the toes of both feet over hers, pinning her in place with a smile that made her heart pound. "Maybe. But I can't go around giving away all my secrets, can I? I might have to make you work for it."

He closed the distance between them, staring at her until their faces were inches apart, then whirled around and returned to the stern as he threw a sly grin over his shoulder.

HOPE LOVED THE SECOND DIVE. Alex led the group on an underwater treasure hunt through a long channel in the reef. The broad crevice was full of nooks and crannies.

He stopped several times to show the group creatures hiding in the cracks with his powerful dive light, only illuminating the animal briefly to avoid stressing it with the light. Alex found lobsters, crabs, and nighttime fish hiding out during the day, their eyes enormous. Turning on her much-smaller light, Hope discovered many of the holes contained animals, including more lobsters and even a sleeping turtle. The time flew by, and much too soon the group was boarding the boat again.

Chilled after the dive, Hope skipped the towel and let the sun dry her bikini-clad skin. Most of the divers were on the sundeck, leaving the main area nearly deserted except for April, who unhooked regulators. Hope walked to the edge of the canopy and reached up to hold the grab bar with both hands. She faced the stern and open ocean, her knees soft to compensate for the boat's movement. Closing her eyes, memories of the last time she'd stood in this same position flooded through her and her toes curled, a delicious shiver running up her body.

Alex soon came up behind her, placing his hands on her hips as he breathed into her ear, "You are absolutely killing me right now."

"Then you know how I feel whenever I'm around you," she said softly. "Though I seem to recall you were on the other side of me the last time."

"I have no idea what has gotten into you today, but I definitely like it."

Hope turned around and pierced him with her eyes. "Nothing has gotten into me—yet."

His face tightened as he inhaled sharply.

A slow smile spread on Hope's face as she glanced down his body, then back to his eyes. "Better get back to work. We wouldn't want to get totally unprofessional here." She whispered in his ear, "That can come later." She moved to her spot and made sure all her things were together. April was much quieter now.

Message received.

The slithering green creature returned to its lair.

AFTER THEY RETURNED to the resort, Alex rinsed wetsuits with a freshwater hose while April dunked the BCDs in a long open-top tank. Hope approached and Alex turned off the hose, placing his hands on her shoulders. "Thanks for coming today. I always have more fun when you're there."

"There's nowhere else I'd rather be."

Quickly, Alex wrapped his arms around her and boosted her up so they were face-to-face, kissing her as he walked in a slow circle. "Any time you want to wear that cover-up, it's fine with me."

"I thought you might approve." She raised a brow. "You do have to let me down at some point, you know."

"Nah. I'm kind of enjoying this."

"So am I. You have no idea how much. But I believe there's still work to be done."

"Oh, all right. You're the boss." He put her down and draped one arm over her shoulders as they walked back to the dive shop.

Hope disengaged herself. "Sorry you had to see that, April. Someone needs to work on his professionalism."

Alex shot her a dazzling, unapologetic grin. "Oh, come on. Nobody's here except April, and she's staff." He turned to April. "You don't care, do you?"

She put on a brave face and smiled. "Of course not. It's nice to see you two together."

Alex winked at Hope. "Told ya." He waved a hand at April. "I can finish up. Go ahead and take off. I'll see you tomorrow."

She didn't put up too much of a fight and soon walked down the pier, a little less bouncy now.

Hope sighed. "Now I feel guilty. That really wasn't very nice. Maybe I shouldn't have come today."

Alex dropped his armful of wetsuits. "What are you talking about?"

Hope had to laugh. "You really have no idea, do you?"

"What?"

"Let's just say April and I set some clear ground rules this morning."

His face was blank. "Huh?"

She encircled his waist with her arms. "Alex, she's more than a little attracted to you. And I wanted it to be crystal clear to her you are already involved with someone. Namely me."

He drew his brows together. "You don't think I'd—"

She placed her index finger on his lips. "No, I don't. But that doesn't mean I enjoy watching her make sheep's eyes at you."

"Sheep's eyes, huh?" He drew her close again and gave her a fluttery kiss. "You're the only woman for me. So that's what all that was about? You were fighting over me?"

"No, I wouldn't say fighting precisely . . ."

"Hmmm. I can't decide whether that makes me feel like a sex object or turns me on."

"Maybe I can help you figure that out."

He grabbed her hand. "Come on. The door to the dive shop has a lock on it."

Chapter Seven

A STRONG AFTERNOON breeze thrashed the palm trees into a frenzy as Hope sprawled on her porch couch, a paperback open on her stomach. She was currently engaged in a battle of wills with Cruz. She refused to bribe him with food, determined to earn his affections only if he offered them freely.

"You know I'm eventually going to wear you down." His floppy ears perked up. "It would save us both a lot of time if you'd just come over here and let me pat your head."

Today he'd trotted up the stairs and sat down at the edge of the deck. Then he lay down in his customary position with his head on his front paws, his eyes never leaving her. Every few minutes, he would scoot a little more toward her. As of now, he was halfway between the stairs and couch, the closest he'd ventured yet. He sat up and scratched behind his ear with a hind leg.

"See? You've probably got mange. If you'd let me touch you, I could give you a bath and take care of that for you."

Cruz yawned in response, then became alert, looking behind him. He turned around and disappeared into the jungle. No longer distracted, Hope couldn't keep her gaze from returning to the azure ocean and blue sky. The peaceful setting presented a sharp contrast to the knot forming in her stomach.

With a sigh, Hope picked up her laptop from the coffee table. Opening the lid, she was immediately presented with an ad for running shoes, further reminding her about starting a running routine. "As much as I'd prefer to think about running again, I probably have something more important to think about." Since Cruz had abandoned her, she was only talking to herself.

Hope brought up the website to check the latest weather. A storm brewing in the Atlantic was starting to look serious. It was now officially a tropical depression and headed straight for the Caribbean. Just looking at the large white mass of clouds on the screen caused her gut to twist. She shut the lid.

"Maybe it will fizzle out or head in another direction. We should know more soon."

SEVERAL DAYS LATER, they had formed a command center in the lobby office. Patti pointed to the resort bookings on Hope's computer. "It looks like three-quarters of our guests have canceled for the next few weeks, so that's good."

Hope nodded. "Could you keep trying to contact all the rest to reschedule them? Offer to rebook them any time in the next year with no penalty fees." Hope ran a hand through her hair. "We have two guys here now who are hardcore divers and don't want to reschedule their flights home. I sent Alex to talk some sense into them."

The television mounted on the wall of the office normally cycled through landscape photos of St. Croix, but they had it tuned to the local news today. The meteorologist was on, and Hope unmuted it.

"Folks, we've got a pretty good storm headed our way. In the past twenty-four hours, it has strengthened into a solid category-one hurricane." Wearing a loud tropical-print shirt, he stopped in front of his map and faced the camera. "And I hate to say it, but we're projecting it to make a direct hit on the south shore of St. Croix. The outer bands are forecasted to hit by tomorrow afternoon, with the brunt of the storm following within hours."

He pointed to the image of the island—the massive storm was just to the south. "The timeline is still fluid. It's starting to increase speed a bit. The airport is planning to close by 5 p.m. tomorrow, folks—but if you need to fly out, call your airline *now*. The airport could very well close sooner."

Hope muted it again and turned to Patti. "At least all the guests were willing to listen to me when I had my emergency meeting this morning. I stressed that everyone needed to call their airlines immediately if they wanted any chance of getting out before the storm. Where do we stand on that?"

"We've got twelve guests here right now. Six are flyin' out today, and four tomorrow mornin'. If Alex can convince the other two, we should be empty by tomorrow."

Footsteps echoed through the empty lobby, and Hope turned as Alex entered the office. "How did it go?"

"They're calling right now. I told them the dive shop was shut down and if they waited any longer, they might not get out for weeks if the airport gets blasted. Hopefully, it's not already too late."

"They were both at the meeting this morning," Hope said. "They know they have to stay at the emergency shelter in Frederiksted if they can't get a flight out. Thanks, Alex."

He nodded. "Tommy and I are going to secure the boat tomorrow morning. He knows a good hiding spot on the north shore. He'll go straight home after."

"I saw Charles with a big pile of lumber and tools. If we can get all hands on deck to get everything boarded up today, I'd like all employees off starting tomorrow."

"Where are you plannin' on stayin', Hope?" Patti alternated her gaze between her and Alex. "Do you want to go to the shelter? Or Gary and I have extra room. You two are welcome to stay with us."

Hope crossed her arms, avoiding Alex's sharp look. "I'm not going anywhere, Patti. I've put my heart and soul into this place —I'm not deserting it now."

"Dear, it's not safe to stay so close to the ocean. The storm surge can be very dangerous." Patti spoke like Hope was a bomb needing to be defused.

"A hurricane is nothing to take lightly," Alex said. "I need to know you're safe."

"Listen guys, I'll be fine. The house is back from the water and elevated. The windows will be shuttered. We're not talking about a category-five storm, plus we should be protected here on the west coast. I'm staying." Hope marched out of the office to organize the preparations.

The day was cloudy and extremely still, with off-the-charts humidity. Hope swore she could feel the air pressure dropping. The employees and remaining guests took on the arduous task of boarding up the resort, wrapping up the kitchen, lobby, and bar, and nailing boards to windows.

Hope filled a wheelbarrow with ice and bottled water and wheeled it around, offering everyone a drink. She swung by the bungalows where Alex and Tommy worked. Each time she did, Alex tried to convince her to leave, but she never stayed long enough to hear him out—she'd made up her mind, anyway.

By early evening, they were nearly done. Hope wheeled her

barrow to the final bungalow porch, breathing heavily. Resting for a moment, she took in the view.

Alex pounded a board over the window, his shirt off and sweat pouring down his back. Hope's breathing wasn't decreasing any as every muscle in his upper body flexed while he wielded the hammer. Finally finishing with the last board, he dropped the hammer and grabbed his shirt, wiping his entire face and head as he leaned against the wall with the other arm.

That snapped her back to reality, and she fished two cold bottles out and handed the first to Tommy, who was still pounding. Nodding his thanks, he drank as she continued to Alex, her eyes now riveted to his chest as beads of sweat rolled down it. Hope looked at him, and her face must have given away her thoughts because he smiled, though his eyes sent a different message.

"Hope, please . . ."

"No. Here, drink some water. You must be parched."

"Thank you." He opened it and drank the entire thing. She looked over to find Tommy's also empty and retrieved more.

"It's five-thirty now. We're all meeting in the dining room at six for a group dinner. Cold sandwiches, I think."

Tommy nodded. "Sounds good."

She held her hand out to Alex. "Let's head to my house and get cleaned up."

Hope rubbed a hand up and down her arm. Alex had the shower knob turned fully to cold as he stood under the water, letting it pour over him. She tiptoed into the shower stall, not eager to get blasted by freezing water. "Can you make it warmer? I hate cold water."

He turned and drew her into his embrace. "I'll keep you warm."

She sighed against his chest, snuggling in and enjoying his closeness, before he spun her around under the showerhead. Hope screamed, and a laughing Alex relented, reaching behind her to turn the knob.

His smile disappeared as he took her face in his hands, rubbing his thumbs over her cheeks. "I'm not going to talk you out of leaving the resort, am I?"

"No. I need to be here. I've worked too hard to just leave. I'm done running away."

The steam swirled around them as he stood motionless with her face cupped in his hands, staring at her.

"Alex . . ."

He sighed, then scanned the master bathroom. "All right. This is a pretty secure room. We can make this our hideout."

"No. You don't have—" Hope quieted at the look on his face.

"Yes, I do. There's no way I'm leaving you to face this alone, and you know that."

"I know." She wrapped her arms around his waist. "Thank you."

The next morning, Hope stood at the counter, tapping her fingers as she watched the toaster. The bread finally popped up, and she was in business. She shuffled over to the window with toast in one hand and coffee in the other.

The morning had dawned in gray, begrudging light, and the wind already whipped the waves into a white froth as a steady rain poured down. Alex was gone before she woke up, leaving the television on with the volume muted. She turned the sound on, and the local newscasters broadcast a steady stream of doom regarding the approaching storm.

It had strengthened to a high category one and might be a category two before the brunt of the hurricane made landfall earlier than expected, late that evening. Finally, the reporters started repeating their predictions of incipient mayhem, so she turned the television off.

After dressing, she dug out her raincoat, pulling on a stocking cap before putting her hood up. The wall clock said it was 7:30, and the resort van was scheduled to leave at 8:00 with the last departing guests. The two men had obtained some of the last seats available on this morning's flight. The airport was now scheduled to close at 10 a.m.

Hope descended the porch steps, and the rain immediately pelted her hood. She pulled it tighter against her face, weaving around the puddles forming on top of the sandy beach. A wind gust pushed against her back, propelling her forward.

As she staggered up the beach, Hope was surprised Charles was outside the toolshed, hammering more plywood over the windows. She ducked under the cover of the shed's eave. "I didn't think you'd be here today."

Charles turned around. His dreadlocks were pulled back with an elastic tie, and he wore his usual staff shirt. "Only for a few minutes. Makin' sure this shed is locked up tight. I use a lot of the equipment in here."

"Thank you. It means a lot to have you helping."

"Well, gotta make sure the resort is safe. Give a reason for the tourists to come back." He gave her a direct look, narrowing his eyes. "What about you? I heard a rumor you're stayin' here. How are you goin' to stay safe?"

"Alex is staying with me."

Charles bit his lip, clearly trying not to laugh. "Oh, that's good then. I'm sure the tour guide can protect you."

Hope's mouth tightened. "I'm sure we'll be fine. Is there a problem?"

"Oh, no. I'd best be on my way now. You take care, hear?" He gave her another long look, then headed toward the parking lot.

Hope shook off the encounter. She had more important things to worry about right now than her surly landscaper. She continued up the beach and back into the increasing rain, Charles quickly forgotten.

Alex walked down the pier toward her, and she stopped to wait. He was bareheaded and dressed in only shorts and a sweatshirt.

Hope waited until he got close, so she didn't need to shout. "Don't you own a raincoat?"

"I don't need it yet. I'm saving it in case I need to go out later when the storm hits."

"You're a stubborn man, you know that?"

"Says the woman who refuses to leave for safety during a hurricane."

She glared at him, making him laugh. He took her hand and rubbed it. "Your hand is freezing! You want me to get you some mittens, or maybe a snowsuit? I thought you were from Chicago."

"My blood is thinner now. And if you're done insulting me, let's go see off the last of the guests."

He bowed over her hand before kissing it, saying, "After you, milady."

Hope rolled her eyes but couldn't help smiling as they made their way to the restaurant, which had been transformed. All traces of humor faded as she took in the changes. Metal hurricane shutters had been pulled down vertically like garage doors, completely enclosing the dining area. The patio was totally cleared, her beloved Edison bulbs and solar lights safely packed away. They entered through a side door, and Hope was grateful to be out of the wind as she took off her raincoat and hat.

The remaining guests were scattered about the dining room finishing breakfast as Patti went from table to table, checking in. Gerold had come in early and prepared a boxed breakfast for everyone before returning home. Hope approached Patti as Alex trailed behind her with a towel, trying to dry off at least somewhat. Patti turned when she saw Alex.

"Is everything ready down at the pier?"

"As ready as it can be. It's out of our hands now."

Clark entered the room and approached Patti. "All the luggage is loaded. We're ready to go." Patti nodded, then got everyone's attention, directing them to follow Clark to the van.

In a matter of minutes, only Patti, Alex, and Hope remained. Patti wrung her hands before drawing Hope into an embrace. "You be careful, child. I'll see you soon." Then she moved to Alex and said, "Ugh, you're all wet." She overcame her aversion, though, and hugged him tightly. Patti murmured, "Keep her safe, Alex."

He looked at Hope as he returned the embrace. "You know I will, Patti."

Then she was gone too, and Hope and Alex were alone. She gathered up the remaining meal boxes to take with them.

Alex put his arm around her as they walked back to the door. "Come on, baby. Let's go to the house and ride this thing out."

Chapter Eight

NIGHT CAME AT 5:30. There was no twilight. The day went from an angry gray half-light to a howling black maelstrom in an instant. The wind didn't blow—it screamed like a malevolent wraith. Hope shut the front door against it, chilled despite the protective shutters drawn over every window. Though she was grateful not to witness the horror outside, the shutters gave her a haunted, claustrophobic feeling.

They stacked an assortment of candles, flashlights, and extra blankets on the kitchen table. Alex turned on the television and proceeded to watch baseball. "We're probably going to lose power, so enjoy the creature comforts while you can. You sure you don't want to watch a movie instead?" She declined, too anxious to pay attention and questioning her decision to stay behind, though she wasn't about to admit that to him.

Her stomach growled, reminding her it would be a good idea to eat something for dinner. Hope made a couple of sandwiches and gathered two drinks to go with them, then returned to the couch. She forced herself to eat, chewing mechanically, her mouth dry. Alex wolfed his down, going back to the kitchen to scrounge for more.

By 9 p.m., the wind was a non-stop wailing banshee. It was like an evil spirit enveloping the house as its pale, skeletal fingers sought entry. Alex read a military thriller on the couch, his feet up on the coffee table, while Hope paced in endless circles. "How can you be so calm?"

He lowered the book. "It's gonna be a long night, so you might as well relax a little. Come sit down." He patted the cushion next to him, rubbing her shoulders after she sat down.

Hope closed her eyes and heaved a big sigh, relaxing at his touch. "Oh, that feels good."

"Yeah, your shoulders are like rocks. Just relax a little—we're safe in the house."

"I'm trying." She forced her muscles to unclench, focusing on Alex's nearness.

The shrieking wind decreased momentarily, and barking filled the void, followed by several loud yelps.

Hope was immediately on her feet and running. "Cruz! Cruz is out there—he sounds hurt!" She threw open the front door. The wind was so strong she could hardly hear Alex yelling behind her.

"What are you doing? You can't be serious right now!"

She staggered into the screaming blackness, the only light coming from fragmentary lightning flashes as she shouted, "Cruz!" Finally, answering barks came from the jungle across her yard, and she sprinted over the sodden ground.

"Hope! Slow down. I can barely see you!" The wind snatched Alex's voice as soon as it came out of his mouth.

She ran down the path, stumbling in the mud as she called the dog's name. The entire sky lit up with lightning and exploded with thunder. Rain washed over her in sheets, and the force of the wind made her reel.

I've lost my mind.

The trees surrounding her thrashed in every direction. In

the flashes of light, they appeared to creep toward her. It even smelled electric. Hope slipped in the mud but righted herself.

Staggering, she looked up to see a flash of yellow.

Cruz leaped into her arms, licking her face and whining. She whirled around and ran into Alex.

"Come on, Hope! Goddammit, we've got to get back. Now!"

Hope took off running back to the house with the dog in her arms and Alex right behind. She slipped again but managed to stay on her feet, rebounding off a tree as she ran.

The sky lit up again with another all-encompassing, thunderous crash, accompanied by a vast groaning sound. Hope screamed. Then she was on the ground, mud all over her chin as Alex grunted behind her. As she sheltered the whimpering dog beneath her, a great weight pushed on her back, compressing her.

"Are you ok?" Alex shouted in her ear.

"Yes, I think so. And I'm not deaf. Stop yelling in my ear."

Cruz wiggled and snorted beneath her, and she could hardly breathe. Alex's body was behind hers, covering her. "Alex—you're squashing me."

"That's because there's a tree on top of me, Hope."

"Oh my God—are you ok?"

"Peachy."

"Stop joking!" She resisted the impulse to dig her elbow into his side, but he finally stopped laughing.

"Ok, we're in a hollow here, so we're not completely trapped. Can you wriggle out from under me?"

"I'll try. Maybe Cruz can get out."

"By all means, make sure the dog is ok. I'll just lie here."

She ignored that. Cruz had been struggling, so she let him go. He crawled out from underneath her, then turned around to lick her face. "Oh Cruz, your breath is awful."

Hope belly crawled through the mud, working her way

through the dense branches. She finally got free before turning around to help pull Alex out from under the tree. Both were dripping wet and blinking from the rain pelting their eyes.

He gave her a quick once-over, all traces of humor gone, then waved an arm toward the house, shouting, "Go, go, go!"

She started running again, with Cruz by her side. As she emerged out of the trees and into the yard, the wind staggered her sideways. Hope bolted across the grass as she dodged debris, then ran up the front steps and burst through the front door with Cruz, Alex right behind her. He whirled around and slammed the door shut, throwing the deadbolt.

Alex crushed her to him. "Oh God. Never do that to me again. I thought I was going to lose you."

"I'm sorry. I couldn't just leave him out there. He sounded so afraid!" Heart hammering, she squeezed his arms, making him wince. Hope looked closer—his right arm was covered in blood.

"You're bleeding!"

"Yeah, I figured I was. You have a first aid kit, right?"

"I'm not quite the Boy Scout you are, but yes, I have one in the bathroom. Let's go."

Cruz sat near the bathroom door as Alex sat down on the closed toilet and took his shirt off to inspect the damage. There was a three-inch gash over his right bicep, the blood running freely down his forearm.

Hope leaned over him, poking and prodding. "Let me clean it up with some peroxide, then I'll put some butterfly bandages on it and wrap it tightly. It doesn't look too deep, so the butterflies should help it scab over."

"Yeah, that'll work."

She grabbed a washcloth from the cabinet and poured half the bottle of peroxide onto it to clean the wound. Alex clenched his jaw but said nothing.

"Was this from the tree?" she asked quietly.

"I imagine so."

Cruz whined, and belly crawled over to place his head on top of Alex's waterlogged shoe, watching him with mournful eyes.

"Looks like we're both sorry, honey." She stopped to kiss him, tears threatening at what she'd caused.

Alex pulled back. "As much as I'd rather keep kissing you, if you don't get the butterflies on that, it'll never stop bleeding."

That snapped her attention back to the job at hand. "Oh! Ok. I'm on it."

A few minutes later she was done, a white gauze bandage wrapped tightly around his bicep.

"Thanks. You did a good job. Now let's get these wet clothes off."

His words brought home that Hope was shivering and soaked, her hair dripping. Her whole front was covered in mud. She looked into his eyes, and her composure broke. "I'm sorry, Alex. This is all my fault. You shouldn't even be here. You should be safe and dry somewhere."

"Oh, hush. This is nothing—I'm fine."

Once again, she was in his arms with tears rolling down her face. It had happened more times than she'd like to admit. "Why am I always crying with you?"

Because you feel safe with him . . .

"Because you've been through a lot these last few months." Alex stroked her hair. "Besides, my life would be terribly sad and dull without you in it."

"You don't think I'm predictable and boring?"

He laughed and held her at arm's length, incredulous. "Hope, I would call you many things, but predictable and boring would be the absolute bottom two choices. What on earth made you ask that?"

"Nothing. Nothing at all."

A smile crept across her face as Alex enfolded her in his arms again. That Hope was gone forever.

As they changed into dry clothes, the power went out, plunging them into black night as Cruz whined nearby. The storm became even louder and more threatening in the darkness.

"Come on. Let's get out to the kitchen for those candles," she said.

Once they had some light established, she filled a bowl with water for Cruz, who lapped it up. Then she took out some lunch meat from the fridge and put it on a plate for him. "There you go, boy. I'd say you earned that." She gave Alex a shaky smile. "He finally let me touch him."

As terrible as the storm had been so far, it was still increasing. They set up a makeshift nest in the master bathroom, pulling the mattress off the bed and placing it on the floor. The smell of wet dog in the close confines soon became overpowering, so Hope threw down some blankets in a corner of her bedroom for Cruz to bed down on. She shut the bathroom door.

Hope set a candle on the counter, the soft light flickering around the room. "You know, if you ignore the fact we're stuck in a room that smells like a wet dog after a tree fell on you during a hurricane, this is actually kind of romantic."

"Any room with you in it is romantic, but I'm glad the dog is in the other room now."

"Agreed."

He scanned the room, making sure it was safe. This man hadn't hesitated to chase after her into a hurricane. Hope moved to him, grabbing a handful of his shirt as she pulled his head down to kiss him.

Alex's mouth was hungry and hot as she ran her hands under his shirt and up his chest. His ribs expanded with his sharp inhalation.

"I think we might need to investigate this mattress further." Her voice was low and husky.

His teeth gleamed in the candlelight as he smiled. "Agreed."

"But I think you've performed quite enough heroics for tonight. In fact, I think it's time you let someone else be in charge for once."

"Oh yes, ma'am." He stepped forward and ran two fingers over her tattoo with a seductive smile.

A massive gust of wind made the house shudder as their mouths melted together.

Chapter Nine

THUNDER CRASHED outside as Hope rested on an elbow and drew her finger down the side of Alex's face. His eyes were still closed as his breath heaved in and out. She actually saw his heart pounding below her. Bending down, she gave him a slow, lingering kiss.

Alex put his left arm around her and pulled her down on top of him. "Oh, woman. The things you do to me. And I'm not just talking about making love, Hope."

"Is that right? Well, the feeling is mutual, you know. You bring things out in me I didn't even know were there." She was leaning down to kiss him again when the shrieking wind increased further.

Hope winced, closing her eyes.

Alex raised a hand to her face. "Hey, you don't need to be afraid. I promised I'd keep you safe."

"I know. I always feel safe with you."

Alex stood and started dressing. "Get some sleep. I'm going to stay up for a bit."

He helped her settle in, then kissed her hair and moved

down to the foot of the mattress, sitting sideways as he leaned against the wall.

Warm and secure, Hope drifted off.

SHE WOKE SOME TIME LATER. The wind was slightly less. Still an invisible evil spirit seeking destruction, but perhaps less hungry now. The candle revealed Alex still sitting in the same position, the faint glow reflected in his eyes.

Hope's eyes were growing heavy again when the night exploded with a tremendous crash as the house juddered around them.

"What was that!" Hope bolted upright, the blanket clutched to her chest.

Alex was already on his feet and nearly at the door. "It's probably a tree hitting the roof. Stay here—I'll check it out." He was back a few minutes later. "Can't tell what it was with the shutters down, but the house is secure. We're fine. Go back to sleep."

"What about you? Aren't you coming?" She pulled her shirt on, settling onto the mattress.

"In a little bit." He sat back down at the foot of the bed.

FINALLY, Hope opened her eyes to a dull, weak light creeping through the single shuttered window. The wind was noticeably lower now. Alex was still at the foot of the mattress, like he hadn't moved at all.

"What time is it?" she asked.

"A little after six. Are you ok?"

Hope sat up, frowning as she tucked the sheet around her. "I am, yes. I slept, Alex. You stayed up all night, didn't you?"

"I wasn't tired." He squeezed her foot through the blankets. "Besides, you snore. There's no way I could have slept."

She kicked him, laughing. "I do not!"

"I couldn't hear the storm over you. Maybe you should see a doctor."

She threw back the covers. "I'm going to make the coffee somehow."

Cruz followed her to the kitchen and drank from his water bowl. "You probably aren't housebroken, are you?" He sat and cocked his head at her. "Hang on. I need coffee before I let you out."

Hope lit several candles before finding a teakettle in a cupboard. She set it on the gas stove and used a match to light the burner. Then she started rooting through the kitchen cabinets. "I know I saw instant coffee in here."

The kettle whistled as she found it, grasping the jar as if it were a priceless treasure. She'd made both cups when Alex came into the kitchen, wearing clean shorts and carrying a T-shirt. Handing him a cup, she said, "It's instant, but it's caffeinated and hot."

"Thanks. That hits the spot. I'm not picky."

"You don't fool me for a minute, you know. I know perfectly well you stayed up all night keeping watch." She wrapped him in a hug. "Thank you. I don't think I could have faced that alone."

Alex tilted her face up. "You never will."

Their kiss was interrupted by Cruz scratching at the front door.

"He's housebroken! I can't believe it." Hope ran to the door and opened it. The dog scurried down the stairs to do his business in the rain, then ran back inside.

As Hope returned to the kitchen, the dim candlelight provided a little illumination as Alex poured water into his second cup of coffee. She moved her gaze to the bandage on his right arm, where there was a dark stain within the white. Then he turned to reveal something else. A purple stain covered his back from his right shoulder to his left flank.

Hope padded up behind him and slid her arms around his waist. "Oh, Alex. Your back is one enormous bruise."

He turned around in her embrace. "It was worth it."

Maybe Hope should apologize again, but he didn't want to hear it. Alex's need to protect ran to the core of him. Instead, she peered at his bicep. "I want to replace that bandage on your arm. You've bled through it."

"If you want. It feels ok this morning."

Stubborn man.

***

WRAPPING the last of the bandage around his arm, Hope stood up. "There. That's much better." The gash had been red and angry, but the butterfly bandages held the wound closed so it could scab over. "Try to keep it dry, ok?"

Alex bent his elbow back and forth. "Thanks. I'm going to go outside to check the perimeter of the house and see what that crash was last night. You stay here—it's still blowing like hell out."

"I'm perfectly capable of being out in the rain, you know."

"Yeah, I noticed that last night."

Warmth crept up her face. "You sure you're doing ok?"

He enfolded her. "Better than ok. An added plus is now maybe Cruz will stop biting me."

"He has never bitten you!"

"Only because I've got fast reflexes." He grinned. "I'll be right back, ok? There's no sense in both of us getting soaked, you know."

"Wear your damn raincoat this time!"

"Yes, ma'am."

He took longer than she expected, making her wish she had gone with him so she knew what was happening. She was contemplating braving the wind when the front door opened and Alex returned, water streaming off of him.

"Yeah, it was a tree." He removed the dripping raincoat as Hope handed him a towel. "I couldn't get close enough to see if it broke through the roof, but I didn't see anything obvious. I rolled up the shutters over the office windows. Since they're on the downwind side, it should be safe enough now that the worst is past. You can go look if you want. I want to check out the ceiling in there, anyway—the tree is above your office."

Hope made her way to the office as Alex went to change clothes yet again. She stood in front of the two side-by-side windows which faced north, her fingers turning white as they gripped the sill.

The yard was covered in driftwood and tree limbs. Someone's bicycle lay on the ground, one wheel spinning. The ocean was a raging chaos of frothy water. Her breath came faster and faster. Alex squeezed her shoulders in his usual silent approach, but Hope was too shocked at the scene in front of her to be startled this time.

"Alex, what happened to the beach?"

"Storm surge. It's receding now. You see the debris line there at the top? It almost made it all the way to your house." Her beautiful white sand beach had disappeared under the furious ocean.

"I had no idea it could do that."

Is this the end? Is it all gone?

He wrapped his arms around her waist and pulled her back to him. "That's why Patti and I tried to talk you into leaving. This isn't bad, as far as hurricanes go."

"Not bad? My God. I wonder if anything is left of the resort."

She wasn't sure she wanted to know. Everything Hope had worked so hard for . . . could just be gone now.

Chapter Ten

THAT AFTERNOON, Hope pressed one hand against the cool glass of her office window as she checked the current state of the storm. The wind had decreased to an angry breeze, and the rain was intermittent. Occasional patches of blue sky peeked through the clouds above.

Hope's stomach was a spiky cluster of nerves as she and Alex bundled into their raincoats and left the house to inspect the damage. They walked up the beach, which was slowly reappearing as the ocean continued to recede.

First, they inspected the four bungalows on the south side of the restaurant. Tree branches, shingles, and driftwood were strewn everywhere, but the shelters themselves were in relatively good shape.

"They seem intact," Alex said. "Some shingles missing, but the plywood over the windows seems to have held. Decks look a little beat up, though. Let's check out the restaurant and lobby."

The heavy-duty doors and shutters had done their job well. The insides of both buildings were undamaged except for water which had swept in under the door frames and left scattered puddles on the tile floors. Hope double-checked the backup generator powering the kitchen's refrigerators and freezers. It automatically came on when the power failed, a regular occurrence on the island.

That's one thing that's gone right, at least.

They continued walking north to survey the other four bungalows. The first three were similar to the others, but the northernmost bungalow, Orchid, had a large tree trunk wedged into its front porch. One end protruded through the covered windows and into the room.

Hope sighed, slumping. "Well, that's going to take some work to remove."

Alex tried again to reassure her and urged her down to the pier, tugging on her hand as he examined the structure.

"Thank God it's still intact," Alex said. The beach end of the pier was submerged in the churning water, as were the stairs leading up to it, so they stood on the sand appraising it. The palapa at the end still stood, though most of the thatch was missing.

Then Hope saw it.

"Oh no! The roof of your apartment is gone!"

"Yeah, I was just looking at that. I don't see it washed up on the beach anywhere. We might have a new artificial reef we can advertise to divers." He gave a crooked smile, trying to make light of it. All four walls of the upper structure stood, but it was as if a giant hand had lifted the roof and taken it elsewhere.

Alex did his best to comfort her, but Hope was an empty husk. Everywhere she turned was ruin. She flopped onto the wet sand, sitting with her arms draped over her knees. "All your things are probably ruined! Oh, honey, this is terrible."

"Come here." Alex pulled her back to her feet and drew her close. "The only thing that truly matters is in my arms right now. What little I have that's valuable is in a watertight box. It's fine, Hope. I've been through worse."

She looked out at the roofless building as rain spit into it. "How are we going to recover from this?"

He cupped her face. "With a lot of hard work. The same way we always do when a storm hits."

"We have insurance that should help defray the costs of this, but—my God. It's just destroyed."

"Storms are a fact of life down here. That is reality. We're a tight-knit group, and we'll get through it together."

She leaned her forehead against his chest, leaning into his strength. "You're pretty good at pep talks, you know that?"

He snorted. "I know some people who might disagree with that, but thank you. You don't have to face it alone—you're surrounded by people who are committed to coming back from this."

"I know. I'm very grateful for everyone." She kissed him, his lips wet from the rain. "Especially you. I just need to have my pity party for a little while longer. Right now, I feel like this entire year has been one obstacle after another."

<hr>

By the next morning, the surf was still pounding the shore, but the ocean had receded enough that the steps to the pier had reemerged. They inspected the stairs, which were sound enough. Clasping hands, they alternated between walking and hopping down the wooden decking, which was loose in places. Several planks were missing altogether. Alex unlocked the door to the compressor/gear storage room, and the smell of wet neoprene immediately enveloped them.

Hope reared back. "Oh man. That smells terrible."

Alex had already entered, walking straight to the large machine dominating half the room. "The gear will dry out." He circled it, inspecting closely. "The good news is the compressor looks ok. That's what I've been the most worried about."

While he inspected the other side of the room, Hope gaped at a large panel of wall missing by the coiled rental regulators, daylight shining through. "Uh, that doesn't look good."

Alex popped his head up from behind the compressor and hurried over. He immediately counted the regulators, his index finger tapping the air. "It's not good. Looks like we're missing four regs."

He sighed, resting his hands on his head. "I can dive under the pier and look for them, but the current and surge could have carried them anywhere and then buried them deep in the sand." He met Hope's eyes. "We're probably going to have to replace at least a couple of these. I'll do my best to find the lost ones, but it's going to be a tall order."

She gulped, scared to ask the question. "How much would it be to replace them?"

"A thousand to twelve hundred bucks a piece."

"Wow. Ok."

"I know." His eyes softened. "Scuba equipment isn't cheap, baby."

"We'll add that to the list of things to be replaced and figure out the priorities later. Let's keep going."

They continued to the dive shop/classroom on the other side of the walkway. Chairs were piled up in one corner, and a high-water stain ran around the perimeter. The three tables were jumbled up along one side.

Finally, they were ready to face Alex's apartment. Amazingly, the locked door was still intact, and Alex entered after unlocking it. Hope followed, squinting at the spitting gray sky above before turning her gaze to the destruction. The apartment was in shambles. His couch was nowhere to be found, and the kitchen cabinets were open, their contents strewn all over the floor.

Alex shuffled around his small home with wide eyes, rubbing his chin over and over. A pile of kindling that must have been the table and chairs lay in the corner. His mattress was waterlogged and torn open, both it and the box frame tilted up on one wall in front of his closet.

At his stunned expression, Hope straightened her back, confident in her decision. Alex would never let her down. She approached him and took both of his cool hands in hers. "Mr. Monroe, this seems like a good time to invite you to move in with me."

He leaned his forehead against hers, a tiny smile rising. "I kind of thought this would be a little more on the romantic side, but I accept, Ms. Collins."

PATTI RETURNED to work the next morning. Hope was sweeping out the restaurant when she walked in, while Alex rearranged the tables and chairs. Patti broke into tears upon seeing both of them safe, and they huddled around each other in the flickering candlelight. Then, in true Patti fashion, she pulled herself together. "Let's get to work, shall we?"

"The roads are clear?" Hope asked.

"Yes. The rest of the island has damage, of course. But it doesn't look like anythin' catastrophic."

"Oh, Patti. I'm still in shock."

Smiling, Patti embraced her, reassuring her the damage wasn't anything they couldn't overcome.

By early afternoon, the power was back on, albeit flickering and intermittent. Clark and Tommy showed up together shortly thereafter, and soon the sounds of chainsaws and hammers could be heard all over the resort. Their first guests were returning in less than a month, so they concentrated on getting the bungalows on the south side of the beach repaired and habitable first.

As Hope left the lobby, Charles was at work, throwing heavy driftwood and debris into a big pile. They nodded to each other as he tossed a huge piece of wood on top. She was pleased he'd returned to work so quickly.

"Looks like you made it through ok," he said, his voice deep and rough.

"We did. Thank you for helping with the clean-up."

"Where else am I gonna be? This place has the best view. Gotta make sure it came through ok." He stared at her, and Hope rushed to the pier, still unsure if she was exaggerating his threat.

The last thing she wanted was to tell Alex and have him get in the landscaper's face. Charles would probably flatten him like a bug. Alex was a tall, strong man, but Charles was a behemoth. Alex must have had some training in fighting when he'd been a SEAL, but that could only carry him so far. And it had been a while now. She shook her head, snapping out of it.

Stop worrying about imaginary problems! You have enough real ones to deal with.

Alex was patching the opening in the gear room wall when Hope entered to inquire about the diving. He shrugged, laying his scraper down. "It'll be lousy for a couple of weeks. It's amazing how much storms stir things up. The water will be cloudy, and the reefs will show some damage. But nature has a way of healing itself." He evaluated the still-calming ocean. "This wasn't a severe enough storm to wreck the reefs. In a month, they'll be ok. In two or three, they'll be back to normal. Or what counts as normal these days."

"I'll check the bookings and contact anyone who's planning on diving to see if they want to reschedule."

After that, Hope returned to check the kitchen and ran into Patti, who was stomping across the tile floor and muttering.

Her stomach plummeted. "What's wrong?"

Patti yelped, raising both hands to her breast. "Oh! I didn't see you there. I was checkin' the northern bungalows. It's terrible how disasters can bring out the worst in people. Two of the televisions are gone."

Hope stopped, her jaw dropping. "Someone stole our TV sets?"

"I'm afraid so. I can't imagine we'll ever get them back."

"No. One more thing to add to the insurance claim."

Patti drew her into a warm embrace. "Don't you fret, child. Before long, we'll be good as new. You just watch."

Hope made her way back to the house and found Tommy on the roof, bending over the tree leaning on the house. He'd brought over a ladder and determined it hadn't broken through, only caused damage to the roof surface. "Let me get a chainsaw, and we'll have it off in a few minutes. Don't you worry."

She smiled and squeezed his arm. Two stolen televisions were a minor annoyance compared to her gratitude. "Thanks for your help, Tommy. You're a lifesaver. I don't know what I'd do without you guys."

Hope turned, taking in the rebuilding that had begun and her deepening relationship with Alex. Finally, a sense of peace wrapped around her like a warm blanket.

They would survive.

Chapter Eleven

OCTOBER . . .

"CLARK, I have told you three times." Hope tried to rein in her exasperation. "The blender is in the box right behind you." She placed her hands on his shoulders, gazing into his wide, nervous eyes. "Just relax. You mix drinks every night—there's nothing new here."

Hope got back on her step ladder to finish hanging the banner above their booth. She and Clark stood in a cavernous, dark ballroom of The Buccaneer Resort. It was one of St. Croix's most storied hotels, and the facility was beautiful, present room notwithstanding. Pale pink with white trim, the facility was softly lit with overhead canister lights. They had done an admirable job of cleaning up and hosting a big event like this less than two weeks following the hurricane, though this room hadn't been their original choice.

Hope tacked up the last corner and stood back to inspect her handiwork. The banner hanging above their booth was dark blue, with *Half Moon Bay Resort* displayed in a large white font next to their logo. Satisfied, she turned her attention back to Clark, who was wringing his hands and taking deep breaths.

He stared at Hope like he was drowning and she was a lifeline. "Thanks. I'm a little nervous, though."

Really? I hadn't noticed.

She held both his hands. "Your drink is incredible. Win or lose, Clark—you deserve to be here. You should be proud of yourself. I sure am. Now, you continue getting ready."

Hope took a deep breath of her own, trying not to wince as she made a mental note to take more ibuprofen at the earliest opportunity. Her cycles had been getting more painful, and she needed to find a new doctor here. One more thing on the to-do list. *Of all the days to get my period . . .*

Her phone buzzed with a text from Gerold stating he was on his way, and she returned her mind to the event. She scanned the ballroom for other bright blue polo shirts. Hope had bought everyone on staff, including herself, new Half Moon Bay Resort polo shirts with each person's name embroidered on the right breast. It was just a coincidence that they were the same shade as Alex's eyes.

She spied Patti standing with a big group of people, probably relatives. Patti was related to practically everyone. Hope approached her. "Well, what do you think?"

Patti looked critically at Clark. "I think he might pass out at any moment."

Hope laughed and pulled her shirt away from her neck. "The fact that it's about a hundred degrees in here isn't helping, I'm sure."

Patti smiled. "I keep expectin' a bear to come in for hibernation. I wonder if there are lights burned out up there?" She peered at the dim lights high overhead.

"Who knows? I think we're set up, so I'm going to get some fresh air before the competition starts."

She went outside to the open-air walkway lined with pink half-circle arches and breathed a long sigh. Even though it was humid and still tonight, it was refreshing compared to the stifling ballroom. Her sandals whispered on the tile floor as Hope walked toward Alex at the end of the hall. He stood alone in a small alcove overlooking the ocean, leaning on a rock wall with his eyes closed.

"Leave it to you to find the ocean."

He opened his eyes and drew her into an embrace. "Hello, gorgeous."

"I wondered where you were. Clark is about to have a nervous breakdown, and I had to get some air for a minute. Though I can see why you'd rather be out here. This is incredible."

Hope leaned forward to peek over the rock wall, which overlooked a vast lawn. It was dark now, but lights were scattered around the grassy expanse and decorated the many trees, bathing the landscape in a soft glow. Waves crashed from the nearby ocean, and the horizon was ablaze in lightning from a distant summer squall.

Alex returned to leaning on his forearms as he watched the storm, his eyes thoughtful. "I'll come back into the hall once the competition starts, but I'd prefer to wait out here until then."

"You don't want to help me talk Clark down off the ledge?"

He threw her a quick smile before sobering. "It's not that. I don't do well in dark, enclosed spaces with lots of strangers, Hope."

She cocked her head at him, then blinked rapidly as she understood. "Oh. I'm sorry—I didn't even think about that. You ok?"

"I'm fine. It's a lot better than it used to be."

Hope leaned on the wall next to him. "How many people here know about your wound?"

"Only you. Well, Steve knew, but he's gone now." Alex continued to stare at the ocean, speaking without looking at her. "You remember the story I told you about the dolphin?"

"Yes, of course." After her diving accident, he'd told her about a personal encounter with a dolphin.

"That happened as I was trying to decide whether to move down here and take this job. I always felt that dolphin was telling me to go back to the ocean. And now here I am." He turned to her. "With you."

Oh, Hope, you are in so deep this time.

She was drawn to him as if he were a magnet. They stood together, holding each other for several minutes while neither said anything.

Hope sighed and said, "I need to go back in, honey. Clark has lost the blender three times already. By now, he's probably forgotten his name." She gave him a quick kiss. "Let me know if you need anything, ok?"

THERE WERE THREE JUDGES, two women and one man, who were all locals. When they reached Clark, his nerves disappeared. Hope wasn't close enough to overhear their conversation, but he visibly relaxed as he made three glasses of Half Moon Hope, smiling and laughing with the judges. A warmth spread across her abdomen as she watched him. The judges gave nothing away as they sampled his drink, making notes on their clipboards before moving on.

It took them another half an hour to sample the remaining entries before they clustered together in one corner to make their final decisions. After fifteen minutes, one handed the master of ceremonies a half-folded piece of paper.

As the results were announced, most of the Half Moon Bay Resort crew grouped in front of Clark's station. Alex had a good view of the proceedings from where he stood near one of the exterior doors.

The crowd's anticipation grew as the master of ceremonies announced the top five placings. A murmuring rose and fell throughout the crowd, punctuated with loud cheers as each placing was announced. They were announcing the top three now, and Clark's name hadn't been mentioned yet. Hope was equally terrified and expectant.

She crossed her fingers.

"In third place, from Castle View Boutique Resort, is Camille Hoskins with Tropical Heatwave."

Across the hall, the crowd in yellow shirts erupted.

"And our Reserve Champion, from Half Moon Bay Resort, is Clark Bailey with Half Moon Hope!" Clark gaped and jumped up and down as their entire crew exploded with a riot of applause. Patti and Hope ran up to be the first to embrace him.

"You did it! Great job, Clark!" Hope didn't hear the first-place announcement and didn't care. Tears rolled down Patti's face. Hope dug a tissue out of her pocket to give her. She looked up as Alex made his way over to them, applauding with a grin. She lifted an eyebrow, and he stopped clapping for a second to flash her an ok signal.

Gerold had elbowed his way in to give Clark a hug. "Congrats, man. You did great."

Alex shook his hand, and Clark stood back with a dazed smile, as if he couldn't believe they were all there.

One judge approached and handed him a tall trophy crowned with a martini glass. "Congratulations, Clark. It was really close. Make sure you enter this contest again. You've got a bright future ahead of you."

Chapter Twelve

THE HIGH MOUNTAINS to the east were bathed in wispy clouds as Hope closed the door to her Jeep. She was finally getting used to driving on the left side of the road—something she hadn't realized they did here before moving to the island. Now that the debris had been cleared from the roadways, she was determined to get back into life and help the local economy a little.

She'd found parking only a block away from her destination, which was lucky for Frederiksted. Walking onto a side street, she sighed as she crossed into the building's shade and passed several colorful shops until she stood in front of Cruzan Running. A bell jingled above her as Hope entered, and the blast of air conditioning sent an icy tendril down her back. The wall to her right was filled floor to ceiling with shoes.

A thirtyish Black woman with long, thin braids came out from behind the counter and said, "How can I help you this afternoon?"

"I'm here to get a new pair of running shoes. I moved here in March and used to run before that. I've missed it, but I definitely need new shoes before I start again."

"Well, you're in the right place. I'm Cindy Pearce. It's nice to meet you." She held her hand out, and Hope introduced herself. The store carried the latest model of her favorite shoe, so Cindy went to see if they had her size in the back.

"So, you live here on the island?" she asked, returning with the shoebox.

"Yes, at Half Moon Bay Resort, just north of here."

"Oh, that's a beautiful resort." She spoke in a lilting Caribbean accent. "Looks like a good place to work."

"Thank you—it is."

"Did you say you live there?"

"Yes, I'm the owner."

Cindy sent her an impressed nod before inspecting the shoes on Hope's feet. "There, now walk around the store a bit and see how they fit."

The shoes were light and bouncy on her feet. "They're perfect. I'll take them."

Cindy rang up the purchase and said, "You know, we have a runnin' club here—you should think about joinin'." She grinned. "We're called the Cruisin' Cruzans. There's a group run every Saturday that leaves from the Frederiksted pier at 9 a.m. You should come. It's very informal. Run whatever pace and distance you like."

"Thanks. I might just do that."

***

It was late afternoon by the time Hope returned home. She entered the cool, inviting interior and looked down at Cruz in front of her, his tail wagging so hard his hindquarters danced. Since the hurricane, the dog had given up the nomadic life, happily sharing the house. He was even warming up to Alex. She smiled and gave him a scratch behind his ears before glancing up at Alex, who was opening a beer bottle in the kitchen.

"You look like a woman who needs a beer."

"No, I'm a woman who needs a kiss."

She was delighted when he came over and fulfilled her request. Having him here to greet her never failed to send a flutter through her. She'd expected a few hiccups after Alex moved in, but they had proved remarkably compatible—or maybe not so remarkable. She had always been a neat, organized person. If anything, Alex exceeded her in this. Hope had never lived with a man before—too afraid to commit. She had no regrets now.

She eyed the bottle in his hand. "A beer sounds ok too."

Alex handed her the open one and retrieved a second for himself. "Shopping trip?"

"Yes. I bought a new pair of running shoes. I used to run a lot in Chicago, and I'd like to take it up again. The woman at the store said they have a group run every Saturday, and I might join them." She set the bag on the kitchen table.

"Good for you. But be careful where you run. Some parts of the island aren't safe, and the roads are narrow and twisty with pretty much no shoulder."

"Oh, I was planning on running at midnight in the most dangerous part of town."

Alex winced. "Sorry."

Hope nodded, acknowledging the apology. She appreciated his protectiveness, but it sometimes came close to coddling, which she didn't appreciate as much.

"I plan to start on one of the treadmills in the fitness center for now. And I like the idea of a group run—that's safer." She crossed to the table and took the box out of the bag. "I'm looking forward to it. I ran a couple of half-marathons in Chicago.

Maybe I can work up to that again." She looked at him. "You want to join me sometime?"

He smiled, but there was something sad about it. "Nah. I used to run, though." Then he laughed. "I used to run *a lot* in SEAL Teams. But I did some races too."

"You ran marathons, didn't you? I don't even need to ask."

"I ran four. I entered several more I had to cancel." Alex crossed the great room to the wall of floor-to-ceiling windows overlooking the ocean.

"That's too bad. How come?"

"My schedule wasn't exactly predicable. I missed several because of deployments."

"Well, I guess that's a good reason."

"It never bothered me too much because I figured there would be plenty of opportunities for races."

She joined him at the window as Cruz made his way over to his bed in the corner, circling three times and laying down with a sigh. Hope nudged Alex with her elbow. "Ok, I need to know. What was your best time?"

He watched the ocean with his arms crossed, his mouth tightening. "My personal record was 2:44."

"Holy shit!" She laughed. "My *half*-marathon PR was 2:05. No more running, though?"

Alex shook his head. "The doctors told me unless I was eager for another hip replacement, my running days were over." He turned and embraced her, his shoulders tense under her fingers. "I'll gladly cheer you on from the sidelines, but I'll stick to swimming."

Hope smiled at him—he despised pity. "Well, you're an incredible swimmer. I imagine you did a fair amount of that in the SEALs too."

"A bit, yes."

He stopped any further conversation with a kiss. Hope

opened her mouth and kissed him deeply, giving him what he needed.

After wrapping her in his arms, Alex held her head against his chest and murmured, "You have no idea how much you help me."

"We're a good team, you know. I never thought I'd trust a man like I do you. I've had to overcome some trauma that scarred me pretty deeply, though more on the inside than outside. Our experiences weren't the same, but I know a little about what you're going through." She met his eyes. "You'll get through this—we'll face it together."

LATER THAT NIGHT, Hope was still awake when Alex moaned in his sleep before jerking awake with a sharp intake of breath. Sighing, he got out of bed, pulling on his boxers and leaving the bedroom. She stared at the closed door, understanding better than most that solitude was sometimes the best thing to chase away a nightmare.

HOPE HAD FINALLY ARRANGED an appointment with her insurance agent to appraise the storm damage, but it still wasn't for two more weeks. She bit back an irritated surge. The man was extremely busy with all the claims on the island right now. And the two of them hadn't exactly hit it off, so she wanted to give him the benefit of the doubt this time.

Alex had been trying to find the lost regulators, and she was reluctant to spend any more out of pocket than she had to. But he'd been scrambling to find enough rental gear for the returning guests, and Hope was close to telling him to replace the lost ones.

But those were problems for another night.

After eating dinner at the resort restaurant, Hope and Alex returned to the house, arranging themselves comfortably on the couch in the great room. Alex was already absorbed in the latest scuba magazine, which detailed the new gear available. He had an insatiable thirst for learning about scuba gear.

It amazed her that this fun-loving, marine life-obsessed man was once an elite Special Forces operator, though she still wasn't sure exactly what that had entailed. Hope was pleased he was opening up about his painful past more readily now. From her own experience, burying things only delayed the day of reckoning. There was no escaping it.

Hope grabbed the remote and flipped through television channels, not really interested in anything. Finally, she settled for a reality show with contestants competing in various adventure sports. The episode was centered around six people having various skydiving adventures. One very excited young man was being interviewed after completing his jump, rocking back and forth in a chair as he used the same term over and over. Hope had no idea what it meant. "I hate it when they don't explain things. What does HALO mean?"

Alex flipped the page, answering without looking at her. "High Altitude, Low Opening." He folded over the magazine and began reading again.

"How on earth do you know that?"

He glanced at her over his magazine with raised brows. "Did you forget the part where I told you I was a SEAL for fifteen years?"

"No, I didn't forget." Her voice started to rise. "What does skydiving have to do with diving and swimming through the water with guns?"

Now he bit his cheek, trying not to laugh. Hope narrowed her eyes at him. "Don't you make fun of me, Alex!"

He sighed and put the magazine on the coffee table before picking up the remote control and turning off the TV. "I would never make fun of you about this." He smiled again. "Not much, anyway. SEAL is an acronym. It stands for SEa, Air, Land. We're trained in all three modes of combat. It's not just diving."

She rubbed a finger over her brow. "Oh. I thought it was mainly water stuff. And, of course, land operations too." She still had the suspicion he was trying not to laugh at her.

"Well, there was a lot of jumping out of airplanes and helicopters and shooting guns too."

"So, it's not named after the animal?"

"No, baby. The military loves acronyms."

"Ok then. You don't mind talking about this?"

He brushed the back of his hand down her face. "No, not with you. It's only that last night . . . Everything before that is ok. I'm very proud of what I did. That's what makes it so hard. SEAL Teams were my whole life."

"I'm proud of you too." She paused, glancing at the dark television. "So, you did that HALO thing they did on the TV show?"

"Not exactly like the TV show." He lifted the corner of his mouth. "Though they seem to be offering that more to civilian skydivers."

She frowned. "Those people were jumping from thirty thousand feet. What was the highest you jumped from?"

"Most were between thirty and forty thousand feet. But some were higher."

"My God, that sounds terrifying."

He grinned at her. "Oh no. It's awesome." He picked up his magazine and opened it again. "It's better when someone isn't shooting at you, though."

Hope sighed, still trying to process these two sides of Alex. "I think this is going to take me some time to sort through."

He darted his gaze back to her. "Take all the time you need. I'm not sure I'll ever sort through what you told me."

That got to her. She took his magazine and set it down, snuggling up against his chest. "I know that was hard for you. I hope you understand you're the exact opposite of Caleb. You protect what you love, not destroy it."

Alex leaned his cheek against her head, but his muscles tightened. "It kills me to think about that bastard hurting you. It's a damn good thing there's a continent and a huge amount of water between him and me. There's nothing I wouldn't do to protect you."

Hope tensed, knowing some men liked to say things like that. But Alex meant every word.

She relaxed her body into him. Hope had spent years desperately looking for safety, but too afraid to get close. And yet she'd found her match in this paradox of a man who'd spent over a decade fighting. She listened to the slow, steady beat of Alex's heart. It was the heart of an honorable man, not a violent one.

Chapter Thirteen

ALEX GRUDGINGLY CONCLUDED he might be beaten. He'd been diving every morning and afternoon when not helping with repairs. Shortly after the storm, he'd thoroughly scoured under the pier, elated when he dug his hands into the sand and came up with the console containing a dive computer. Following the attached hose, he uncovered the entire regulator.

But after many subsequent dives, each more frustrating than the previous, that had been his only success. He'd even gone into Frederiksted to borrow a metal detector from a friend who owned a dive shop, which had proved less helpful than he'd hoped. It had successfully located a multitude of soda cans and beer-bottle tops, but no regulators. He'd performed a succession of grid patterns to be methodical, searching nearly the entire beach area from the pier to the house reef.

The other three were gone, but he didn't want to tell Hope. That was why he'd been inspecting the perfectly fine compressor for half an hour after returning from his dive and only started home when the sun dropped below the horizon.

A glance at his roofless apartment sent a flash through his mind—Hope tearing out into the hurricane after Cruz. A faint smile came to his face. She could be a bit impulsive, but he couldn't fault her courage. Or her loyalty. The bruise on his back had been annoying but hadn't affected him much, and it was a distant memory now, several weeks after the storm.

When he had examined his wrecked apartment, the one positive finding had been his closet. The mattress wedged against it had largely protected his belongings. He'd simply grabbed everything worth salvaging and transferred it all to Hope's house. His house too, now. Alex was plenty secure enough not to be threatened by moving into his girlfriend's home. And the nights had been more than worth it.

Ambling down the beach, his smile fell as he tried to work out the best way to tell her they needed to replace the lost regs.

As he passed the last bungalow, Charles was locking up the toolshed. Alex exchanged a hard look with him, but no words were passed as the landscaper left for the day. The two men hadn't had any more tense encounters, but there was no love lost between them. Charles did his job and was cordial to the guests and other staff, so Alex was resigned to accept him.

Unless he put a toe out of line—then the big man would hear from him in spades.

Alex climbed up the porch steps, and as he opened the slider, the most amazing aroma enveloped him. Hope stood in front of the range stirring a tall stockpot, and his bad mood slipped away at the sight of her. "Oh, that smells incredible. What on earth do you have going on there?"

She turned around with a smile, and his own appeared in response. "You won't believe it! I finally got Gerold to teach me how to make his lobster bisque." She set the spoon down and came over to wrap her arms around his waist. He brushed his lips against hers, then deepened the kiss as emotion flooded through him.

"I swiped a couple chicken breasts from the kitchen, and I

have a wonderful dinner planned for us tonight." Cruz came over and allowed Alex to pat his head.

"Well, if it tastes half as good as it smells, it's better than I deserve. You'll probably want to give Cruz the chicken and me the dog food. I struck out again." He sighed, the failure rankling him. "Maybe I can give it one last shot tomorrow."

"That's what you said last night." She squeezed him tighter. "You said from the start you didn't think you'd be able to find them. Enough's enough. Order new regulators, honey." Her smile grew. "And I think dog food is an upgrade for Cruz. He's perfectly happy with that."

Alex poured two glasses of wine. "I hate making you spend the money on this. Don't want you to start calling me Damn Fishmonger."

Hope laughed, a sound that reminded him of waterfalls. "I don't think you need to worry about that. And actually, our dear Frank has been on his best behavior ever since I had my little chat with him."

"Ok, I'll order two regs. I think we can get by without the other two for now."

"No, order all four. We might as well do it all at once. That's why I have insurance." She stirred the pot again. "I'm running expenses on my credit card for now, but I'm going to have to do battle with my insurance troll soon. Though to be fair, I'm sure he has plenty to deal with right now."

"All right, Boss Lady. I'll call Gordon tomorrow. I need to get his metal detector back to him at some point, anyway."

"You're not going to order them yourself?"

"No, he does a lot of volume, so he can get better prices than me." He took a long drink of wine, his taste buds lighting up with the rich smoothness.

.   .   .

They ate at the table on the back porch, and the dinner was every bit as good as she promised. Hope was an incredible amateur chef and helped Gerold from time to time. Alex was finishing his chicken Cordon bleu when she put half of hers on his plate. "I can't eat this—you take it."

"You sure?"

"Definitely. You have quite the appetite, Mr. Monroe."

"Only for you." He was relieved to hear her tease. During dinner, her upbeat mood had changed to a pensive quietness.

Hope darted a glance at him before resting her chin in her palm as she watched the ocean. "How long will it take to get those regulators in?"

"Probably a week. I'll ask Gordon to put a rush on it. We've got the first group of six divers coming soon, and I'd like to have the new gear by then. They need to rent equipment." He put down his fork. "Ok, I'm done. That was a lot of food."

"Let's sit on the couch." She poured the rest of the wine into their glasses and sat next to him, still quiet as she stared at the horizon.

"I scoured almost the whole area between the pier and the house reef twice, looking for those regs," he said as she nodded, dropping her gaze to the floor. A knot formed in his stomach. "You've been awful quiet. You doing ok?"

"Yes." She hesitated, taking a breath. "But we've been together for a while now, and there's something I'd like to know."

"Ask away."

She met his eyes, serious. "Will you tell me about your wife?"

His stomach lurched. *Why? It's certainly a legitimate question.* "Of course. I wasn't keeping it from you or anything. It was just a really long time ago." He took a sip of wine. "We were high school sweethearts. I enlisted in the Navy right after we graduated, so I'd be leaving home soon. We decided on the spur of the moment. Within a couple of days, we had the marriage license and an appointment at the county courthouse. We didn't even tell our parents until after we were married." He snorted. "They were *not* happy."

"No, I wouldn't think so."

"She went with me to Basic." He looked at Hope. "Wasn't that far from Chicago, actually. There was trouble from the start. She was miserable away from home. I got stationed in San Diego, and she hated it, never feeling like she fit in. And I moved around a lot in the first couple of years. She moved back home after we'd been married for a year, and we got divorced about a year after that. It wasn't her fault—she wasn't cut out to be a military wife. We should have broken up when I enlisted."

Alex sighed. These were more memories he didn't enjoy looking back on. "I took it hard at the time. In retrospect, getting married was a really stupid decision, but I wanted to make it work. It made me pretty wary about relationships while I was active duty, though."

The corner of her mouth turned up as she settled closer. "I guess it's a good thing you're not active duty anymore."

"And I'm not eighteen, either. I'd like to think I've learned a thing or two over the years." He leaned in and pressed his lips to hers, wanting Hope to understand how different she was.

She kissed him back fully before pulling back. "Do you keep in touch at all?"

He shook his head. "I don't even know where she lives. It's ancient history. I don't even think about it anymore." He turned to Hope, relieved she wasn't upset, and a warmth spread through him, rapidly building to something stronger. "I'd much rather think about you."

Alex placed their wine glasses on the coffee table and took her in his arms.

Several days later, Alex sat at his workbench in the stuffy gear room, working on his third BCD of the afternoon. A light gust blew through the open window, and he sighed at the wonderful cooling effect. The first guests arrived the following day, and he was making sure the rental equipment was fully operational after the storm. He put down the inflator hose as his phone rang. The display read Gordon, so he eagerly picked up.

"Hey, Gordon. Tell me you've got good news for me."

"Yep, the computers came in this morning, the last things I was waiting for. October seventh—how's that for record time? Apparently, we're a priority due to the hurricane. I've got all three regs built up, so they're ready to go." He paused. "I'm hoping to join a buddy of mine for a dive under the Frederiksted pier tomorrow. A cruise ship just left, so there might be some valuables down there. Is there any chance you might be able to come down here tonight to pick these up and drop off my metal detector?"

It was 5:45 p.m. "Sure. I can probably be down there within the hour. That ok?"

"Works for me. I've got gear to wrench on 'til you get here."

"Are you ever going to move to a better part of town?"

"Hey, you try paying rent on this island." Gordon laughed. "And those break-ins happened two years ago, you chicken."

"Oh, shut up. I'll be there soon."

Alex retrieved the metal detector, locked the door of the gear room, and grabbed a couple of sandwiches from the kitchen. As he walked through the sliding glass door, Hope sat at the kitchen table with her laptop open. "Hey, our regs are ready to go. Gordon needs me to come down there now and pick them up."

"I should probably go with you. I'll need to submit the

receipt to the insurance company, so the credit-card slip should have my signature."

He set the sandwiches on the table with a frown. "I'm not real happy about you walking around down there after dark. The area is a little sketchy."

Hope grinned at him. "I seem to recall we did a lot more than walk in Frederiksted after dark recently."

He couldn't resist kissing her after that, then turned serious. "That was a different part of town. But I imagine it'll be safe enough early on a Thursday evening, so let's go. I grabbed a couple of sandwiches—we can eat on the way."

"Perfect. I've been cooped up all afternoon, trying to figure out if we should remodel the bungalows now since we're going to have contractors working anyway. The three we need for the guests are habitable, so at least that's ready." She stood up and smacked him in the chest with a sandwich, making him smile. "Come on, I'll drive. It'll be fun."

Chapter Fourteen

HOPE DROVE DOWN THE DARK, narrow street, but the nearest parking was in a lot several blocks from the dive shop. They were soon walking toward the store, and what Alex had meant about this part of town being shabbier became clear. There were few streetlights, and most of those were burned out, giving the area a deserted, ominous feel.

She tried to ignore the sensation of being watched, and her good mood dimmed. The shops were closed, heavy metal grates pulled down over their storefronts. Hope turned to Alex, who walked alertly, scanning his eyes back and forth as he carried the metal detector in one hand. He kept the other hand pressed to the small of her back as they walked.

He's protective, I'll give him that.

They approached a store. Two metal grates were pulled down over the large windows, but the glass door was still unobstructed, and the lights were on inside. *Emerald Isle Scuba* was written in big letters on one window, and there was a red and white dive flag painted on the door.

Alex opened the door and they entered. "Hey, Gordon! Where you at?"

"Comin'!" A middle-aged man with a Georgia accent appeared from the back room, carrying several one-foot square padded regulator bags with a dive flag emblazoned on each. Hope resisted the urge to wince. He wore a loud yellow and green Hawaiian shirt and blue shorts.

Alex handed Gordon the metal detector, which he set behind the counter. He gave Hope a quick smile before turning back to Alex with a smirk. "Oh, so you brought some muscle to protect you after all, huh?" He set the bags on the glass counter that ran across the back of the shop.

"Very funny." Alex unzipped a bag to reveal a coiled regulator. He picked it up and inspected it, clearly satisfied as he put it back and zipped the bag. "Nice job. You even managed not to put the second stage on upside down this time." He grinned as Gordon shot him a dirty look. "And she's not the muscle—she's the boss, so show some respect, ok?"

Hope introduced herself, and they shook hands. "What's the damage?"

Gordon moved to the cash register. "Ok, get ready. That'll be $4,400. And I didn't even charge for building up the regs."

Alex snorted. "I certainly hope not."

Hope's stomach dropped to her ankles at the total. She ran the credit card through the machine with a sigh.

Gordon smiled at her. "If it makes you feel any better, Alex picked out good stuff. High quality, but nothing unnecessary. It'll make a good impression on guests and be able to take a beating."

Hope winked at Alex before turning back to Gordon. "You don't have to tell me that. I have the utmost faith in him."

They finished the transaction, and she tucked the receipt into her wallet as Alex picked up the four bags. Saying their goodbyes, they headed out the door.

It was after 7 p.m., and night had fallen. Two streets away, cars went by in a steady stream of traffic, brightly lit by street-lights. But here, Hope immediately tensed as they walked down the dark street. With its trash-strewn alleys, the area had a spooky vibe to it.

As Hope looked up, a thin alley cat hissed at her from a rooftop, then ran away. There were no other people on the street, and Alex once again walked softly, making nearly no sound. Though capable of looking after herself, she was relieved he was there.

As the breeze blew a lonely piece of newspaper into an alley to their left, a large man stepped out, standing six feet away and facing them. Hope's heart leaped into her throat as she and Alex stopped.

It was Charles.

"Nice night for a walk?" His subtle menace was amplified a thousand-fold tonight. The Caribbean lilt to his voice was the only thing musical about him. She'd already known he was huge, but seeing Alex near him brought home the difference. Charles probably outweighed him by fifty pounds.

"I watched you go into the dive shop and thought it might be worth my while to hang 'round a bit—see what you came out with. I know you've been doin' a lot of work on your fancy, fine resort." Charles dropped his gaze to the square bags Alex carried in his right hand. "Glad I did. Those look like regulator bags. I can get lots of money for what's in those, and I'm always lookin' for a little extra cash."

Charles gave Hope a smile that made her blood run cold. "And I've been watchin' *you* for a while now. You're just the icin' on the cake tonight."

Alex spoke in an even tone. "Don't do anything you'll regret,

Charles. I'm not giving you these regs." Then his voice became iron. "And I'm sure as *hell* not letting you anywhere near Hope."

"Is that a fact?" Charles reached behind him and pulled a pistol out of the back of his pants, pointing it at Alex. "This here says different."

Hope gasped as her heart threatened to explode out of her chest. The pistol was dark and menacing—she had no doubt Charles could use it.

Alex stood up straight, his face hard. "Do I look scared? It's not too late to turn around and walk away, you know. You don't want to do this." He still spoke evenly, but he was like a drawn bow, coiled tension ready to be released.

Charles's face contorted into snide laughter. "Oh, yeah. Big man dive guide. Do I look scared of *you?*" He shook his head, then dropped the comic routine, becoming threatening again. "I'm gonna give you one more chance. Put the bags on the ground and walk away, Diver Boy. You're no match for me and you know it. So, you go your way, and me and this . . . delicious piece will go ours."

Snakes crawled in Hope's gut at his leer.

Alex's voice strengthened. "Look, Charles, I used to hunt people down for a living—people a hell of a lot more dangerous than you. This is a very bad idea. But I don't want to hurt you, so I'm putting the bags down, ok?"

You don't want to hurt him?

Alex bent down and placed the regulators on the ground with his left arm held out, blocking Hope. As he stood up, he took a step closer to her, slightly crouched, weight on the balls of his feet. He was beginning to alarm Hope.

"You followed half the directions, asshole. You forget I'm the one with the gun here?" Charles glared, his voice hard and rough like sharp splinters.

Then he smiled—a grim rictus of menace. "Or maybe you want a demonstration?"

As Charles moved the gun toward Hope, Alex exploded into motion. He moved so fast Hope couldn't believe it. Within a few steps, he grabbed the giant man's right wrist with his left hand, forcing the gun up. Then, lightning-fast, Alex punched him in the face with his right fist three times in rapid succession. Blood exploded as Charles's nose broke.

Roaring, he head-butted Alex in the forehead, making him stagger back.

He lost his grip on the giant man's wrist, then regained his balance.

Two things happened simultaneously. Alex kicked out with his left leg and swept it sideways at Charles's legs, wiping him out at the knees. And as Charles began to fall, he roared again, and the gun discharged. Alex threw a savage elbow under his jaw as Charles's feet were swept aside, and the hulking man's eyes rolled up into his head as he fell unconscious to the sidewalk.

Alex stood balanced on both legs, standing over him with his right fist clenched and watching intently. Hope stood rooted to the spot behind, both hands pressed to her chest as she stared at Alex in horrified fascination.

A dark-red stain on the back of his left shoulder was steadily growing.

Alex whirled around. "Are you ok?"

She gaped at him, her mouth opening and closing—the matching red stain on the front of his shoulder was smaller but also growing.

"Hope! Are you all right?"

She just nodded, taking a couple of jerky steps forward. She tried to speak, and her voice came out in a squeak. "Alex, your shoulder."

Beads of sweat broke out on his face as he nodded and looked down at it. "Yeah, looks like he got me." He turned and kicked the gun away from Charles's hand, who didn't react at all. "Better call 911. I hit him pretty good, but he could come to soon."

He turned back to Hope. "I think I'll sit down now."

With that, Alex slumped abruptly to the ground.

Chapter Fifteen

BREATHING IN GASPS, Hope fumbled her phone out of her purse and dialed as she rushed toward Alex. Her hands shook so badly she could barely touch the three digits. The dispatcher answered right away, and Hope asked for an ambulance and the police.

Alex sat on the sidewalk with both legs outstretched. She knelt next to him. "Stay awake! Help is coming, but don't you dare pass out on me."

No, no, no! He's going to be fine—he has to be!

Sweat poured down his ashen face, but he managed a smile. "I'm still here. Can't let you have all the fun."

The police car and ambulance arrived together, lights and sirens ablaze. Hope had managed to get Alex's shirt pulled over his head and good shoulder, pressing it against the wound. Two police officers approached with guns drawn. One was tall and Black, and the other was short and white. Hope glared at them. "Point your damn guns at him!" She indicated the still-unconscious Charles. "He shot Alex, and he was trying to rob us!"

Alex gestured to Charles's gun with his good arm, his eyes now glassy. "I kicked his gun away. Nobody touched it but him."

Tall Guy, whose name tag read Perkins, quickly moved over to secure the gun, placing it in an evidence bag.

The paramedics approached, and one started working on Alex. He turned to his partner. "Call dispatch and get a second ambulance for that guy." The paramedics quickly got Alex strapped to a stretcher. His hair was drenched with sweat, but he was staying awake.

The paramedic glanced at Hope as they moved toward the ambulance. "Do you have a car so you can follow us to the hospital?"

"Yes, it's on the next block." Everything was in ultra-crisp color, every detail enhanced—the red on Alex's shirt, the flashing lights of the police car, the blue of the uniforms.

"Wait," Alex called from the back of the ambulance, using a commanding tone of voice that made everyone turn to him. "Please walk her to her car. We've had enough excitement tonight."

Short Guy blinked. His nametag read Watson. "Of course."

Then they shut the doors to the back of the ambulance. Hope moved to pick up the regulator bags when Officer Watson stopped her. "I'm sorry, ma'am. You'll have to leave those. They're part of the investigation for now."

"Ok, fine. Let's go." Hope hurried, the man having to trot to keep up with her. With an armed police officer at her side, the street was much less threatening. She quickly made it to her car and thanked the officer. Starting the ignition, she lined up behind the ambulance, following it to the hospital.

Hope's head spun as she drove. She had just discovered knowing Alex had been a SEAL and seeing him in action were two very different things. Hope had massively underestimated him, just as Charles had.

She watched through the rear windows as one paramedic hurried around in the back of the ambulance. But Alex wasn't visible, which only increased her dread. She gripped the wheel with clenched fingers, refusing to succumb to the fear.

She soon reached the hospital, parking in the lot while the ambulance continued to the direct entrance. The emergency-room clerk took her information but wouldn't let her back to see Alex. So she had to wait, a ball of restless, panicky energy perched on the end of a hard plastic chair, and tapping her feet on the tile floor.

A nurse came and got her at about 9 p.m. Alex was in a curtained bay of the emergency room with no other patients nearby. Hope tried to take a deep breath, but the antiseptic smell made her nauseated. She closed her eyes, fighting the swirling emotions. Visions of the night Caleb had beaten her flashed through her head.

Stop it—this isn't about you.

Forcing away the thoughts, she shook out her trembling hands and opened the curtain.

ALEX LAY on the bed with his eyes closed, but he opened them and smiled when he recognized her. He was pale but no longer sweating, and his eyes were alert. Shirtless, he had a large bandage with ice packs applied around his left shoulder. That arm rested in a sling. An adhesive bandage was secured at the top of his forehead, near his hairline.

Heart finally calming, Hope gripped his face tightly in both hands and kissed him, trying not to cry as relief filled her. "You look a lot better than the last time I saw you."

"Feeling better." He searched her face. "You ok, baby?"

"I'm fine." A laugh escaped that sounded slightly unhinged. "I'm not the one who got shot." Then, desperate for something safe to talk about, she said, "Would you believe they made me leave the regulators at the scene? All that and we still don't have them."

He smiled and shook his head. "It's been quite a night."

Around 9:30 p.m., the two police officers were back. Officer Perkins smiled at Alex. "Glad you're doin' ok." He glanced at Hope. "Sorry you had to meet Charles. We recognized him as soon as we saw him lyin' on the ground. That guy is serious trouble."

Hope briefly closed her eyes and ran a hand through her tangled hair. "Actually, we've met. He works as a landscaper at my resort. We were trying to give him a new chance in life."

Perkins shook his head. "No good deed goes unpunished." He pulled out his writing pad. Hope and Alex each gave him their statements.

"This is enough for us to get started. Hopefully Charles will be going away for a long time after this," Watson said. "We'll probably have some follow-up questions in a few more days."

By 11 P.M., the medical staff declared they were done with Alex. "The bullet went clean through and cauterized a lot of the vessels as it passed," the doctor said. "I cleaned up some bleeders and stitched up the entry and exit points. Your vitals have been stable the whole time, and you seem to have the pain tolerance of a horse."

Hope snorted. "More like a mule, I think." She relaxed when Alex smiled.

"It isn't a bad idea to keep you here overnight, just to be safe," the doctor said. "Or you can go home if you feel strong enough. I'll leave it up to you."

Alex clenched his jaw, a sign Hope knew well. "I'm going home. Tonight."

"The police told me they're done here. We'll get your discharge paperwork going and get you out of here."

Soon, Hope was driving her Jeep around to the front of the hospital. Alex swung into the passenger seat, leaning back against the headrest. She was relieved the doctor let him go home—the hospital wasn't a fond place for him. He had refused pain medication but was stable, and his usual good humor had come back as they waited. The ride back to the resort was quiet as he kept his eyes closed.

Hope parked in the garage and tried to help Alex out of the Jeep, but he insisted he was perfectly capable. After unlocking the front door, Hope steered him to the bedroom, flipping back the blankets on his side of the bed. "Here. I want you in bed right now."

"Ok, but you might need to be on top tonight."

"You've just been shot. This is hardly the time for jokes." Hope pulled the covers over the top of him and propped him up on the pillows as she sat on the edge of the bed.

"I can't really think of a better time."

"Your middle name is stubborn, isn't it?"

"No, it's Theodore. I'm pretty sure my parents hated me."

Finally, Hope started laughing.

"There it is! Now I can stop." Alex gave her a small smile in return.

Then she cupped his face in both hands, pressing a gentle kiss to his lips that lengthened into something much deeper. "You scared the hell out of me tonight." Hope darted her eyes all over his face, confirming he was really ok.

"I know. I'm sorry. But I'm all right—really."

The lines in his forehead had deepened. "I'll get you some ibuprofen, since you refused anything stronger."

"Ibuprofen's fine. They gave me narcotics when I was at the hospital in Germany. I stopped before I got to liking them too much. The way they numbed my pain was . . . dangerous. I'll stay away from those things."

Hope nodded. "I'll be right back."

She padded out to the kitchen, filling a glass with water and retrieving the bottle of ibuprofen from the cabinet. It slipped through her fingers and fell with a rattle onto the counter as Hope took a massive gasping sob. Her breath started coming faster and faster, and she slammed her hand down on the cool granite. "Stop it! Don't you dare fall apart now."

Hope stood straight and forced herself to breathe through her nose, slowing each inhale and calming herself. Then she picked up the pill bottle and shook it. It was close to empty, so she made a mental note to buy more since she wouldn't be the only one using it now. Picking up the glass and pill bottle, she marched back to the bedroom.

Alex was sound asleep, his head turned slightly as his chest rose and fell in deep, silent breaths.

Hope set the glass and bottle on his nightstand, sitting in a chair in the corner as she pressed both hands between her knees and concentrated on the pressure to help her keep it together. Fat, silent tears slid down her face, but those were all right. It was the loud, soul-wrenching variety she was trying to avoid.

Alex lay in the bed, his left arm in its sling and the ice packs still in place. The lines in his forehead had smoothed a bit in sleep.

Hope sat in the corner watching him, her love and relief expressing themselves in her silent tears. Trying to understand the mind of a man who had been shot yet joked about it afterward—to put her at ease.

And most of all, trying to come to terms with the fact that the man she loved had run *toward* a loaded gun without hesitation to defend her.

Eventually, the tears extinguished themselves, and Hope

fell into bed. She reached out to stroke Alex's face before pulling back at the last moment, not wanting to wake him. Instead, she whispered, "Sleep well, my love. God knows you've earned it."

Chapter Sixteen

THE PAIN WOKE HIM.

It was a hot, gnawing throb in his left shoulder, coupled with a strong headache. Except that was wrong—his shoulder hadn't been wounded.

Alex broke out in a cold sweat as he opened his eyes, rushing his right hand to his hip. Confused, it took him a moment to understand he was in a large bedroom with the blinds closed across from him, not the hospital room he'd lived in for months in Germany.

And his hip didn't hurt—it was definitely the shoulder.

He wrinkled his brow, trying to make sense of his surroundings and why his hip and abdomen felt fine.

With a flash, his tangled mind came fully awake, and he breathed a relieved sigh.

I'm in St. Croix, not Germany. This is the house I share with Hope.

The previous evening came back in the next flash. His rushing that asshole Charles and knocking him out, but getting shot in the process. Alex's heart was still beating fast, and he rubbed his right hand hard against the scarred hip, forcing himself to believe it was healthy now. This pain was something new.

But Alex was no stranger to pain.

He turned his head to the left, revealing Hope asleep, facing him, and his heart slowed at last. Relief spread over his body like a warm blanket. She was safe—nothing else mattered.

Pain could be mastered.

Alex cracked a small smile as pride rose, spreading through his chest. It had all come back when he'd needed it—he'd acted without hesitation, his actions automatic. And very effective.

Even though the shoulder wound was minor compared to his combat injuries, it was still a gunshot wound—his first! Alex closed his eyes and tried not to laugh. Fifteen years as a SEAL, and his first shot was courtesy of a thug on a dark street. At least Alex had the last laugh—Charles was in jail.

The police had explained that Charles's broken nose had been set in the emergency room, but he'd had no serious injuries otherwise, so they led him to the local lockup to await charges. Officer Perkins had mentioned the phrase *attempted manslaughter*. Charles was in a lot of trouble.

The shoulder throbbed now.

Alex looked at the clock, smiling faintly at the full glass of water and bottle of ibuprofen next to it. It was only 4 a.m., but he was up for good at this point.

Alex tossed back the covers with his right hand and sat up. He was still dressed in the shorts he'd worn to Gordon's dive shop. The hospital had given him some snap-shut smock thing, but he'd ripped it off before getting in bed.

He managed to pick up both the pill bottle and water glass and padded into the bathroom, where he removed the sling and now-dry cooling packs to reveal a mass of gauze wrapped around his shoulder. Looking in the mirror, he spotted a bandage on his forehead too, near the hairline, which must have been from being head-butted.

Alex was supposed to leave the bandage alone for the first two days and always wear the sling, so he put it back on. After entering the closet, he changed into clean shorts and managed to pull a T-shirt over his head and right arm. He returned to the vanity, but now he couldn't open the ibuprofen bottle since one arm was tucked inside his shirt.

"Screw it. Shirtless it is."

Tossing the shirt on the closet floor, he suppressed a frustrated sigh before opening the bottle. He took several tablets before heading for the kitchen and life-giving coffee. Today he needed it.

It was still pitch dark, but a strong impulse pulled him toward the ocean, so he retrieved a zip-up hoodie from the coat closet, tossing it around his shoulders before taking his steaming mug to sit on the porch. Cruz rose from his bed in the corner of the great room to follow Alex, settling at his feet.

The early morning smelled fresh and salty. Alex inhaled deeply, still feeling somewhat in shock. He closed his eyes and listened to the eternal push and pull of the waves. It soothed him, as always.

Just before 5:00 a.m., the slider opened.

"You ok, honey?" Hope asked.

"Good morning. Come join me." He patted the couch on his right, then drew Hope in, taking a long breath of her hair—it always smelled wonderful. "I'm doing fine. Slept like a rock."

She curled her legs beside her, holding her coffee mug in both hands. "I saw the ibuprofen in the bathroom. Did you get some?"

"Yeah. The pain's better now."

Hope sat there with her eyes closed for a long moment before rushing her mug to the coffee table and burying her face in his good shoulder. "What if that bullet had been a few inches lower?"

"It wasn't, so stop thinking about it." He drew her closer and kissed the top of her head, needing the reassurance as much as she did. "I'll be fine. Good as new in a couple of months."

Hope sat up, watching him closely as streaks of tears ran down her cheeks. "You know how much I love you. Please tell me you know that."

Alex wiped her face, his heart twisting at this woman who loved him completely for who he was. He needed her to help him meld the man he used to be with the one he was now. "Yes, I know. Because it's as much as I love you."

By mid-morning, Alex and Hope were walking up the beach toward the resort after discussing their plan. Alex glanced to his left at the pier. *Surface Interval* was out for the morning trip, and they'd already met with Tommy and Robert. "Thank God Robert and April have been filling in more. I'm glad he was working today. I'll get hold of April and ask her to fill in too for a while."

"Alex, I want to put Robert on the payroll. Permanently. It's going to be weeks before you can lead dives again, and he deserves a steady position here."

"He does. He has been a huge help to me—to us."

Alex's old apartment was still roofless, but they'd made quick repairs to the gear room and dive shop, and Hope was blocking availability so they didn't get overbooked. They entered the lobby, and Hope nodded to Martine, releasing the steadying arm she'd held around Alex's waist. "Alex and I have to talk to Patti, and we have an announcement for the rest of the staff. Could you please call everyone and get them here in the lobby?" Martine nodded, lowering her brow as they entered the office and shut the door.

Patti was at her desk, shuffling through an employee schedule—the landscaper's schedule, of all things. She raised her head, her brows climbing at seeing them both.

Alex sat on the corner of her desk as Hope stood behind. "Morning, Patti. You need to know about something, and I want to tell you in private before we fill in the rest of the employees."

Patti straightened in her chair, her gaze fixed on his zipped-closed sweatshirt. His shoulder bulged with several bags of frozen vegetables Hope had wrapped around it.

"What's wrong?"

After trying to figure out how to phrase it, he dove right in. "Hope and I had a little excitement last night. When we picked up the new regulators in town, we ran into Charles." He paused, meeting her eyes. "It wasn't a friendly meeting. He ended up in jail, and I got shot in the shoulder."

"WHAT?" Patti rocketed to her feet and her eyes became glassy, but Hope moved quickly, putting an arm around her and firmly sitting her down. Hope perched on the chair arm, keeping an arm around her shoulders.

"Are you all right?" Patti whispered.

He took her cool hand, squeezing it. "I'll be fine. The bullet went completely through."

Patti stared at him, her eyes bulging as tears streaked down her face. "What happened, Alex?"

He gave her an abbreviated version that glossed over the fight. Patti cried harder, and Hope tightened the arm around her.

Patti raised both shaking hands to her temples and rubbed. "This is all my fault! If I hadn't hired him, it would have never happened."

Alex shifted on the desk. Now was the part he'd been dreading. Of course he didn't blame Patti, but getting her to see that might be a different story.

"If you're to blame, then so am I," Hope said. "I was all for hiring him. Don't beat yourself up."

Alex leaned closer. "You're the heart and soul of this place, Patti. No one could ever blame you for trying to help someone. Least of all me." He gave her hand one final squeeze before standing, dizziness washing over him. "We need to tell the rest of the staff. Martine's getting them together now."

Alex opened the office door to find all the staff on duty that morning milling about the lobby, speaking in hushed voices. They quieted and turned to him as one, every pair of eyes worried. He faced them in front of the check-in desk with Hope at his side, a protective arm around his waist again. Patti crept out of the office to stand next to Martine.

"Sorry if this seems mysterious," Alex said. "But I only want to say this once, so we wanted to talk to everyone working this morning."

Alex repeated what he'd told Patti, once again assuring everyone he was not badly injured. Gerold's eyes traveled up and down his body, and it took several rounds of assurances before the group was convinced.

He scanned the assemblage before him. "I already talked to Robert and Tommy, but needless to say, this is going to affect the dive operation for a while. At least with most of the bungalows being out of commission, we should be able to cover things with only one divemaster."

Patti stared at the bruised and swollen knuckles of his right hand, then lifted her gaze to his. She'd stopped crying, but tracks of tears were still visible on her face. "Are you *sure* you're all right?"

"Yes." With a smile, he crossed the distance and wiped her face. "This wasn't your fault, ok?"

She nodded, but the doubt was clear in her eyes. Alex straightened with a sigh and reached for Hope's hand. "We need to get back to the house. I'll take the boss with me so you guys can get back to work without her looking over your shoulder."

Hands clasped, Alex and Hope walked down the beach so he could begin the process of healing.

Chapter Seventeen

AFTER THE SHOOTING, Hope worked long days as she tried to organize the repairs necessary for the resort. This also allowed her a little distance from the caged lion Alex became as his confined existence began to chafe more. He'd spent the first couple of days getting the dive operation situated. Robert immediately agreed to help however he could, thrilled to be on the payroll, and April was willing to fill in when Robert needed time off. But once that project was handled, Alex's agitation increased.

For Hope, job one had been getting her insurance claim for the hurricane damage approved. She'd expected an epic battle with her local agent, but that had proved not to be the case.

Mr. Janssen, a small, diffident man, had shown up to inspect the property dressed in a brown suit with a bow tie but wearing sensible rubber boots. From the wide-eyed looks and terrified glances he threw over his shoulder as they inspected the storm damage, Hope surmised he was still traumatized from their earlier encounter, when she'd camped out in his office and refused to leave until he approved the claim for their new boat.

Janssen studied the blue sky from the interior of Alex's

former apartment with a fussy scowl and proclaimed, "This won't do at all."

"No," Hope replied. "A roof would be rather beneficial." When she explained her designs for the space, he nodded quickly.

"Yes, it's an excellent location for that. I'll review your policy and process a claim as soon as possible. Because you have resort damage and dive-operation damage, there will most likely be separate payments."

He soon finished and left via the front lobby, throwing one last glance over his shoulder, perhaps verifying Hope wasn't about to bite him on the back of the neck. Instead, she waved a friendly goodbye. Breathing a sigh, she was almost disappointed at how easy it had been.

I guess if I want to face a formidable opponent, I can always go home.

Alex had proved a model patient—for exactly forty-eight hours. Two nights after the shooting, Hope had peeled away the thick gauze wrapping and the pads underneath to reveal his swollen purple and yellow shoulder.

She winced at the sight. "Oh, honey. That looks awful."

Alex shrugged to test his mobility, and then pumped his fist open and closed. "Actually, it feels a lot better without the dressing. Another week and I can get the stitches out. I'll head back to the dive shop tomorrow and see what I can do to keep busy."

Hope snapped her head up. "You can't go back to work three days after getting shot!"

Alex stiffened as he narrowed his eyes, and Hope's stomach sank.

"I'm not planning on leading dives. I just want to keep busy."

"At least take a week. Only one week. Please?"

He held her gaze steadily, and Hope raised her brows in a

beseeching request. Finally, Alex relented with a scowl. "Fine. A week. But fair warning—you wanted this." His eyes softened as he lifted the corner of his mouth. "Don't blame me if I get cranky."

His words were prophetic.

Hope had always thought there was something feline about Alex. He moved with the graceful, confident power of a great cat. Beautiful to look at, but with the promise of lethal ferocity if needed. Of course, now that she knew his background, that made a lot more sense. At this point, he most reminded her of a lion kept in a too-small cage, pacing back and forth while staring intensely at his keeper.

Fortunately, Alex didn't look at Hope like he wanted to attack her. It was more like he was trying to get around her, though he did bark at her from time to time. Not that she blamed him—it was a frustrating situation. And she certainly couldn't forget he was in this situation because he'd been protecting her.

No, a little irritation was perfectly acceptable.

But it was strange. Alex would snap at her before a look of regret would come over his face, followed a few times by something almost like self-loathing. Hope must be imagining that—Alex couldn't possibly hate himself after what he'd done.

A WEEK after she'd removed his bandage, Hope woke and moved to the porch with her coffee. The sky was changing from deep indigo to soft blue, and a pale light heralded dawn. Alex paced back and forth over the wooden planks. Cruz sat in the corner with his ears flattened, not inclined to approach Alex.

Hope took a sip, trying to be positive. "Only a couple of days until your stitches come out."

"About goddamn time."

She stifled a sigh, keeping her own irritation from rising—that wouldn't help. "Then you can get back to some of your normal activities. You won't have to worry about keeping your shoulder dry anymore."

He whipped his head over to her and stopped in his tracks. "I could go back to some of my routine now. I'm not looking to swim for miles. I only want to work on some gear. This is ridiculous." He resumed pacing, his eyes blazing. "I'm not a goddamn invalid. It's my shoulder—and my *left* shoulder at that." He hissed a frustrated sigh through clenched teeth. "I'm going for a walk on the beach."

He whirled around and stomped off the porch.

Hope took a deep breath, turning to Cruz in his corner, his tail tucked. "Isn't he just a peach to be around right now?" He whined in agreement. "Poor man. This is so hard for him." Hope was well aware Alex had woken in the middle of the night a couple of times since the shooting, then gone outside for a while before returning to bed.

He hadn't talked about it, and she was hesitant to bring it up, but it was reasonable to assume Alex's present situation was bringing up bad memories of when he'd almost been killed and the year-long recovery that had followed. The tension in his frame was evident as he stalked up the beach.

He knows you're here for him. He'll talk when he's ready.

Hope stretched her calf, still sore and tight from yesterday's treadmill run. Better to skip the workout this morning and just shower and eat at the house before work.

Hope was buttering some toast when the slider opened behind her. Alex walked toward her, that strange look like deep shame clenched on his face. He pushed her plate away and gathered her in, enfolding her in his right arm as he kissed the top of her head. Hope melted into him as always, basking in his warm strength.

"Please forgive me," he whispered against her head.

Hope pulled back. "For what?"

"I've got no right to snap at you. I'm so sorry. I really hate myself right now."

"It's ok. You're allowed to be a little irritable right now."

He shook his head and pulled her close again. "Your words kept repeating in my head. Over and over—the whole time I walked."

"What words?"

He swallowed audibly, glancing at the floor as his arms dropped to his sides. "That he was always sorry. That you made excuses for him."

Hope's blood turned to ice at what he said. She held his face with both hands, willing him to listen. "Don't you *dare* compare yourself to Caleb." Watching the haunted look in his eyes, she understood now where the self-loathing was coming from. "You could *not* be more different. What you just said proves it."

"I'd never do that to you."

"I know that."

"Do you? Deep down? Hope, I've had to be a very violent man in the past. I've shot people—killed them. I never enjoyed it, but I don't regret it, either."

"I know who you are. I'm ok, Alex." She softened into his embrace again.

"You wouldn't be human if you weren't a little grouchy right now," she continued. "And maybe it is time for you to go back to work a little—be productive."

"I think that's a very good idea."

She arched a brow at him. "If I agree to let you go back to work, will you promise not to compare yourself to my asshole ex-boyfriend anymore?"

"Deal."

"Then you have my blessing. Please take it easy, ok?"

His shoulders fell, his relief obvious. "I won't overdo it, but I can't just sit around here anymore. There's plenty I can do, and it will help me get my strength back, anyway."

Hope tilted her head, a slow smile coming to her face. "Well, I'm all for you getting your strength back. There are some definite benefits to that."

So SHE'D SET Alex free, and his strain eased immediately.

Soon, contractors appeared at the resort. A roof rose over his apartment, now destined for a new life, and thorough repairs were made to both the dive shop and the gear storage/air compressor room. They were still limiting bookings, making do with modest repairs while Hope decided on the major enhancements she wanted to make with the insurance money.

Life at Half Moon Bay Resort was returning to normal.

Chapter Eighteen

NOVEMBER . . .

Warmth radiated through her, and it wasn't from the gentle sun. It was happiness. Hope sat on the side bench of *Surface Interval* in front of her tank while Alex gave the dive briefing. He stood on the stern platform, his wetsuit fully zipped as water beaded off his head and face.

The long wooden dock loomed behind him, colorful fish darting around the wooden pilings supporting the massive jetty. The tourist agency had decorated the end of the pier with an enormous cornucopia. Thanksgiving was less than two weeks away.

Alex had recently begun leading dives again, allowing Robert some much-deserved days off. Today, they had a group of three couples, plus Hope. Alex was animated, his happiness bursting through at being back in the water. As he held his arms out from his sides, describing the size of a coral head, his left arm was lower than the right—but getting stronger every day.

"This long structure next to us is the Frederiksted pier,"

Alex said. "We have perfect conditions today with no wind to create surface surge or chop. While you're diving, look closely at the wooden pilings—they are *covered* in life."

He walked around the group with a fish book, pointing out the life they were likely to see. Hope was amazed at his knowledge of marine life. Occasionally she'd give him a description of a fish she'd seen, trying to stump him. She never had.

She clutched her mask, drumming her heels on the fiberglass deck. Alex had mentioned this dive multiple times, but she'd never done it. The group was soon in the water, descending through the clear, warm ocean. Hope studied the wide-spaced wooden pilings in front of her. Schools of fish flitted about everywhere—she hardly knew where to look. Alex had explained the site was a favorite artificial reef, and as long as a big cruise ship wasn't in port, it was a popular dive.

Looking into the deeper water, Hope spotted half a dozen long silver fish, four to five feet long and built for speed with torpedo-shaped bodies. *Definitely the tarpon he told us about.* The fish hung motionless in the water, content to watch the divers, who gave them a respectful distance.

Hope swam over to a vertical dark-brown wooden beam, inspecting it closely. A thick carpet of purple covered an area, precious eggs guarded by a black-striped sergeant major. The fish flitted its tail back and forth to cool them and keep them at an optimal temperature.

Around the other side of the wooden beam, half a dozen crabs scurried up and down the piling, their claws pinching on any available food. Hope shook her head. Alex was right—it was a complete world here, each piling housing its own ecosystem.

She relaxed and floated in the water, enjoying the sense of weightlessness, and turned her gaze once again to the large tarpon hanging near the slope leading to deeper water. Hope's gaze sharpened at movement behind them as an enormous black-and-white shape swooped over the coral on the distant slope.

She'd never seen one before but recognized it immediately, whirling to get Alex's attention. He was some distance away, showing some minuscule creature with his metal pointer. Hope's fins churned the water as she sped toward him, shaking his arm with both hands. When he turned to her, she yanked him around toward the slope, jabbing her finger at the creature. Alex widened his eyes in recognition and gave her a double ok for sighting it.

He banged his tank with the pointer and beckoned with both hands for the group to follow, motioning everyone to stay as low as possible near the surface of the coral. They swam toward the slope, skirting the tarpon, and Alex arranged the group to his liking. Everyone settled deeper than the creature and just above the coral surface, holding on to a dead section if necessary. Alex was next to Hope and grasped her free hand, squeezing it as the manta glided straight toward them.

The huge ray was twelve feet across, black on its flat top and white with black patterns and spots underneath. It passed inches from Hope's head as the rush of water in its wake raised her from her perch. The manta performed a graceful barrel roll and came in for another pass, hovering nearly motionless above a large coral head as a multitude of tiny cleaner fish rose to clean the massive ray.

It swept forward again with a flap of its expansive wings, gliding once again over Hope's and Alex's heads as the cleaner fish returned to their home. The manta passed so close her hair waved in the current as it swept overhead, effortless grace in action.

Alex squeezed her hand again, and Hope turned as he signaled for her to stay low, then he backed away to check on the others. The manta made another pass at a different angle, a stubby tail trailing behind it. This time, it slowly glided over the heads of one of the couples in the group. Alex was between them, writing on his dive slate and explaining the manta's behavior.

After more than ten minutes, the manta was apparently clean enough, and with elegant sweeps of its powerful wings, disappeared into the depths. A sad pang twisted in Hope's gut as she watched it go. Alex signaled the dive was over, and the group began to ascend.

Before long, they were back on board and slowly motoring to the next dive site. As the divers helped themselves to cold drinks, Alex passed around containers of fresh fruit and cookies to enthusiastic cheers. It was a happy group on the boat today.

"Mantas are rare. We got really lucky today," Alex said, his blue eyes crinkling.

Hope was pleased he wore his wetsuit stripped down to the waist as usual, not self-conscious about his wound. It was a livid red circle on the front and back of his shoulder, and he didn't have the full range of motion yet. But all six guest divers were tourists from the mainland who knew nothing of the shooting.

Recently, a couple of locals had been on board and remarked about it, but Alex had told them he was doing much better and changed the subject. Several articles in the local newspaper had followed the shooting, so it was common knowledge amongst those who lived there.

But he and Hope were a long way from being finished with the ordeal.

Alex changed over to fresh tanks for their second dive then stood on the stern platform, where Hope joined him. "That was an incredible dive," she said.

"Wasn't it? I never get tired of it. I always find something new on that one. And the manta was a bonus."

"Is there anything you don't know about the life down there?" she asked with a teasing smile.

"Plenty. New species are being discovered all the time." His smile faded. "But there's a lot disappearing now too."

Hope had realized early on that Alex was a highly intelligent man, but his knowledge of marine life amazed her. "Well, today has been pretty fantastic."

His smile was back. "Especially with you here."

AFTER RETURNING TO THE RESORT, Hope stepped out from under the palapa and regarded the resort pier, leaving Alex and Tommy to finish removing equipment from the dive boat. "Tommy!" she said with a laugh. "Turn that music off. This is supposed to be a tranquil, relaxing place, you know."

He groaned, but the reggae was soon replaced by the breeze whispering through the new thatch of the palapa next to her. Hope closed her eyes, inhaling the fresh, nutty scent.

The sun was directly overhead now, and its warmth soaked into the wood under her flip-flops. She stopped for a moment to admire the effects of some extremely hard work, pride rising in her chest. The resort showed definite signs of recovery now, and the pier was good as new.

The project manager for the remodel crew had inspected both the compressor/gear storage room and the dive shop, declaring the compressor room only needed minor repairs. But the drywall in the dive shop had been completely replaced, and she and Alex had painted both rooms themselves. The damaged and missing boards of the pier had been replaced by the closest color match she could find.

Hope tightened her ponytail as she stopped at the bottom of the stairs next to the dive shop, looking up at the resort's biggest project. At the top of the stairs, there was now a fifteen-foot square deck. A covered roof was being constructed to attach it to the building. With a satisfied sigh, Hope climbed to the top and opened the door. The scent of fresh paint met her as soon as she walked in, and she proceeded a few steps, leaving the door open to let out the stuffy heat. The construction crew had left for the day, their supplies stacked in the corner.

To her left, a counter had just been installed, and along the wall behind it were upper and lower cabinets. A sink bisected the counter. In front of her was a large expanse of bare room—there was little hint of its previous incarnation. Hope stepped forward and closed her eyes, taking a deep breath as she inhaled the new scent of the room's possibilities.

She squeaked when a pair of arms slid around her waist, laughter coming from behind her. "Alex, I will *never* get used to that."

He nuzzled her neck. "Sorry. When your life depends on being quiet, I guess it just becomes second nature. To be honest, I never really noticed it until you got here."

She turned around and stood on her tiptoes to kiss him. "Well, I'm highly in favor of anything that keeps you alive. Even if it scares me half to death every time you sneak up on me. Though, at this point, I suspect you're doing it on purpose."

"I'll never tell." He moved to run a hand over the countertop as he glanced around. "This is turning out well. Not sure I like the idea of you getting all fancy with my old apartment, though. I can't come crawling back up here if people are using it to get manicures and massages and stuff. Now what am I supposed to do if you kick me out?"

"Not a chance." Hope crossed to him, sliding her arms around his waist. "Not every girl gets to snuggle up with a former Navy SEAL, you know. I kind of like having you in my bed to keep me warm and safe at night."

His smile faded. "I'll always keep you safe. Never doubt that."

She leaned into his chest. "I don't."

If she'd ever had any doubts about that, they were long gone. Hope held him close for a few moments before pulling back to walk further into the room, a smile spreading on her face. "It's nice to have a roof back on this again. You know, we made a good painting team."

"Yeah, once you finally admitted wielding a paintbrush wasn't going to kill me. There's nothing wrong with my right arm, you know."

Hope shook her head and raised an eyebrow at him. "You really were a horrible convalescent, you know that?"

"Yeah, I know. But you promised you forgave me." He winked at her, leaning against the wall.

"I did." She continued into what had once been Alex's bedroom. "This is going to be the massage room. I'm having the deck built up and covered to make an outdoor massage area too." Just outside the room was the full bath the contractors had remodeled and brought up to date. "I'm sure the guests will appreciate having a closer bathroom to the dive boat ."

"Yeah, as long as I remember to lock the door when I shower after a dive."

Hope smiled and slid up to him again. "Oh? And would you lock the door on everyone?" She kissed his neck and smelled the ocean salt. Opening her mouth and tasting him, she smiled as his breath caught and he tightened his hold.

"You always get full shower privileges." Then, with a deep sigh, Alex pulled back and squeezed her shoulders. "I only came up here to say thanks for coming on the dive. Now you've got me all distracted."

Hope laughed. "Sorry, but you have quite the effect on me."

"Never apologize for that."

Hope sobered and wrapped him in a tight embrace. "I'm so glad you're healthy again—to have you back doing what you love."

"Thanks, baby. It's good to be back." He straightened. "Besides, it was pretty minor as far as gunshots go. Only a little flesh wound—not even worth bragging about." She let him deflect the situation with humor.

Then his smile faded, and a look of bare need came over him. Hope responded and their mouths came together, wet and insistent. They hadn't deprived themselves since the shooting— Alex was quick to point out *that* part of him worked just fine. But his wound had necessitated a rearrangement of things, and he'd only recently been able to put weight on that shoulder again. He very much wanted things back to normal in all ways.

Reluctantly, she broke off their kiss. "Tommy's probably wondering what happened to you."

"That's because you keep distracting me. But you're right—I need to get back to work. I'll see you later."

After he left, Hope ran a hand over the newly installed counter, which would be the check-in area of the new facility. She had wanted to offer spa services for a while. But the cost had been a major factor, and the resort didn't have any unused buildings capable of housing even a small facility. The hurricane and Alex moving in with her provided the perfect opportunity. Even at small resorts, guests expected spa and massage services, and she was happy to be close to providing that.

"Even hurricanes can have a silver lining."

Chapter Nineteen

HOPE STOOD in the resort lobby, rifling through the bundle of mail. As she headed toward the office, her breath caught when she spied the large tan envelope. *Here at last!* She'd begun to despair of it never coming. Hope set the rest of the mail down on her desk before whirling toward Patti, who manned the front desk just outside. "Do you have a second to help me with something?"

Patti turned to her with a smile. "Of course. What do you need?"

Hope held up the envelope with a broad smile. "I've got a surprise for Clark. Let's head to the bar."

"Well now, this sounds mysterious. Count me in."

They exited the lobby and made their way around the restaurant to the pool bar, where light calypso music played. It was one o'clock, so most of the guests were still at the restaurant eating lunch, but a few were in the pool, ordering drinks from Clark at the swim-up bar.

He nodded to Patti. "Afternoon, Auntie."

"How's it going today, Clark?" Hope asked, hiding the envelope behind her back.

Clark beamed, his silver tooth shining. "Better than I deserve, as always."

"Oh, you deserve it, Clark. I have a little surprise for you."

"Oh?"

With a flourish, Hope produced the oversized envelope and tore the tab off one end to open it. "I've asked Patti to give me a hand with this." Hope removed the folded black plastic from the envelope and gave one end to Patti, who tried to figure out what it was. "This is for you, Clark."

Hope walked away from Patti across the sand floor, stringing out a banner so it hung between them. Two feet tall by ten feet long, it read in bright blue print, *Half Moon Bay Resort, Home of St. Croix's Reserve Champion Mixologist Clark Bailey!* "Do you like it? I thought we could hang it up above the bar, facing the tables."

Patti peered at it. "Hope, that's wonderful! What a great idea."

Clark blinked rapidly. "Thank you, Hope. This means so much to me."

Hope turned her gaze to the bare expanse of wood above the bar as she tapped her fingers on the banner. "I wonder if I should get Tommy. We probably need more than push pins to attach this, or the wind will destroy it. He'll know what to do." She folded the banner and set it on the bar. "Hang on. I'll be right back."

As she started toward the palapa, laughter emanated from the compressor room. Seeing Alex and Tommy leaning against the compressor, Hope called out, "Tommy! Do you have a minute? I need you."

"Sure thing," he called back.

Alex looked at her. "Hey, what about me?"

Hope chewed on her cheek, appraising Alex's tall form. "Yeah, you might come in handy too. Come on, guys. Let's go."

She turned and walked back down the pier, the two men obediently following. As Hope neared the steps, she looked back at Alex. Sure enough, his eyes had been glued to her butt. Meeting her gaze, he smiled and shrugged, realizing he'd been caught looking, then offered his elbow as they descended the stairs.

At the bar, she and Patti once again strung the sign between them. "I want to hang this above the bar, and I thought you would have a good idea of how to attach it so it's windproof, Tommy."

"Oh, yeah. Let me go to the toolshed. We'll get this up in no time." Tommy headed off to get his supplies.

Alex smiled at Hope. "When did you get this?"

"Just now. I ordered it almost two months ago—it took forever."

After returning, Tommy and Alex spread the banner out between them. As Alex reached up with his left arm to hold it in place, Patti's face tightened as she hesitantly stepped forward. Hope placed a hand on her arm and shook her head, saying quietly, "He's fine."

She dropped her gaze to the ground. "I know, but I can't help myself."

Patti was still coming to terms with the shooting. It didn't matter that Alex repeatedly told her he didn't hold her responsible. Patti had plenty of blame for herself.

Charles had a large contingent of family on Antigua, where he had spent a portion of his life, and the judge declared him a flight risk. That and his prior convictions caused him to deny bail, so their former landscaper was now a resident of the local jail until his trial.

The two police officers had followed up with Alex and Hope, solidifying the case against Charles. Hope had recently received a phone call from the prosecuting attorney informing them Charles's attorney had recently been granted a delay from the trial's original date of late January. It was now slated for mid-March.

After Alex returned to work part-time, Patti had driven him to distraction with her fussy mothering. And now that he was back full time, his patience wore thin.

Fifteen minutes later, Tommy and Alex had the banner firmly attached above the bar. Clark wiped his eyes as they stood back to admire it.

"You deserve this, Clark," Hope said. "We're very lucky to have you. We're getting more locals at the bar now, and that's because of you. Things are really looking up around here."

As ALEX and Tommy left the bar, Hope walked beside them. On impulse, she turned to the two men. "You guys want to see the new bungalow?"

They both nodded, and the group continued walking on the soft white sand before finally stopping in front of the Orchid bungalow. Each of the eight bungalows was named after a tropical flower or tree found on the island. The tree through its front windows had long since been removed, though the resulting damage made Orchid the obvious choice for her test subject.

Hope marveled at the rich, multi-hued wooden structure before her. Once the design was finished, the others would be remodeled one at a time to lessen the effects of construction on the guests—another reason she'd started with this one, which was the furthest from the restaurant and pool on the northern side.

Tommy turned to her. "I'm goin' to check the new breaker panel. I'll meet you two inside." He continued toward the back of the structure as Hope and Alex gaped at the new bungalow.

Even before the hurricane, each exterior had been weathered and worn, the wood slightly peeling. She'd had the exterior hardwood of Orchid sanded down and stained with a premium product the contractor had recommended. The result was spectacular. The stain highlighted the many shades of brown, red, gray, and tan natural to the tropical hardwood. Worth every penny.

Alex propped his hands on his hips and gave a low whistle. "This is *nice*, baby."

They climbed the steps on the side of the porch to stand inside the covered area, now open and expansive. He looked around him. "You got rid of the bug screens."

Hope turned to him with a smile. "I did. They detracted from the view—it's much more open now. And we don't have an insect problem, so they were unnecessary." She took in the darker, glossy stained floors, which contrasted the lighter walls.

Hope opened the main door, also richly stained wood, and entered the sizeable room. The wood tone of the floor was rich and inviting, and the interior walls were painted a modern white. It smelled of a fresh start.

The furniture had recently been delivered. Though kept clean, the old furniture had been worn and stained, and the contrast now was dramatic. Two queen beds took up half the room, facing a large window showcasing the full ocean view. This bungalow and one on the south side were set up with two beds, while the other six contained a single king-size bed. The new linens for the bed were modern white striped, and a blue runner lay across the foot of the bed.

Alex crossed to a bed and bounced his hands on it a few times before turning to her with a smug grin. "New mattresses? Should we try them out?"

"Yes, they are new, and we already have. All the bungalow mattresses are the same as the one on our bed. Settle down."

Alex gave a disappointed mew before proceeding to the living area.

Tommy entered the bungalow, wiping his face with a handkerchief. "The new panel looks good. I'm glad you updated all the wirin'."

"I updated everything, except the wood structure itself."

Across the room, a sleeper sofa and a loveseat sat at a ninety-degree angle to each other with a coffee table in front. Gone were the worn and stained floral rattan furniture. The new fabric was a soft green, and two blue-and-white striped accent chairs faced the loveseat. Tommy sat down, bouncing a few times on the couch.

"Don't break it, Tommy. Boss Lady spent some serious change here. She'll take the repairs out of your paycheck, you know." Alex opened the closet doors, peeking at the expansive interior.

Hope moved to the bathroom. With satisfaction welling, she ran a hand over the double white quartz-topped vanity. It was cool and silky to the touch. The most extensive part of the refresh stood before her—an oversized walk-in shower with walls tiled in modern white rectangles with small blue glass tile accents scattered throughout. The shower floor was flattened river rock.

Alex appeared behind her and placed both hands on her shoulders, squeezing. "It looks totally different in here. I'm no expert on design, but I think it's great."

"Ditto," Tommy added.

The new bungalow was modern and ocean tranquil. She was thrilled with it.

Returning to the main room, Tommy inspected the bare white walls. "You leavin' the walls blank?"

"No, but I haven't decided what to do with them yet. I have an idea, but I want to think on it a bit more."

He nodded, moving back to the porch. She and Alex followed as Hope locked the bungalow behind her. The two men headed back to the pier while Hope rested against the railing and stared at the palm trees waving in the breeze. As Alex walked away, a smile slowly crept across her face. The trial loomed on the horizon, but he was on the mend, and so was their happy little resort.

Chapter Twenty

ALEX OPENED HIS EYES. He generally went from sound asleep to wide awake in an instant, and today was no different. The clock informed him it was 5:30 a.m.. He nearly always woke before Hope, which afforded him the luxury of watching her sleep sometimes. It was still dark, but enough light filtered in to reveal she was sleeping on her back with her head turned away. Just her jawline was visible on her face, and her chestnut hair fanned out on the pillow. With a sigh, he rolled over and got out of bed. If he stayed any longer, he would start thinking about other things, and the poor woman deserved some sleep.

Especially after last night.

Alex smiled sheepishly, glad to be fully on the mend. He was slightly embarrassed by his apparently endless appetite for her, but Hope was enthusiastic about the situation, so that was comforting.

Walking out to the kitchen, Alex took two mugs out of the cabinet, setting Hope's on the counter while he put his under the dispenser of the coffee machine. Hot coffee in hand, he moved to the windows, where a soft light now appeared. Cruz let out a long, whining yawn and got up from his bed. Alex let him out, then stood watching the dawn break and at peace as he stared at the ocean.

Thirty minutes later, he was starting his second cup when Hope began moving about in the bedroom, and he got busy with her coffee. When she appeared, Alex held out her mug. "Good morning."

She took a sip and smiled, sliding up to him as he automatically wrapped his arms around her. "Morning, love. Thanks for the coffee."

They moved to the porch couch. The sky was now more blue than black. "Looks like a nice day. You want to swim with me this morning?"

"Yes, that sounds like fun. I'm glad you're back at it."

He drained his coffee. "Let me stretch my shoulder while you finish."

At the doorway of the master bathroom, he raised his left arm above his head and pressed his shoulder into the frame. The pain was mostly gone now, though some stiffness remained, and his range of motion improved every day. As he walked by the mirror, he glimpsed the circular red scar.

That would take longer to fade.

Later, Alex sat in the elevated wheelhouse of *Surface Interval*, a copy of the dive-staff schedule open on his lap. The bubbles of Robert's group were some distance off, so there was still plenty of time. Returning his attention to the folder in front of him, he raised his bare feet to rest against the console in front of him.

He was arranging the regular schedule so both he and Tommy could get one day off each week. Robert would fill in for him leading the dives, and Alex would fill in for Tommy as boat captain, as he was now.

Alex had started slowly but found plenty to keep himself occupied while he healed as he serviced all the resort scuba gear. Despite Patti trying to coddle him. He was eternally grateful to be in love with a woman who understood him so well—that he needed to stay busy.

He snorted.

She was probably just trying to keep you away.

Being wounded had brought back some bad memories, though he didn't regret his actions for a second. And working on the scuba equipment had served another important purpose, providing a productive outlet for his emotions instead of burying them as he used to.

He looked up again, and the group's bubbles were much nearer to the boat. *Enough thinking—time for action.* He closed the folder with its schedule and tucked it under his arm, then descended before sliding the folder into his dry bag. Once again fully focused on his job, he walked to the stern to lower the ladders.

Soon enough, Robert was handing him a pair of orange fins. *These would be Warren's.* Alex hurried to put them in Warren's spot on the boat, returning as the man climbed the ladder to get back on. Taking a firm hold on the regulator's first stage at the top of the tank, Alex helped steer the man back to his spot, steadying him to make walking while wearing heavy scuba equipment easier on the bobbing boat. Warren turned around to sit down, trying to slide his tank into the vertical tank holder, but he was off a little.

"A little more to your left, keep going—there," Alex said, and there was a loud *whoosh* as the tank slid home. He couldn't help a small smirk as he let go of the brand-new regulator Warren used. The police had finally released them, and all four were getting regular use.

"Thanks, Alex." Warren, who had been a guest at Half

Moon Bay several times, removed his mask and placed it in his box below the bench, water dripping from his salt-and-pepper hair. "Captain Alex, huh?" he asked with a laugh. "I didn't know you could drive the boat."

Alex raised his eyebrows. "Oh, yeah. I've had my learner's permit for a week now. I've only crashed twice." He grinned and went to help the next diver. He had to admit it was a lot of fun changing things up between leading dives and driving the boat. He'd had his captain's license for years but had hardly ever driven until recently.

Robert made his way on board with his fins tucked underneath his arm and slid into the tank holder closest to the stern, water beading on his shaved head. He'd been born on St. Croix, and Alex had known him for years. "Well, you didn't get lost today, so that's already an improvement."

"Hey, that only happened a few times. Good dive?"

Robert nodded as several divers started talking at once, describing what they'd seen. The high point was seeing two spotted moray eels out swimming along the reef.

Warren turned to Alex. "Looks like the reefs are coming back from the hurricane, but you can still see the damage."

"Yeah, it will take some time to heal."

"You've been here a while. How's the overall health of the ocean here?"

He hesitated, choosing his words. "Like most reefs, there is a decrease in the corals and the amount of fish. But we're working here at a local level to mitigate that as much as possible. And I might start some projects at the resort too."

"Good way to keep guests coming back. You know more about those critters down there than any other dive guide I've ever been around. You should give lectures or something," Warren said, then laughed.

Alex smiled. "I might just do that sometime. Sounds like you guys had a successful morning. Let's head back for lunch."

He climbed up to the wheelhouse as Robert unmoored the boat, and soon they were on their way back. Thoughts and ideas swirled in Alex's head as the wind blew through his hair. There was nothing like getting shot to make a man think about life. He'd always loved the ocean—maybe it was time to step up and use the knowledge he'd gained.

HE AND ROBERT were nearly done rinsing the gear when Alex told him to take off for the day.

"You sure, man? I don't mind finishin' if you want to have lunch with Hope."

"Nah. Our schedules almost never work out for lunch. Go ahead—I got this."

He entered the dive shop and woke the computer to check the upcoming dive schedule, shaking his head with a smile at how much busier they were becoming. Hope had all the bungalows available except the one being remodeled, and the days of only needing one dive guide were getting rarer. They were getting regular bookings from locals and tourists from nearby facilities that didn't have dive operations.

The door opened and Alex glanced up, stifling a sigh as Patti entered. Even her steps were tentative. Normally Patti went around the resort like it was her stomping grounds, but she'd become much more cautious around him since the shooting. She needed time to forgive herself, and checking up on him was her main way of going about it.

"Everythin' go ok on the boat this mornin'?"

He kept his voice soft and teasing. "Yes, Patti. I've had my captain's license for years, you know. I can drive the boat without crashing it."

"I know. I just worry about you."

"Please stop blaming yourself. Some people can't be saved."

"He *shot* you! Of course it was my fault. It was my idea to hire him."

Alex leaned forward, pointing at her to reinforce his words. "Listen to me. It was sheer coincidence we were all down there at the same time. If someone else had come out of that dive shop, Charles would have robbed them instead."

And they might not have known how to fight.

He came around the counter and embraced Patti. "I'm fine. So is Hope. None of us could've known he was going to cause that kind of trouble."

She pulled back, inspecting her fingernails. "I know. I just don't understand how he could have done it."

"That's on him. You did everything you could to help the guy." Privately, Alex knew exactly why he'd done it. Charles had made it clear from the start he thought Alex was an easy mark, and no doubt he was used to intimidating everyone in his path. When Charles spotted them downtown, he simply took advantage of the situation.

Not quite the easy mark you thought I was, huh, Charles?

A great swell of pride rose inside as Alex ushered Patti back out, reassured once again. And maybe a tiny bit of his old swagger was back now.

Chapter Twenty-One

HOPE AND CINDY sat at Tropical Bean, a trendy outdoor coffee café, after their Saturday morning run. It faced a brick side street and resounded with the pleasant chatter of a popular restaurant. Pumpkins and turkeys decorated the tables and displays, the big day only a week away. Hope had been running regularly with the group, and Cindy had been very welcoming. In addition to working at the running store, she oversaw the Saturday group runs. She and Hope had visited the café for a post-run treat for several weeks now and had developed a friendship.

"How far did you run this mornin'?" Cindy asked her.

"Five miles!" Hope sipped her iced coffee, proud of herself. "I'm thinking about signing up for a 10K at some point. I'd like a goal to shoot for, though I'm not in your league."

Cindy waved her off with a laugh. "Runnin' is one of the few things I have a talent for. We have lots of events here on the island. I'm sure you'll find something that works for you. In fact, we've got a charity event next month—a Christmas-themed race. There are several distances, and it raises money for the local humane society. If you ran five miles today, you should be able to finish the 10K no problem."

Hope laughed. "Easy for you to say—it's still over six miles. But that might just work. Are you from St. Croix?"

"My family is from St. Thomas, but I moved here after high school. I like the slower pace here, though you'd never know that when a cruise ship is in port. I've started school again—takin' classes at the community college. I'm studyin' to become a physical therapy assistant."

"Oh, you'll be great at that! You've got the perfect personality for it. I'm not nearly patient enough."

Cindy shooed away a nearby pigeon eyeing their table. "Anyone special in your life?"

Hope's face broke out in a wide smile.

I really am too old to act like a love-sick teenager every time I think about him.

"Yes, I'm in a relationship. I met him soon after I arrived, and we've been together since the summer."

"Maybe the two of you can do something with my boyfriend and me some time. I've been with Marcus for a year now."

"I'd love to! I'll talk to Alex about it. It would be good for us to make some new friends." She laughed as the pigeon took to the air and landed on Cindy's chair arm. Her lip curled in disgust as she snapped her napkin at it. "Ok, I think maybe it's time to go. See you next week."

WHEN HOPE GOT BACK to the resort, she headed straight for the kitchen. A high-end road bike was locked in a rack, and Hope smiled at Gerold's persistence. An avid cyclist, he rode to and from work every day—rain or shine. He also spent most of his days off riding, which she would have preferred not to know.

She didn't like the idea of her star chef riding on the narrow, dangerous roads.

As she entered the kitchen, he was chopping a bell pepper with lightning-quick strokes. "Gerold, I talked to Alex, and he's fine helping me on Thanksgiving Day. If you want to get the meal started for the guests, I'd be happy to finish it for you so you can get home. Charlotte is already planning to work so she and I can handle the service, and I'm not afraid to recruit Alex if necessary."

Gerold finished slicing and wiped his hands on his hand towel. "You sure? I don't want to desert you on an important holiday."

"I'm sure. I'd like as many people off as possible. You deserve it. The resort only has six guests booked on Thanksgiving Day, so Charlotte and I can easily handle it."

With the holiday dinner settled, she mingled with guests for a bit in the restaurant before sitting down to eat. She was perusing Gerold's winter menu when her phone rang.

"Hi, Hope, it's John Strickland. I trust you're doing well?"

She bristled at the reporter's chummy tone. He'd written an article describing the boat sinking ordeal, and a few more had followed after the shooting. "I'm well but rather busy, Mr. Strickland. How can I help you?"

"I wanted to ask about any new thoughts you might have regarding Charles. I'm sure that must have been a terrible ordeal, and you can't be happy about the trial delay. Would you like to comment?"

The tablecloth bunched in Hope's fist. "No, I would not. It would be inappropriate considering it's an open case."

"Well, let's talk about Alex. Your dive guide seems like a pretty interesting guy."

Hope's water glass began tipping back and forth, so she unclenched her hand and it steadied. Alex had gained some unwanted notoriety, but she'd be damned if she added to it. "What about him? He's a wonderful guide."

Strickland laughed. "I'm sure he is. Maybe I'll come out there and dive with him. We could have a beer afterward."

Over my dead body.

"Mr. Strickland, I'm afraid I need to go. I really have nothing to say on the matter." Hope hung up and took a deep breath. Strickland had always been polite, but she didn't like his persistence. Determined to shake off the unsettling conversation but mindful of what she had already accomplished that morning, Hope ordered an iced tea.

Clark brought it over with a frown. "Iced tea? Really? You need to try my latest."

"I just finished running, Clark! I haven't had anything since except coffee, and I'm about to bounce off the walls. If I drink any alcohol, you'll have to pick me up off the floor."

"Ah—that's no excuse!"

"Is it better than Half Moon Hope?"

He winced. "Well, maybe not. That was a good one. I'm still workin' on it."

"Clark . . . you've set my expectations very high. Let me know when it's ready—when I'm not fresh off a run!"

Alex was in the resort pool, teaching a scuba refresher course. Charlotte brought her fish sandwich, and Hope ate with gusto. She took a sip of iced tea as Alex finished up with his students, exuding an unconscious charisma that made him all the more alluring.

Heat crept up Hope's neck, and she closed her eyes, remembering the previous night. She looked back up, and Alex was staring right at her with a sexy, private smile.

Are you reading my mind right now?

His smile got bigger, causing the same response in her. His students had removed their tanks and left them next to the pool. Alex did the same and came over, tossing a towel over his seat to keep it dry. "I'd love to know what you were thinking about."

"The same thing you were, I'd bet." Hope used the throaty voice he loved.

"We'll have to compare notes later, then."

They did their best to maintain a professional demeanor anytime either of them was working, but from the smiles they received from guests and staff alike, she wasn't sure how effective they were.

Alex snagged a tortilla chip off her plate as Hope slapped his hand. "How was your run this morning?"

"Good. I'm firmly in the middle of the pack—right where I want to be. I'm getting to be good friends with Cindy. We had coffee again afterward. She's seeing someone too, and we talked about the four of us getting together sometime. That sound ok to you?"

He stole another chip, eluding her slap this time, and Hope pushed the plate toward him with a sigh. He scowled at her. "I'm not gonna eat your sandwich. I only want some chips. And yes, just let me know what you two ladies work out, and I'll show up."

"Excellent. And there's more here than I can eat. I insist. I don't want my dive guide wasting away."

Alex darted his eyes to hers, a definite gleam in them. "Better make sure you keep me well fed, Boss Lady. I'm expending a lot more calories these days, you know."

"Eat up, then."

He took another chip and sat back in his chair. "Nope. Not eating your lunch after you did a long run."

Hope gave up. "Charlotte! Tell Gerold we need another fish sandwich. Alex is being stubborn again."

"Nothin' new there. Second order comin' right out."

Hope faced Alex again with a smug smile. "See? Problem solved."

HOPE SWAM AT A STEADY PACE, watching a starfish on the sandy bottom as her body sliced through the water. She had joined Alex on his morning swims as a way of providing an inducement.

Where is he?

Hope took another breath to her left, expecting to see Alex at any moment. Three strokes later she repeated this to the right, but still no sign of him.

As his shoulder healed, Alex started to work more on his stamina and speed in the water. Hope would dive into the water first, and he would wait before swimming to catch her. As he got stronger, her lead at the beginning increased. Hope blew a snort of bubbles out of her nose, remembering their early days when Alex had been holding back on their swims. Now she was getting an idea of how good a swimmer he really was.

They'd begun early, and dawn had just broken with a pink sky to the east. This was definitely the largest head start he'd given her so far, and she smiled, pleased he was healing so well. She continued looking for him on each side but kept her same steady pace in the water and was far south of the resort now.

Hope caught a movement below her.

As she looked toward her feet, Alex gained on her, swimming underwater but facing up. He was a couple of feet beneath her, using smooth dolphin kicks to propel himself. He wore swim goggles today and glided forward underneath her with his arms outstretched and clasped above his head. The position caused every muscle in his chest and abdomen to be defined in sharp relief, and an electric current ran through her. She couldn't look away.

Her heart rate skyrocketed as his body slowly rose toward her. He pulled his arms down to cup her head and pressed the length of their bodies together as his lips met hers. They paused their forward movement as they shared a long, liquid kiss. Desire rippled through her as she draped her arms around him, his skin slick in the water.

He brushed his tongue over hers. Hope moaned in response—but she needed to breathe *now*. She pulled him upright and broke their kiss to take a fast, deep breath, almost a gasp, before jerking him back to her mouth, kissing him hard as she wrapped her legs around him. He smiled against her lips.

"Oh my God, you turned me on just now," she breathed into his ear.

"In case you haven't noticed, you did the same to me." He ground against her—she could feel it all right.

With her lips locked to his, she ripped her goggles off and wrapped them around her wrist before adding his as well. Alex's hands were underneath her, holding her to him as his legs continued to tread water and keep them afloat. He moved both hands closer to the center of her, stroking as he kissed her. He slipped one hand beneath her bikini bottoms, and her body convulsed as she attacked his mouth.

With two quick tugs, Alex untied the sides of her bikini bottoms, handing them to her. "Here. You might want this back later."

Then he moved his hand to fumble with his board shorts. He shifted her position a little, and in one sharp movement, he was inside her. Hope moaned against his mouth. She took a quick glance toward the distant pier, but they were alone as they started moving together.

"You're going to have to do most of the work here," he

mouthed against her ear. "I need to keep our heads above water."

"Oh, shut up and kiss me."

He did. Thoroughly.

As they continued, she tipped back to look at Alex's face. The sun rose over the mountains to the east, casting his features in a golden sheen. His eyes were half open, intent on her as his breathing increased with the force of her movements. Then he darted his head forward, crushing her mouth to his again.

Her breathing was as ragged as his as she stroked her hands across his submerged back, wanting to feel every inch of skin. She buried her head in his neck, tasting the salt on his skin before she clamped her lips together, not wanting to wake up the whole island, and gasping through her nose as she tightened her hold. Her climax rolled through her, wave after wave.

Soon after, he moaned, and his body jerked in her arms. Hope lifted her head back to see him with his head tipped back, eyes closed and mouth open—every line in his face smoothed out. He relaxed, staying in that position and taking deep breaths as his legs continued to tread beneath them.

She smiled and nuzzled his ear. "Did they teach you that in SEAL training?"

A deep laugh burst out of him, echoing off the water. "No, they most certainly did not."

Hope toweled off under the palapa and replaced her black fishnet cover-up. She unwrapped Alex's goggles from her wrist and held them out. "Do you want these back?"

He had just finished towel-drying his hair and grinned at her. "You keep them. I'd rather keep the memory."

She wrapped both hands around his head and pulled him down. His mouth was hot and salty, and Hope wanted to eat him alive. She walked him backward against the wall of the dive shop, giving them some privacy as she ran her hands over his chest. Finally, she broke away. "Why did you wear goggles today?"

He moved to her ear and tugged the lobe in his teeth. "I wanted to make sure I saw you this morning."

Delighted laughter bubbled through. "You planned that?"

"Not exactly—let's say it was a spur-of-the-moment decision. Besides, it was your fault. You can't expect me to behave myself when you wear that cover-up." He moved to her mouth again.

They had been kissing a while when a voice said, "Aren't you two sick of each other yet?" She broke away as Tommy walked by them, shaking his head and laughing.

"Oops, caught in the act." Hope shot Alex a sideways glance and caught his answering grin as Tommy continued toward the boat.

Alex sobered, his gaze sharpening as he drew an index finger over her tattoo. "I love the colors in this. The turquoise in the cocoon and butterfly."

Hope shook her head, amazed at the difference in her life. "That's a fairly new change, actually. It used to be green. I got the colors changed right before I moved down here. I thought the light blue was better for a tropical location. And it even matches your eyes."

A corner of Alex's mouth twitched. "Mixing your old life with your new one. Like a certain other activity coming up. You excited?"

"Yes, I am! I've been working hard on my running. Now I'll find out if it's going to pay off," she added with a laugh. "But we've both got a full day ahead of us. We better get going. Ready for breakfast?"

"Got what you wanted, so now you're back to bossing me around. Let's go, baby."

152

Chapter Twenty-Two

DECEMBER . . .

A FESTIVE EXPECTANCY filled the warm morning air as the excited crowd milled around. Downtown Frederiksted was festooned with holiday lights and fully decorated palm trees. Hope was running a 10K in the annual Santa Dash. They encouraged Christmas-themed costumes, and her answer was a tank top with a large print of Rudolph's head. His nose was a red light that blinked on and off.

Alex winced at her. "At least I can pick out who you are."

"I think it's cute. Be nice."

"And you think I have bad taste in clothes."

Hope checked her watch. Again. It was now 8:50 a.m., and she craned her head around as she looked for Cindy and Marcus. The starting area was more crowded than she had expected, but she couldn't be missing them. They were also running the 10K, and Hope was excited for the four of them to finally meet.

Someone walked by in a full reindeer costume, and Alex's head followed. "That guy is gonna get *hot*."

Hope laughed, leaning on him as she stretched her hip. "It is so odd to be running a December race in a tank top and shorts. I can't get over it." She looked around one more time, then breathed a frustrated sigh. "Well, I'd better get to the start line. Maybe we'll find them after the race." She stood on her toes to kiss Alex. "Don't expect any world records from me. I'm happy just to finish this."

"Your time doesn't matter. Have fun and don't step in any reindeer poop."

Hope made her way to the start line and seeded herself in the middle of the pack, her nerves jangling. The starting gun went off, and she began at a measured pace, bumping elbows with other runners in the pack. She didn't have a set goal but was hoping to stay under a ten-and-a-half-minute pace. Shortly after starting, she checked her watch, and she was running slightly over a ten-minute mile pace.

This works—settle in here.

The first part of the course ran along the oceanfront, and her nerves settled as the sunlight sparkled on the turquoise water. Hope couldn't help but compare it to the last race she had run in downtown Chicago. It had been in the middle of summer and also hot and humid. She grinned. *The scenery is sure better now.*

Then a familiar voice called out, "Hi, Hope!" as Cindy and a dark-haired man sped past her, laughing. She shouted over her shoulder, "We were late. Good job. Keep it up!"

Hope waved and kept on. Cindy was a much stronger runner than she was, and the man was keeping up. Now Hope really wanted to meet up with them at the finish. This had to be Marcus.

At the halfway point, she ran along a series of rolling hills east of Frederiksted. It was a steady up and down—a difficult part of the race mentally. She looked at her GPS and found she was just under her goal pace. Looking to her left, she grinned at a tan cow in a pasture, idly watching her as it chewed grass.

She started feeling the heat about mile five and dumped a cup of water over her head as she passed through an aid station. The course turned back toward Frederiksted. *Almost there. Keep going. One foot in front of the other . . .*

As she neared town, the crowd started picking up again, and the cheering urged her on. Checking her GPS one last time, she was at a 10:20 pace.

At the six-mile mark, Hope turned onto Strand Street, the main thoroughfare of Frederiksted, which had been shut down for the race. Energized by the crowd and with only a short distance left, she picked up her pace.

She turned a corner, and the finish line was just ahead.

"Great job, Hope! Go get it, baby!"

Alex stood to her right, applauding as he cheered her on. Grinning, she increased her pace and crossed the finish line, raising her arms in triumph.

Hope continued walking and fished a cold bottle of water out of a barrel, taking a long drink, very proud of herself. The race ended in a clean, grassy park, and the finished runners walked around to cool down.

Cindy stood nearby, and Hope approached with a smile, excited to finally meet her man. "Great job, guys!"

They exchanged high fives as Hope caught her breath, and Cindy introduced Marcus. He looked around thirty, his dark hair and trimmed beard contrasting his pale skin, and was nearly Cindy's height of five feet, seven inches. Both were a little taller than Hope. "You guys were late, huh?"

Marcus sent a sideways glance at Cindy. "Yeah, someone

had a last-minute porta-potty stop." He rolled his eyes as Hope laughed.

Cindy looked at Hope, opening her mouth to speak, then widened her eyes as her gaze drifted up and to Hope's right. Hope turned around as Alex approached with a smile lighting up his face. Their eyes met, and her own smile grew in return as he drew her into an embrace. "Ugh! I'm all sweaty, and I probably smell."

His mouth was next to her ear. "You're sexy as hell to me right now."

Hope laughed, smacking his chest as she turned to make introductions. Cindy's warm brown eyes sparkled as she shook Alex's hand. Marcus craned his neck as he looked up at him, his mouth tight as they shook hands.

Alex slid an arm around Hope's shoulder and smiled at all three. "Congratulations, everyone. Great way to spend a Saturday morning."

"But not for you?" Marcus asked.

"Nah, running's not my thing. I'm a great cheerleader, though."

Marcus grinned, even as his eyes cooled. "Hey, don't sell yourself short. They have a one-mile Reindeer Kiddo Dash. You could do that."

Alex's arm tensed around Hope's shoulders as he narrowed his eyes slightly. "Is that right? Well, maybe I have a goal for next year."

"There's a picnic table open. Let's go sit down." Cindy steered Marcus over as Hope and Alex followed. Hope shot a quick look at him, but Alex kept his eyes straight ahead.

They settled down, and Marcus turned to Hope. "So, Cindy tells me you own Half Moon Bay Resort?" Hope nodded. "That's impressive. Good for you."

"Thanks. It's the best thing that has ever happened to me." She pressed her leg against Alex's. "What do you do, Marcus?"

"I'm an IT consultant. I own my own company and work from home, so I'm able to set my own hours. The business is really taking off now—it's pretty successful. Before long, I'll be hiring employees." He laughed before turning to Alex. "What about you, man? What do you do?"

"I'm just the resort dive guide."

Marcus flicked his eyes to Hope, then back to Alex as he grinned, his eyes even colder. "Oh. Looks like things have worked out pretty well for you."

Alex's leg bounced next to hers, the rhythm getting faster and faster. "Well, we can't all be IT consultants." His face was bland, his mask fully in place.

Uh-oh, it's starting to smell like testosterone around here.

"Hey, don't worry about it. Cindy and I both dive—maybe we can join you guys sometime. I've logged plenty of dives. I know my way around underwater."

"Would you be able to fit another two divers on your boat?" Cindy asked.

Hope stretched her back, easing the stiffening muscles. "Sure. We have two guys who lead dives, Alex and Robert, so we can add extra people no problem. That's a great idea—the two of you can buddy up with me."

Marcus had been looking at the horizon and drumming his fingers on the table. "Hope, your resort had the boat sinking and rescue, right?" Hope nodded as he shifted his gaze to her. "Oh! And that shooting—I read something about that in the paper. Wow. I can't wait to talk to that guy. What's the name of the other divemaster again?"

Hope sat there, blinking.

Cindy, what are you doing with this tool?

Chapter Twenty-Three

"HIS NAME IS ROBERT, and he's a class act," Alex said softly. "I'm lucky to work with him."

Hope watched him, her irritation growing. His tail practically twitched as he evaluated his prey. She took a breath to speak when Alex squeezed her knee.

Ok, fine. Play your stupid game.

"Excellent—I can't wait," Marcus said. "Cindy can work out the details with you, Hope. So, you own the resort, right?"

Again, Hope nodded. *Didn't you hear me the first time?*

"Do you have a business degree or MBA? I just finished my bachelor's in information science, and I'm almost done with project management. I've thought about going after an MBA next."

"Well, I've got a business degree, but I can't say I've needed it much. I depend more on street smarts and people skills."

Which you are sorely lacking.

"What about you, Alex?"

"Told ya. I just lead dives and wrench on scuba gear."

"That's a pretty important job," Cindy said, shooting Marcus a pleading look.

He kissed her before turning back to Alex. "Some friends and I play paintball on the weekends—we're looking for more people. You want to join us sometime? I can show you the ropes."

Alex's brows flew halfway up his forehead. "Paintball? Like with paint guns?"

"Yeah. They aren't loud or anything—I can teach you."

"I don't know, sounds kinda dangerous."

"Well, I can protect you if you need it." Marcus laughed. "I'm a good shot. You could learn a lot from me."

"Nah, I'll pass. Guns scare me."

Hope was grinding her teeth now.

"Ok, suit yourself." Losing interest, Marcus turned to Cindy. "Let's go, babe. I need a shower. Worked up a real sweat."

The couple walked away with their hands clasped as Hope shook her head. "Well, he's certainly horrible. What in the world is Cindy doing with him?" She turned to Alex, her voice tight. "And what the hell is up with you? Why did you let him think Robert did all that and not you?"

Alex snorted and crossed his arms. "I don't need my ego boosted by some two-bit pissant with a Napoleon complex. Diving with him should be a real treat."

"You didn't exactly make much of an effort yourself," Hope snapped as Alex sat there watching a runner dressed as a Christmas tree walk by. "I really thought Cindy would have better taste. He certainly has a high opinion of himself. As if a college degree makes him a better person."

Alex whipped his head around. "What's that supposed to mean?"

"It means he's an insufferable ass, and whether someone has a degree has no bearing on what kind of person they are."

A red flush rose up his cheeks. "So I'm just a dumb sailor? A grunt who couldn't possibly be smart enough to go to college?"

White-hot fury sliced through Hope's gut. "Don't put words in my mouth! Don't you *dare* take your anger at him out on me. What's wrong with you? God, Alex—you enlisted right after high school. That doesn't leave a convenient four-year gap for college, now does it?"

He grimaced and rubbed a hand over his face. "I'm sorry. You're right. You're the last person I should be snapping at. Come on, let's walk for a bit." He held his hand out to help her stiff body up from the table, and they walked toward the waterfront. Hope dropped his hand and put some distance between them, still upset.

They reached the brick promenade that followed the oceanfront along town. "I got assigned to SEAL Team Four when I was almost twenty. It wasn't too much later that I discovered I liked giving orders better than taking them." Hope snorted, which brought a small smile to his face. "My commanding officer thought I might be good in more of a leadership position, so he had me start working toward OCS—that's Officer Candidate School."

She nodded, moving a little closer to him as they reached the long town pier and started walking down the center of it. A cruise ship was on the horizon, heading into port.

"You need a four-year degree to be an officer. I was stationed in Virginia Beach, and there were several military colleges around, so I enrolled in one and took classes around my training and deployment schedule. I worked hard and got my bachelor's, and finished OCS. I liked my classes so much I went back and ended up with a master's degree in marine biology."

"I guess that explains why I've never been able to stump you in identifying anything on a dive."

"I'm sorry. I know I can be awful sometimes."

"You have your prickly moments. Marine biology is definitely a good fit for you." Hope took his hand, and he squeezed back tightly.

"Later, I started taking classes in military history. I was working toward a degree when I got injured, and that was the end of that."

He turned Hope toward the side of the pier and put his hands on her shoulders as people continued to move around them. "One of the things I love most about you is that you always stand up to me. You never take any of my crap. Please, don't ever change that."

"You might feel differently if I haul off and kick you in the shins or something."

He shrugged a shoulder. "I'm sure I'd deserve it."

"You're expressly forbidden from killing Marcus when we dive with them, you know."

The remaining tension melted out of him as warm laughter broke through. "Well, that takes all the fun out of it."

Hope stretched her back, wincing, and his flush returned. "I haven't even congratulated you for running a great race."

She shifted her gaze to his. "Oh, I thought you forgot all about the fact I ran a six-mile race this morning—maybe you were still drowning in testosterone."

He held his lower leg out. "Go ahead. You'll feel better."

"Don't tempt me." Then she snorted. "'Guns scare me.' Are you going to scream like a little girl if a bee flies on the boat while we're all together?"

"That's a great idea! I could accidentally knock Marcus overboard in the process." He pressed a soft kiss against her lips before resting his forehead against hers. "I'm sorry."

"Thank you for telling me all that. I know it's not easy for you to talk about."

"It's getting better. The more I talk about it, the easier it gets. With you, anyway."

She pulled back and tilted her head. "You have a natural authority about you. I've wondered before if you might have been an officer. What was your rank?"

"My highest rank was commander—that's the Navy equivalent of a major."

The cruise ship was nearing the pier and gave a loud blast of its horn. Hope jumped, yelping, while Alex didn't react at all.

"Nothing frightens you, does it?"

"I've been watching it approach since we started up the boardwalk." He stroked her cheek. "And to answer your question, yes. The thought of something happening to you scares the hell out of me."

LATER THAT EVENING, Hope swept into their bathroom to get undressed and found Alex standing in front of the vanity. He leaned on both palms, staring at two small boxes open on the granite surface. She had a momentary flashback to when she'd seen him in a similar position the morning after the boat sinking. There was no pain evident in his posture tonight, but the tension was equal. His shoulders and jaw were rigid as he studied the boxes.

They were like large jewelry boxes hinged open on one end. Each contained a medal attached to a ribbon and nestled in the velvet interior. Narrowing her vision on the medal closest to her, she tried to cover her sharp inhale.

Hope didn't know much about military medals, but even she recognized the Purple Heart. She didn't know the significance of the other one. It was a gold-plated cross, all four arms equal in length and hanging from a blue and white ribbon.

At her gasp, Alex vaulted upright, his mask coming over his face.

"What are you doing, honey?" Hope asked.

"Checking out a couple of my medals." His voice was flat and clipped. "I haven't even looked at my Purple Heart since I got it."

She encircled his waist, leaning into him. "Well, you certainly earned that. What's the other one?"

He exhaled through his nose and snapped both boxes shut. "It's just another medal. I got it as a consolation prize for the same op I got the Purple Heart on. The last one." He grabbed both boxes and turned away, replacing them in a box in the corner of the closet, before taking Hope in his arms. "I'm sorry. I can't talk about this yet."

"I'm sorry I intruded."

He cupped her face in his hands. "You never intrude. Never. I left the door open, didn't I?" He gave her a tight smile before drawing her close again.

"I'm not surprised the conversation we had this afternoon brought back some memories for you." She paused, then looked up into his blue eyes. "I know you have nightmares sometimes, and you go onto the porch to regroup. I used to have them too, so I understand sometimes you need to be alone to get it back together. Mine stopped a long time ago. But I was alone during that time, and there were times when I would have given anything to have someone there to hold me and tell me everything was going to be all right. If you ever want that, I'm here for you."

He pulled her tightly to him, murmuring against her hair, "Thank you."

At the same time, they reached for each other, their kiss tender to start. But soon it deepened, becoming feverish. Hope's blood warmed by the second, knowing what Alex needed. She swiped her tongue over his as he grabbed her hair with both hands, pulling her harder against him.

His mouth moved to her ear. "So, how stiff and sore are you after your race?"

"I'm not that sore." She pressed her hips against him with a seductive smile. "And I think you're stiff enough for both of us."

Chapter Twenty-Four

THE SUN GLITTERED across the azure water as Hope ran in the middle of the pack during her usual group run. This morning she and Cindy ran together, which was a nice, easy pace for Cindy. "You know, if you and Marcus want to dive with us, you might want to do it soon. We're about to get really busy at Christmas and New Year's."

"I've been thinkin' about that. I'd love to dive again—it has been several years." Cindy took a drink from her water bottle. "But Marcus and I are both so busy right now with the holidays. Let's plan for next month. We don't have any dive equipment, though—is that ok?"

"Oh yeah. We have everything available. Alex can set you up."

Cindy frowned while shooting a quick glance Hope's way. "By the way, I thought Marcus was kind of rude to Alex when we met at the race, though he didn't seem too bothered by it." Hope kept her face neutral. "I'm sorry. Marcus can be kind of a jerk sometimes."

"Well, maybe they'll get along better when we're diving."

Or at least Marcus will have his damn mouth plugged with a regulator some of the time.

AFTER LUNCH, Hope stepped into the lobby, admiring the transformation. The large room was now a winter wonderland. A tall Christmas tree with wrapped boxes underneath decorated one corner. Next to it stood a false fireplace with stockings hanging from it. The stockings were embroidered with the names Hope, Alex, Patti, Tommy, Gerold, Clark, and Martine.

There had been hardly any Christmas decorations in storage at the resort. Patti explained that in previous years, Steve and Susan had hung a length of garland from the front desk with a couple of sad strings of Christmas lights, which was *not* acceptable to Hope. A trip to Christiansted had solved the problem, and she'd come back with a plethora of yuletide cheer. If guests chose to spend part of their holidays at Half Moon Bay, Hope wanted them to feel at home and like the resort appreciated them.

Her smile fell as she moved her gaze to the front desk and took in Martine's sickly, wan expression.

"Martine, you look a little tired. I can take over if you want to cut out a little early."

"I'm ok. I hate to just leave." She swallowed hard and turned slightly green.

Hope squeezed her arm. "Go on. I'm caught up and can man the desk for a while."

Martine didn't protest further and was soon on her way home. As she shuffled away, Hope made a mental note to put out feelers for an additional front-desk associate soon—she had a good idea what Martine's issue was.

Hope woke the frontdesk computer and opened her email,

scrolling through the list. A new email pinged, and she inhaled sharply at the sender's name.

Two bungalows had now been renovated, but they still had bare walls while Hope decided what to adorn them with. After considerable thought, she'd arrived at her answer and sought out Alex at the dive shop. "I've never seen you with an underwater camera. Do you take pictures?"

He shook his head. "That's never really interested me. Why, you thinking of taking it up?"

"No. I'd like to buy some quality underwater photos of St. Croix, and above-water landscapes of the island would be great too. I want to blow them up and hang them on the walls of the remodeled bungalows."

Alex smiled, straightening from the glass counter. "That's a great idea. And you're in luck. One of the best photographers on the island just happens to work for you—Robert."

So Robert had become her next quarry, and she'd discussed the project with him a week ago. "I'd like to buy at least fifty images from you, maybe more."

He beamed at her and started pacing in the dive shop. "You don't need to pay me. I'll put my watermark on them. It'll be free publicity for me—I'd love to have my images hangin' on the walls here." She could practically see his wheels spinning. "I'll pick out my best images. I'll try to get you a hundred and send you a link where you can access them."

Now, here they were.

Hope clicked on the link and opened the images, her jaw dropping lower with each one. She cycled through beautiful sunlit coral gardens, stunning images of fish and other sea creatures, as well as photos of St. Croix itself—Frederiksted, Christiansted, the mountains, beaches, and many sunsets.

"These are perfect!"

Robert must have sent several hundred pictures, each more

brilliant than the last. She'd have her work cut out for her deciding which ones to use.

LATER THAT WEEK, she and Alex snuggled up on their back porch as the waves washed against the nighttime beach, a crescent moon peeking above the western horizon.

"I'm glad you're doing better," he said. "I hate seeing you in pain."

She smiled and kissed him. "Thanks, honey. I'm getting back to normal now." She'd had a rough couple of days, but once again ibuprofen had come to her rescue.

"I saw you at the front desk again. You've been doing that a lot lately."

"Patti and I both think Martine is probably pregnant, but she hasn't said anything. And, of course, we can't ask her. I hope she starts feeling better soon."

She paused, a nervous flutter alighted in her stomach. It was time to broach a subject she'd been meaning to bring up for a while now. "Maybe it's time to talk about this, Alex."

"What's that?"

"Well, this might be one of those awkward conversations, ok? There's a reason my periods are so bad—I've got a condition called a fibroid uterus. The IUD I have is for medical reasons as much as birth control. Well, probably more for medical reasons at this point." She snuck a glance at him and he didn't look ready to bolt off the deck, which she took as a good sign.

Straightening, Hope watched him closely. "This is definitely not a conversation you have at the beginning of a new relationship, but we're not exactly there anymore, are we? Anyway, the last time I saw my doctor in Chicago, he said I was going to need a hysterectomy in the next few years. And if my periods continue like this one, it may be sooner."

She paused, more at ease now—he watched her intently but didn't look upset. "You've never mentioned a strong desire to have children, but I wanted you to know. That's not in my future."

"I like kids just fine, but my life hasn't exactly worked out in that area. I'm in my forties now. I figure that ship has sailed and I'm ok with that." He reached for her hand, and her shoulders loosened. "I need *you* to be healthy—that's my priority. But I'm glad you told me."

Hope met his eyes and squeezed his hand, emphasizing her words. "Alex, I don't ever intend to keep anything from you again. I mean it."

"I don't either. I'll never lie to you. I know I need to come to terms with what happened in Syria. And I'm starting to." He gave her a small smile. "I've told you more about it than anyone else on earth."

"I know. And I'm not trying to pressure you, either. I've never even had this conversation with a man before." Crickets sang in a peaceful chorus around them, and she inhaled the sharp, salty air before turning back. "I also want you to know I'm really happy with things just the way they are."

"So am I."

She relaxed into him again, relieved to have that conversation done with. "It's hard to believe how fast time goes by. We got through Thanksgiving, but now we've got Christmas season coming." She patted his chest. "Thanks for your help with Thanksgiving. It was fun, having a big table with the guests and eating together. Made me feel good."

"It was. I liked it too."

"Patti and I are splitting holidays, so I'll have Christmas off.

Next year, we'll switch. The bookings are really picking up, and we've got a pretty full dive boat the next few weeks, don't we?"

"Yes," Alex said. "We've got a few days here and there without many divers, but it's packed otherwise. Both Robert and April are working so we can cover it all. The holidays are always busy, and so is winter in general."

Hope tucked her legs next to her as Cruz curled up at her feet. "I can't believe Christmas is almost here."

Alex shot her a sideways glance. "I'm kind of at a loss about what to get you. What do you get a woman who owns her own resort? Running shorts seem pretty unoriginal."

She gave him a tender smile. "This one's easy for me. I don't want anything. I mean it. I've already been given so much—and you're number one on that list. Waking up with you each morning is the best gift I've ever received. Well, it would be if you didn't get up at o-dark-thirty every morning."

Alex laughed and drew her tighter against his chest. "I've always been an early riser. But I know what you mean. And I feel the same way about Christmas. There's nothing you could get me that would come close to what I get every day just being around you. Knowing you're here for me."

Hope snuggled closer to him, swinging her foot. A fast-moving cloud streaked away from the moon, leaving the beach in front of them awash in soft light.

Chapter Twenty-Five

HOPE AWOKE LYING on her side on Christmas morning. Alex had fitted himself behind her and was stroking one of her breasts. She opened her eyes as early light filtered into the room and bit back a grin. He'd probably been lying there for an hour, hoping she'd wake before he couldn't take it anymore. She continued to ignore him, still smiling.

He breathed a row of kisses across the back of her neck as he ground against her. "I can tell you're awake, you know—your breathing changed. Turns out, I have a Christmas gift for you after all."

She laughed, the game lost. "I noticed that. And maybe I have something just for you too. I need to use the restroom before we get too distracted." She threw back the covers. "Don't go anywhere."

"No chance of that." He looked her up and down, his eyes smoldering.

She brushed her teeth before sliding back into bed and wrapping herself in his warmth, kissing him deeply.

"Hey, no fair. You brushed your teeth."

"Oh, stop it. I know you washed your mouth out with that big glass of water you keep on your nightstand. I can't taste a thing." She ran a finger across his stubble. "But if it concerns you, I'd be happy to share some of my toothpaste with you."

Making a rumbling noise deep in his chest, he pulled her toward him, and they got busy.

AFTER, Hope lay with her head against his chest, listening to his steady, loyal heart. She idly stroked his right hip, softly tracing the mass of scar tissue and its raised ridges, pleased that he didn't tense or react anymore. It was fully light now, the day dawning soft and blue.

"I worked last Christmas," she said. "Chicago got slammed with this huge snowstorm, and the hotel was booked solid with people who were only trying to get home." She couldn't hold back a laugh, her shoulders shaking. "It was awful. Everyone was so cranky, not that I blame them. I went home after my shift and drank a whole bottle of wine by myself."

Alex joined her laughter. "Tommy and I always have Christmas off. We set it up the same every year—I line up a bunch of tanks and leave the gear room unlocked, and the guests can dive the house reef whenever they want on Christmas Day. Last year I stocked up on food on Christmas Eve and hid out in my apartment all day. I can be very mature when necessary, you know. To be honest, I would have preferred to have a normal day with a boat dive." He kissed her forehead. "I feel a bit differently this year."

"Isn't it incredible? Of course, my life couldn't be more different, but even your life is light years from where you were a year ago." She kissed his chest and stretched out along the length of his body, then started laughing. "Again? Really?"

"Just ignore it. It'll go away."

A flush spread up his face from his bright red neck to the tips of his ears. Hope raised up on one elbow. "Are you embarrassed right now?"

"I'm almost forty-one years old, for God's sake. I've got no self-control around you."

"You say that like it's a bad thing." She reached her hand down.

"Well, if you keep doing that, it definitely won't go away."

"Refer to my previous comment."

She climbed on top of him.

HOPE CRADLED Alex's head against her shoulder as she gazed at the ocean outside the bedroom. They had to get up sometime. "I've never made my French toast for you, have I? I think I have everything I need." She tilted his face up. "I make amazing French toast. Exactly what we need to ramp this day to a whole new level."

His small smile grew into a face-splitting grin. "Well, I'm not sure this day can get much better, but I accept your challenge. How can I help?"

"Well, you can be in charge of the eggs and bacon. Mr. Monroe, I remember you making me a fabulous post-hurricane breakfast. But I'm going to top you this time. You'd best prepare yourself."

"You can top me anytime."

An hour later, they surveyed the table, having completely destroyed the kitchen. The feast lay before them—a huge platter of French toast, bacon, scrambled eggs, and a variety of cut-up fruit. With a smile, Hope swept to the refrigerator and removed a pitcher of orange juice and a bottle of champagne. She handed the latter to Alex. "You already know how I feel about opening these." He popped the cork, the two of them sharing a smile before he set the bottle back on the counter.

"Get over here." He pulled her in for a kiss.

"Oh no, I'm on to your tricks now. We worked too hard on this, and I'm not letting it get cold." Hope took two flutes out of the cabinet and made their mimosas, and they sat at the table.

She held up her glass. "To spending Christmas with my love."

He clinked his glass to hers. "Beats the hell out of last year, even with the girly drink."

They dug in, Alex eventually eating six pieces of French toast. "You ok diving this afternoon?"

"Sure, sounds like fun. Though it might be hard to share you after our morning together."

Amusement glinted in his eyes. "I thought you might be sick of me by now. Mary and Ben are great to be around. I've known them for several years."

"I'm looking forward to it, and very relieved they came back. It's a change for me—I'm usually only with you or a whole group. Adding just a pair will be nice."

The prospect of diving with another couple brought to mind another topic, and she grinned at Alex. "Speaking of a change in dive partners, Cindy and Marcus want to join the boat in early January. I looked at the bookings and found a day, so they're working their schedules around to make it work."

Alex tipped his head back. "Great. Can't wait."

Hope held her tongue. She wasn't sure what to expect when Marcus and Cindy realized Alex was the man involved in the rescue and shooting, but she would let things play out. The gunshot scar on his shoulder was still very visible, and he spent a significant amount of time on dive trips shirtless, so they were bound to notice it. And Marcus was particularly interested.

The whole situation reminded her of a lion lying crouched, his paw softly trapping the tail of a mouse. Hope's concern was what might happen if the lion unsheathed his claws. Though she was sure Alex wouldn't throw Marcus overboard.

Mostly sure, anyway.

THAT AFTERNOON, Hope sat under the palapa, tugging on her wetsuit. Lined up next to her were four fully assembled tanks. Alex walked toward her wearing his wetsuit, two others folded over one arm. Hope glanced behind him as a couple climbed the steps onto the pier.

Alex tossed the wetsuits over a bench. "I think that's everything. We should be ready to go."

Hope waited until the couple approached, then stood to embrace the dark-haired woman. "Mary! It's great to see you again. Welcome back." Hope moved to hug Mary's husband, Ben.

"We are so happy to be here!" Mary said. "We barely beat an ice storm out of Atlanta. We probably wouldn't have made it out if we'd left a few hours later."

"I used to live in Chicago. I am *not* missing that right now."

Mary and Ben exchanged a friendly nod with Alex. They'd been on the dive boat yesterday and were regular guests at Half Moon Bay. Their last visit had included the fateful day when the boat sank, and Hope was relieved they didn't hold the accident against the resort.

"Let's get geared up, and we'll jump off the dock here," Alex said. "Then we'll make our way over the sand to the house reef and see what we can find there. We'll head back when someone gets to five hundred psi. I'm looking at you, Ben."

Ben laughed, swiping a hand over his balding head. "Ok, ok.

I guess I'm that guy today. You're bigger than me though, Alex, but you never seem to run low on air."

"That's because he doesn't breathe," Hope added. "I'm pretty sure he has gills."

As they swam over the sandy area, they were lucky enough to discover two green sea turtles eating seagrass. Their long, scaly necks stretched out as their beaks cropped the grass. Hope exchanged a smile with Alex. Turtles were always a special find for her.

As they meandered along the house reef, Hope was delighted to see her old friends, the pair of French angelfish. She always looked for the large gray fish with bright yellow accents here on the house reef—and usually found them. Of course, it was impossible to tell if it was always the same pair.

Wanting to point them out, she turned to Alex, only to find him hovering several feet away, his arms crossed as his eyes scanned the reef. His head slowly swept back and forth, and his brow was furrowed.

What is he thinking about?

When they climbed back up to the pier, it was mid-afternoon. Mary turned to Hope and Alex. "Patti told us Christmas dinner was going to be served at 4 p.m. I don't know what you two have planned, but we'd love it if you joined us."

Hope was touched, and Alex's eyes softened as he nodded at her. "We'd love to."

***

Hope wore silvery dangling earrings, which went well with her black floral-print dress. Her hair was flat-ironed, and she touched up her lipstick.

"Can you help me out here?"

Hope turned to the closet. Alex stood shirtless, wearing black slacks as he held a shirt in each hand. "Are either of these good?" His left hand held a dark-red button-down shirt she'd recently bought him, and the right, a plain white T-shirt. Hope bit back a smile—Alex was good at so many things, but fashion wasn't among them.

"I think the dark-red shirt would be perfect." She ambled up to him and slid her hands up the warm skin of his chest. "Though I'm rather partial to the current view."

"Twice this morning wasn't enough for you?"

"Never enough."

"Good to know. Guess I'd better eat a big dinner, then." He gave her a crooked smile before pulling the shirt over his head. He turned, cupping her face as he softly kissed her. "You look incredible, by the way."

"Thank you, love. Shall we join our guests?"

Mary and Ben were already seated at a table for four near the beach when Hope and Alex entered the dining room. Ben cracked a huge smile at Alex as they sat. "I don't think I've ever seen you in anything but board shorts and a T-shirt."

"Hope makes me dress up once in a while."

"It's worth it," she added. "You do clean up rather well."

Patti approached the table, her smile brilliant against her dark skin. Charlotte had the holiday off since she worked Thanksgiving, and Gerold was doing the cooking tonight. "You four look like you've had a good day. Would you like some wine?"

After deciding they were in the mood for white, Hope turned to her. "Have Gerold pick out that dry Riesling. That will go with either the ham or turkey. Thanks, Patti."

After Patti poured their glasses, they raised them and toasted a wonderful day. "I'm so glad you came back here to spend Christmas," Hope said. "After spending four hours in the open ocean, I wouldn't blame you if you never wanted to come back."

"That was a scary experience, but we figure lightning won't strike twice." Mary moved her gaze to Alex. "We never really got a chance to talk to you afterward. Only when we tried to give you a tip, and you shut us down flat." A small smile crossed her face at that. "Thanks, Alex. I think that whole ordeal might have gone very differently if we'd been with someone else."

He stiffened, uncomfortable with praise at something he considered his duty. Hope squeezed his hand, and he relaxed, tossing a smile her way. "You're welcome. I'm not eager to repeat it either, but it's good to keep sharp on emergency procedures. And you guys were all great to work with."

Ben laughed. "Except that one guy who was obsessed with turtles. I thought you two might throw some punches. But you shut him down quick—that was a different side of you for sure."

"I had to get control of the situation. That's all."

"It was a little more than that," Mary said. "I didn't realize you were in the military. Before that day, anyway. Even if you hadn't said anything, it was pretty obvious."

Hope hadn't heard any of this before and was fascinated. Mary turned to her. "He started barking orders at us, especially the turtle man. It worked—we settled right down."

Hope glanced at Alex, pleased he wasn't shutting down even though the conversation had moved into difficult territory. But she didn't want things becoming too uncomfortable for him —it was time for a change in subject. "I have learned in no uncertain terms that Alex is a very handy man to have around when things go sideways. And he's the one who found the new boat too."

Ben's face lit up, nearly bouncing in his seat as he extolled the virtues of *Surface Interval.* Alex turned to Hope, and their eyes held. She winked at him, the acknowledgment clear in his eyes that she'd just rescued him. He leaned over and gave her a quick kiss. Hope picked up her wineglass as Mary smiled at her.

"How long have you two been together, anyway?" Mary asked.

Hope set her glass down, laughing. "Actually, the day the boat sank was the start of it."

Mary's brows rose, and she set her fork down. "Really? You're kidding! I thought you'd been a couple longer than that. I watched when you two reunited on the pier." She broke into a dreamy smile. "That was something else! Alex, everyone instinctively got out of your way while Hope ran into your arms. It was incredibly romantic."

Alex leaned back in his chair with a rueful smile as he shook his head. "Yeah, romantic until I crawled up to my apartment and fell into an exhausted coma. But it's in the past now."

AFTER DINNER, Hope and Alex walked hand in hand down the beach. A soft breeze ruffled Hope's dress, and clouds played hide-and-seek with the moon overhead as Hope replayed their day in her head, smiling at the memory of the angelfish. That jogged her memory, and she turned to Alex. "I watched you on the house reef—you were unhappy about something."

"I was evaluating the health of the reef. The corals are deteriorating, and the hurricane didn't help. It reminded me I need to get going on my coral project someday." His face lit up as it did anytime he discussed diving. "I'm going to start a coral nursery on my old apartment roof and plant them on the house reef. Assuming I can find the roof."

"That's a great idea! I've been wondering about how we can differentiate ourselves from other resorts. An environmental focus could help with that."

"It's not an overnight project, but I'd like to give it a go. I was glad we spotted some turtles for you this afternoon—I know they're your favorite."

"Not a bad day, was it?"

"One of the best." He draped an arm over her shoulder. "Merry Christmas, baby."

Chapter Twenty-Six

JANUARY . . .

THE MORNING WAS sunny with a light breeze as Hope walked down the wooden pier with Cindy and Marcus, who carried an underwater camera in one hand. "Let's head into the dive shop so Alex can get you set up with your equipment," Hope said. She opened the door and ushered them into the brightly lit space.

Alex stood behind the counter, laughing with a middle-aged couple who were repeat divers. The wife, Laura, was braiding her blond hair into a tail. She nodded at Hope before stepping out of the way.

After checking their certification cards, Alex placed two clipboards in front of Cindy and Marcus. "Ok, guys, you need to sign your lives away so Boss Lady can sleep at night."

They filled out the standard liability and medical waivers as Hope responded, "There are plenty of things that keep me up at night." She gave Alex a long look, knowing no one else could see it. His eyes held hers for a long moment, then he gathered the clipboards and headed around the counter.

"Ok, let's head to the gear room." Beckoning them, he walked out the door. "I've already got your tanks on the boat, so we just need to get you wetsuits, masks, and fins."

The smell of neoprene enveloped them as they entered the room. After giving him their shoe sizes, Alex grabbed two pairs of fins and set out an assortment of masks. "Place the mask firmly against your face and inhale. It should stick tight with no leaks. Pick the one that feels most comfortable." Cindy and Marcus tried several and made their selections before collecting their wetsuits from Alex.

"When was the last time you guys dove, anyway?" He started putting the excess masks back in the cubbies.

"It's been a while, but we're fine. It's not like you get rusty or anything," Marcus said.

Alex turned around. "How long ago is a while?"

"About five years for me," he said, then looked at Cindy.

"Around three, I guess."

Alex glanced at the camera in Marcus's hand. "Well, I would have been happy to give you a refresher in the pool, but it's too late now. Let's head to the boat, and I'll go over the equipment with you." His jaw was tight, though Hope didn't know why he was concerned about Marcus's camera.

The four of them climbed aboard and Hope left them at the stern, where Alex demonstrated the particulars of the gear. Making her way to the covered bow area, she learned Laura and her husband Wayne would be the other divers in their group. As they chatted, Cindy asked Alex several questions, while Marcus watched closely at first before losing interest. The other group of six divers came aboard at once, and they were ready to go.

Hope's tank was next to Cindy's. "Ready to go?"

"I sure hope so. This BCD is a lot different from the last one I used—nicer."

"Alex always orders good equipment, so you don't need to worry about that."

Robert and Alex stood under the canopy, heads together and likely determining the dive site. Alex nodded and climbed up to the wheelhouse. Handing Marcus his beach bag, Cindy took his hand, and they made their way to the bow. Hope tagged along, showing them the dry area, then moved off a bit to enjoy some sun as they approached Robert.

"It's great to meet you," Marcus said. "I hope we're diving with you?"

"Huh? I thought you guys were with Hope." Cindy nodded as Robert laughed. "Then you're definitely divin' with Alex. There's no way he'll let her dive with me if he's in the water."

Marcus's face fell. "That's too bad, man. I was looking forward to seeing you in action. It's great to meet you, though. Maybe we can talk later." He shook Robert's hand again.

"Thanks. That's nice to hear." Hope kept a straight face as Robert's brow wrinkled. "Uh, I need to talk to Tommy. We'll be at the site soon."

Hope removed her staff T-shirt and board shorts, standing in a sporty blue one-piece. "Let's get into our wetsuits."

They headed toward their tanks as Alex shouted down from the bridge, "We're getting close! Time to start getting ready." Wayne and Laura sat on the other side of Marcus as Alex and Robert returned to the main deck.

Robert pointed to the other group of six. "You guys are with me—we'll be the first group in the water."

Tommy slowed the boat as Alex quickly grabbed his mask and fins and made his way to the bow. "While Alex is moorin' the boat, I'll give the dive briefin'." The divers listened as Robert described the topography of the site, as well as the fish and creatures they might see.

"And I need to give special mention to one critter we're likely to see, so listen up. This site is famous for a very curious green moray eel named Oscar, and he likes divers. Now listen, it can be a little freaky to have a six-foot predator doing circles around you. So, if he comes up to you, just chill, ok? Don't make any sudden movements and if he gets too friendly, Alex or I will come over and get his attention. That's about it. Questions?" No one had any. "Ok, my group—get into your tanks so we can get wet!"

As Robert's group got ready, the other group sat back down. Marcus grumbled to Cindy, "If we were with Robert, we'd be in the water first. This sucks."

"Marcus, who cares? Hope said we'd be the first group on the second dive." Cindy got up and sprayed defogger solution in her mask as her hands shook.

Alex climbed back aboard, water dripping from his wetsuit as Robert's group descended. "He told you about Oscar, right?" They all nodded. "Did he tell you to keep your fingers to yourselves?"

Hope arched a brow. "Huh?"

"Oscar can get close to people." Alex crossed his arms and put his hands in his armpits. "If he approaches you, keep your hands in. As long as you stay cool, you'll be fine. But don't go waving your hands around. It makes him nervous. Keep your fingers tight—I've seen people get bit who didn't listen. This is a really rare opportunity to get close to a moray, so enjoy it if we see him."

Laura and Wayne stood up first. "We've seen Oscar before. It's pretty cool," Wayne said.

Cindy took a deep breath and blew it out, drumming her heels on the deck.

"You ok?" Hope asked.

"I hate to admit it, but I'm really nervous." She gave a shaky laugh. "I wish we'd taken that refresher now. I'm not too eager to meet a moray face-to-face, either."

Hope didn't disagree with her on that one, but she wanted to be reassuring. "It'll be fine. Alex won't let anything happen to us. He has done this more times than we can imagine."

Tommy grabbed Marcus's camera out of the bucket and helped him and Cindy to the platform as Alex helped Hope. Soon the group was descending. Hope looked for Cindy and Marcus, finding them slightly below. Marcus faced away, photographing an angelfish but sinking easily. Cindy was rigid and trying to vent her BCD with a pinched expression. Hope descended past her quickly, but Cindy couldn't sink any more. She turned to Marcus, who still faced away.

Alex swam to her, pulling out a square lead weight and zipping it into her BCD. Now she could sink, but she fiddled with her inflator and her mask, kicking constantly. Alex looked at Hope and tapped his index fingers together lengthwise, the signal for buddy, and pointed to Cindy. He wanted Hope to stay close, which was just as well since Marcus had moved off to photograph a sea fan, his fins kicking the sand into a cloudy froth.

Alex frowned before turning around and leading the group down to sixty feet. Hope and Cindy stayed close together. Cindy still didn't look comfortable, checking her computer every few minutes and fidgeting while not really looking at the scenery.

Twenty minutes into the dive, Alex turned around for an air check. Cindy had half a tank, much less than Hope. Alex had to bang his tank several times to get Marcus's attention, who indicated he also had half a tank. Alex gave him the buddy signal and pointed to Cindy. Marcus responded with an ok, then went back to taking pictures.

Alex narrowed his eyes before turning to lead the group through a broad channel at forty feet. He found a brilliant red giant crab over two feet wide and hovered nearby as Laura marveled at it.

Marcus was off to the side, photographing a brown and white spotted boxfish. His fins repeatedly slapped the coral, and Alex took off toward him, wrenching his fins off the reef. He shook his head and glared at Marcus, who had turned around to see what was going on.

After Laura moved off, Hope motioned Cindy, who shook her head, not interested in the crab. Her eyes were enlarged, and her clenched fists broadcast her uneasiness. Marcus practically pushed her out of the way to photograph the crab.

Appalled, Hope asked Cindy if she was ok, and she responded with a so-so. Hope grasped her hand, squeezing tightly. It had always comforted her when Alex held hers on bad dives. Cindy clenched back, and the two continued on, swimming side by side as she tried unsuccessfully to interest her in their surroundings. Then Hope saw it.

A long flash of green.

Chapter Twenty-Seven

OSCAR WAS A BRILLIANT EMERALD HUE, six feet of smooth undulating predator coming straight at Hope and Cindy. His mouth opened and closed as he breathed, revealing rows of razor-sharp teeth. Hope froze and rushed both hands to her armpits, rigid from head to toe. Cindy followed suit as Oscar swam up to them. Marcus hurried in, frantically taking pictures of the spectacle. Hope fought off an irritated surge at Marcus, trying to concentrate on Oscar and Cindy.

The eel swam in circles around the two women. Oscar's proximity allowed Hope a close-up view of his needle-like teeth. The eel swam in a loop around them. His velvety skin caressed the back of Hope's hand, sending a shiver down her spine. She turned to Cindy, who had her eyes clamped shut as rapid bursts of bubbles exhaled from her regulator.

Uh-oh, Cindy. Hang in there.

Hope gently grasped both Cindy's arms, and her eyes flew open and then steadied when she realized it was Hope and not Oscar. Marcus was practically in their faces, shutter clicking—Hope wanted to punch him as Oscar swam between Cindy's legs and then Hope's. She kept a tight hold, and Cindy moaned, which further escalated Hope's own dread as she tried to calm her. Oscar had turned his attention back to Cindy, rubbing his body up her leg.

Marcus lined up next to her, kicking and waving his camera. Oscar ignored him, moving once again to Hope and sliding across her stomach as she tried not to shudder. Marcus whipped his free hand back and forth in front of him.

Lightning-fast, Oscar bolted toward the motion, his mouth snapping shut and barely missing the man's outstretched fingers. Marcus jerked his hand to his armpit, his eyes wide behind his mask as a froth of bubbles exhaled from his regulator.

Then Alex appeared.

He shoved Marcus back hard before reaching out and softly stroking under Oscar's body. The eel immediately turned toward Alex, who began moving his fins in smooth sweeping motions, rapidly backing up and drawing the eel away.

Wait! You can go backwards underwater?

The eel circled Alex as he slowly backed up, his arms now close to his body.

Hope's hand was sore from the strength of Cindy's grip, but she relaxed it now that Alex had drawn off the eel. Marcus glared at him, watching as the eel moved away.

When Alex got about twenty feet away, he rotated up vertically. By this point, Oscar had his body wrapped around him, and they watched each other face to face. Alex was completely relaxed, his legs crossed at the ankles and fins motionless an inch above the sand. Man and eel regarded each other, both at ease. Glancing at Laura and Wayne and tilting his head, Alex invited them to approach before turning back to Oscar with a smile. They swam over as Hope looked at Cindy, who watched Alex with wide eyes.

At least she's not about to panic anymore.

Alex hovered motionless in the water, and soon the eel lost

interest, moving to Wayne and Laura. They also remained still, and after circling them several times, Oscar started to swim away. Marcus swam hard, chasing the eel and taking more photos. But Oscar possessed eminent good sense and didn't want anything to do with him.

The green eel sped off, disappearing into the reef.

By then, Alex had come up to Cindy again, making sure she was ok. Her breathing was more normal now, and her eyes more relaxed. He gave everyone the safety-stop signal, and they moved to fifteen feet. Hope held Cindy's hand and gave her a smile while Marcus hovered nearby, flicking through his camera.

BACK ON BOARD, Hope sat next to Cindy while Alex finished getting out of his tank. Excited, Marcus talked with Wayne and Laura about the eel while the other group sunned themselves on the bow deck.

"Hopefully I got some great shots of that eel with Cindy," Marcus said, water droplets flinging from his brown hair. "That was fantastic!"

"I'm not sure Cindy would agree," Alex said softly, his jaw set.

Marcus laughed. "Yeah, she looked scared shitless!"

Alex's eyes flashed. "And that didn't concern you at all?"

Uh-oh, keep it together, honey.

"Oh, come on. She's fine."

Hope stood up, hand out, and Alex darted his eyes to her. He took her hint and turned around, reaching behind to yank his zipper down and ripping his wetsuit to his waist as he began changing Laura's gear over to a fresh tank for the second dive.

Marcus inspected his camera, then dropped it back in the

freshwater bucket. "Oh, man. Too bad you weren't filming me, Cindy. Did you guys see he almost bit me?" He giggled, then tapped his hip. "You know, I gotta say, Alex, you sure managed to hog him after you elbowed me out of the way. He curled himself all around you. I kind of got ripped off there."

Oh shit.

Alex whirled around and loomed over Marcus, more than six inches taller, his eyes blazing even as his voice stayed soft with icy control. "That's because I had to draw him off of Cindy, who *you* should have been looking out for. Instead, Hope spent the dive looking out for her. Maybe you should spend less time paying attention to your camera and more time on Cindy?"

Marcus stumbled backward. His eyes had been riveted to Alex's shoulder during this little speech. His scar was even more livid after being submerged, and Cindy had noticed it too.

Hope stood up. "Enough. Both of you. Cindy is quite capable of looking out for herself. She just had a bad dive. Let's move on, shall we?"

Cindy pulled her wetsuit down, beads of water rolling down her ebony skin. "She's right. I'm fine. But thanks for gettin' that eel away, Alex. That was a bit much."

Alex's expression softened, and he nodded, turning back to the tanks.

Marcus stood there blinking at the even larger scar now visible on the back of Alex's shoulder. "What the hell, man? It was you that rescued those people and then got shot, not the other guy. Why did you deny it?"

Alex turned around, straightening to his full height. "I never denied it. I never said anything, one way or the other. You just made a very fast assumption. Let's drop it—I've got work to do." He turned back to the next tank.

Great, now it falls to me to smooth things out. Dammit, Alex!

"I'm thirsty," Hope lied. "Come on, you two. Let's get something to drink and give Alex some room to work." She moved forward and opened the lid of the cooler, trying to ignore Marcus's grumblings. "Look, Marcus. You took an instant dislike to Alex when you met him. It didn't exactly make him want to open up to you, ok?"

"Well, I never would've talked to him like that if I'd known who he was!"

"Marcus, be quiet. You're makin' it worse." Cindy sighed. "They're right—you're actin' like an asshole. Maybe on the second dive you can pay attention to whether I'm alive or dead. That would be nice."

Marcus widened his eyes as his face crumpled. "I'm sorry. I was just excited. I'll leave the camera on the boat for the next dive. Promise." He kissed her as Hope tried not to roll her eyes. Cindy wasn't smiling, but she might have forgiven him. Hope had no idea what she saw in him.

Ok, it seems to have blown over with these two—time to check the other one.

"There's probably room on the bow if you guys want to get some sun," Hope said before making her way back to Alex, who was attaching the last regulator to its tank. "Well, I think that dive went really well. It's been a lovely morning."

"I'm not apologizing this time." Alex sent a furious glare Marcus's way. "That guy's a prick. And she could have gotten into serious trouble if you hadn't been looking out for her. Marcus was oblivious. I overheard him saying he's leaving the damn camera on the boat next dive, thank God."

Then he straightened, taking a deep breath after finishing with the last tank. He turned to her, his gaze moving slowly from her feet up to her face. A slow smile rose, his flash of anger apparently forgotten. "You were great on that dive, by the way. Perfect buddy in action."

Hope parked both hands on her hips, trying to stare him down. "Oh, you think you're going to smile and flash those baby blues at me, and everything will be fine, huh?"

Alex grinned more and lowered his sunglasses to peer above them. Despite her best efforts, she smiled back—as usual, his charm was irresistible. "You're impossible."

He glanced around and drew her in, quickly swiping his tongue over hers. "You're amazing, you know that? I've gotta go talk to Tommy about the second site." He patted her butt, then climbed up the ladder, leaving her breathless and smiling.

How does he do that?

Cindy was on the bow, watching, and made her way back to Hope. "I was hoping Marcus would act a little more like an adult this time. Looks like I was wrong."

Hope's smile fell. "It's ok. I'm glad you know about Alex now, though. That was awkward for me. I didn't want to keep it from you, Cindy. But Alex wanted to keep it quiet—he doesn't care much for the limelight."

"You don't owe me any explanations."

Hope opened her mouth a few times before voicing the question. "Cindy, are you happy with Marcus?"

"I used to be. Now, I'm not so sure. Before his business became successful, he was . . . different, not so arrogant."

"Well, maybe you guys can talk it out." *Or maybe you're seeing his true colors now.*

Cindy glanced at Alex. "I don't know why I didn't realize earlier you were the one involved in that shootin'. That must have been awful."

"It was."

"I can't even imagine what it must be like to be with a man who would take a bullet for you."

Hope drifted her eyes up to the wheelhouse, where Alex, Robert, and Tommy were clustered, all laughing. Alex stood tall and strong, a man who would never put his own desires before her safety.

He turned his head and lowered his sunglasses again to watch her, waggling his eyebrows outrageously. She broke into a wide smile, fighting back a laugh. "I can't believe it myself sometimes."

Chapter Twenty-Eight

ALEX SWUNG his tank and BCD off his right shoulder and onto the floor next to the compressor. He'd gone for a very early swim, so he had time for a quick dive before work, heading over to his old apartment roof to check the new coral transplants he'd started. It was now near the end of the month, and his big project was well established.

It had taken him several dives to find the roof. It lay in forty feet of water and well north of the pier. He was impressed by how far it had been blown by the hurricane. After discovering it, he'd spent some thoroughly enjoyable dives planning his new coral nursery. He'd built a few frames out of PVC and hung small coral fragments from them.

Many were growing well, a few were already dead, and more were in between—time would tell. Still, they were doing something important with this project. Even in the five years he'd been here, the reefs had deteriorated. Whatever he could do to decrease that was a boon.

A small spotted moray had taken up residence under the roof, reminding him of the Oscar-Marcus debacle. *Freaking idiot.* He had a slow fuse, but Alex didn't suffer fools easily. Hopefully, Cindy would wise up sooner rather than later.

Alex turned to grab his backup BCD when his phone rang on the workbench. He frowned at the unknown number before answering. "Monroe."

"Hi, Alex. This is John Strickland from the *St. Croix Chronicle.* Charles Reed's trial is going to start before long. I was wondering if you had any comments?"

Alex hissed through his teeth, now regretting answering. "Look, I told you when you called last month. I'm not going to comment on an open case."

"I figured since you'll be testifying, you might want to tell your side of things."

"That's what the trial is for."

"Ok, ok. You sure have a way of finding trouble, though, don't you? First your dive boat sinks and you're the hero who saves everyone, then you get shot trying to defend your girlfriend."

"What's your point?"

"Oh, what I said. Seems like Reed picked the wrong guy to mess with that night. You know, I saw him when I had an interview at the jail one day. He's huge! Yet you managed to knock him cold with only a few punches. You just throw a lucky jab?"

"I'm not talking to you, Strickland."

"Well, I guess we'll find out at the trial, huh?"

"Go to hell." Alex hung up.

He took a deep breath. This was the second time the reporter had called him, wanting a statement about Charles. He'd tried to be a bit more polite the last time, but obviously that hadn't worked.

Life was going really well for Alex, and he just needed the trial done with, especially his testimony. His fingers were crossed he'd be able to keep his past out of it and talk only about that night, and he'd said as much to Hope.

She'd looked steadily back at him and said, "I hope so too."

A knot of unease had twisted in his stomach at her look, like she wondered how likely that was. But it was no use worrying about things still in the future.

The trial would come no matter what.

Fortunately, Patti was coming to terms with it a little more. Last week, Alex had ventured up to the lobby office to talk to Hope, instead finding Patti there alone while Hope dealt with a guest emergency in person.

Patti sat at her desk, fiddling with a pen. "I went to visit Charles. In jail."

"Oh? How did that go?"

She glanced up at him before dropping her gaze back to the pen. "Painfully. But necessary. He was all full of innocent sincerity. I didn't buy it for a second. He said you jumped him, and the gun went off accidentally."

Alex snorted. "Yeah, because I usually go around dark streets attacking people holding guns."

"I told him I knew he was the one who stole the two televisions from the bungalows after the hurricane." She sighed. "And then I told him he wasn't family to me anymore, and he'd never hear from me again."

Alex walked around the desk, taking both her hands and drawing her into an embrace. "I'm sorry, Patti. I know your family means everything to you."

She wiped a tear and met his eyes. "Yes. That's why I said what I did. Charles *isn't* family anymore. But you always will be. It wasn't even a hard choice to make."

"Thank you. That's a choice you should never have needed to make."

Now, Alex pocketed the phone and grabbed his regulator—

he'd already set up all the guests' equipment on the boat. As he neared the door, he pressed his left arm against the door frame on impulse. He'd had a great swim that morning, but the shoulder had already tightened up a bit. Now he stretched it out again. Patience was the key, and Alex had firsthand experience that recovering from injury was generally a slower process than expected.

Fortunately, at this point he could do most of what he needed to, and he was grateful. The doctor had told him at his final checkup two months after the shooting to go back to his usual activities but to listen to his body. So he'd started up his weight-training program again, lowering the weight substantially on the left arm. But now he was improving. Not as good as the right, but getting there.

As Alex climbed aboard with his backup BCD, April was already at work setting up her kit. He nodded hello as he tugged the tank strap over his own cylinder. He tried and failed to bite back the smile, remembering the dive where Hope had tagged along and staked her claim on him. Of course, it didn't say much in his favor about how clueless he'd been to what was going on.

Admittedly, it pleased him—he'd never had a woman be territorial around him. He couldn't really express to Hope that compared to her, April was the moon trying to shine against the sun. All she had to do was look at him with those big golden eyes, and he was putty in her hands.

IT WAS A GOOD MORNING—ALL the divers had enjoyed themselves, and so had the crew. He, April, and Tommy made quick work of cleaning up after the trip, and Alex wanted to cement their good teamwork. "Why don't we head up to the kitchen and have lunch together?"

April looked surprised but happy. "Sounds good to me," she said, moving into the bow to make sure nothing was left behind.

Alex treated her the same as he always had, but even he could detect a change in her attitude toward him since she had realized he and Hope were together. If Tommy were at lunch too, that would take any awkwardness out of the situation. And talking Tommy into a meal wasn't usually a problem.

Unless he wanted to rub salt into a wound.

"Ah, I don't know," Tommy said. "I was thinking about skipping lunch so I could leave early today. Maybe you two should go without me."

Even though Alex had been oblivious to how April had felt about him, apparently Tommy had been completely aware, and he never missed an opportunity to remind Alex.

"Yeah," Alex said. "I know you usually skip lunch."

Tommy treated Alex to a full shit-eating grin. "But I am kinda hungry, so I guess I can make an exception today."

"Well, I don't want you to faint dead away, so let's go," Alex said, then called April back before leading the way up the pier to the kitchen. The three of them walked in to find Gerold grilling several hamburgers.

"Oh, that smells pretty good, Gerold. I can't wait," Tommy said. "You finally learn to cook a hamburger?"

"I guess so. We're totally sold out now. These are the last of them today—for the guests." Tommy opened his eyes wide, and Gerold laughed at his stricken expression.

April went to the refrigerator and pulled out a chicken Caesar salad in a clamshell container. "I'm set. You make great salads, Gerold."

"Thank you. It's nice when someone appreciates a salad."

Tommy stood with his hands on his hips, aghast. "What are Alex and I supposed to do now? We can't eat *salad*."

"Agreed," Alex added.

Gerold stared at Tommy and Alex, then pointed his spatula at them. "You two don't deserve me, but I happened to save some extra meat, so I have enough to make three more." He turned to April. "You want a burger instead?"

"No, this salad's fantastic. I'm good."

Gerold shrugged, so Tommy piped in, patting his belly with a grin. "I'll take two."

"Figures."

He had them all squared away soon enough, with two hamburgers for Tommy plus an order of fries for him and Alex.

"Your new sous chef seems to be good," Alex said.

"Yeah," Gerold replied. "Pauline's fresh out of school, but that just means she doesn't have a bunch of bad habits to unlearn. She's gonna work out fine."

They ate with plenty of good-natured joking. With Tommy and Gerold there, Alex didn't worry about April. Which was good because he still caught her looking his way every once in a while. Like now.

"It's good to see you fully recovered, Alex," April said.

"Great to be back. Sorry about your hours getting cut, though." For good measure, he added, "I was a pretty surly patient. I'm sure Hope wanted me back at work as much as I did."

Tommy snorted. "More, I'll bet."

At his mention of Hope, April went back to the remnants of her salad, and Alex breathed a relieved sigh.

A timer went off, and Gerold pulled a tray of his secret-recipe cookies out of the oven while April rose with a smile to wash her plate. "I'm going to finish up. I need to get going."

Tommy added, "I'll join you. Priscilla has an appointment this afternoon, so I need to get home." The two left to finish up as Tommy got a laugh out of her even before the kitchen door closed behind them.

Alex stared at the cookies, keeping one eye on Gerold, who continued cooking for the guests. Finally, Alex made his move, lightly stepping to the counter and lifting two off the sheet.

"Six minutes!" Gerold exclaimed. "I thought you'd be less than five, man. What a disappointment. I must be losin' my touch."

"Oh, you're timing me now?" Alex said as he took a bite of the warm cookie—heaven in his mouth.

"You're very predictable where food's concerned."

"Yeah, bite me." Alex leaned back against the counter. The double swinging doors from the dining room opened, and he brightened as Hope entered. Today she was dressed in a business-like navy-blue dress, with her hair up in a clip. She managed to look both professional and sexy as hell.

She gave Alex a private smile and a wink before turning her attention to Gerold. "Ok, Gerold, I'm here. What did you want to see me about?"

He smiled at her over the stainless-steel table where he scored a mango. "Pauline's doin' a great job, and we're trading off on the cookin' classes now. I wanted to make sure it was all right with you if I rearranged my schedule for the next few months to have three mornings off a week. I'll work lunch and dinner those days."

"Of course. You and Pauline can work out your schedules however you want."

"Perfect! I got a new road bike, and I need to start puttin' some miles in. We're headin' into race season—gotta get ready, you know."

Hope moved to stir a stockpot of soup. "Anything you're training for?"

"There's a century ride—a hundred miles—at the end of the summer that I'd like to get ready for. And a fifty-miler next month I'm thinkin' about."

"Oh, is it part of that big sports festival in March? My friend Cindy told me about it a few weeks ago. She's thinking of doing the half-marathon."

He shook his head. "They don't have bike-only races in that one—only the two triathlon distances. I'd love to do the bike course for the half-Ironman distance. It's pretty famous. But I'm not up for the other two legs of the race."

Alex covertly lifted another cookie as Hope's face went blank. She dropped the spoon into the soup, and he could practically see the lightbulb over her head as she whirled around. "Gerold, you're a genius! We could form a Half Moon Bay Resort team and enter the triathlon!" She glanced at Alex before turning back to him. "Alex could swim, you can bike, and I can run. I had some friends in Chicago who were triathlon fanatics. The Half Ironman is a 1.2-mile swim, a 56-mile bike ride, and a 13.1-mile run."

She paused, the corner of her mouth dropping. "Well, it would be a test for me, that's for sure. I haven't been able to get my run over eight miles since I keep running out of gas—but I'm sure I could finish. You could bike that easily, and Alex could swim a mile with both hands tied. What do you think?"

"I think it's a great idea!" Gerold's grin showed off his perfectly white teeth. He turned to Alex. "You interested?"

"Count me in! Sounds like fun." Alex wiggled his fingers at her. "I think I'll leave my hands free if that's ok. Guess it's time to start working on my speed."

He grinned at Hope, pleased she'd thought of the idea. No doubt she'd figure out a way to profit from it too since they were doing it as a resort team.

Alex couldn't wait to see what the three of them could accomplish together.

Chapter Twenty-Nine

SEVERAL PEOPLE AMBLED down the Frederiksted pier, the absence of a cruise ship ensuring a pleasant stroll in the warm sunshine. Hope sat at Red Fort Grill, tearing her gaze from the long wooden structure back to the menu before her.

This outdoor restaurant was one of her and Cindy's favorite lunch spots, though if a cruise ship was in port, they chose somewhere further from the waterfront since Red Fort's proximity to the pier guaranteed a throng of diners. But today was peaceful and beautifully tropical. Rattan tables and chairs were scattered about, accompanied by tiki torches, unlit during the heat of the day.

"Sorry I'm late." Cindy sat down with a rush.

"I just got here myself. Trying to decide what looks good." They made their selections and ordered when the server brought Hope's iced tea.

"Your running's goin' really well." Cindy's face was tight today. "How long did you run on Saturday?"

Hope smiled, laying both palms on the table as she leaned forward. "Ten miles! I'm going to hold it there for a while. I was wiped out. Are you going to do that half-marathon?"

"I think so. I've got time to train for it. You?"

"Believe it or not, Alex, Gerold, and I are entering as a team for the long-course triathlon. I'm going to do the run! Hopefully, I have time to train. We're getting so busy now that the holidays are over, and I've got all the bungalows open except the one being remodeled. It's a good problem to have, but Alex and I have both been working nonstop. I thought hiring Robert would take some of the pressure off him, but I'm starting to wonder if we need to hire another divemaster." Cindy had looked down when she mentioned Alex. "Is everything ok?"

She returned her gaze to Hope, tears glittering in her eyes. "I broke up with Marcus last night."

Thank God. It's about time. "Oh, Cindy. I'm so sorry. You doing ok?"

"Yeah. I shouldn't even be upset, but I am. We've hardly seen each other since we went divin', and I never got over how he acted that day. I haven't been happy for a while—it was time to end it."

"It's still hard, though, isn't it?"

Cindy nodded, digging a tissue out of her purse. "It is. You're lucky, Hope. You and Alex seem happy together."

"I'm very lucky. But you wouldn't believe how many frogs I had to kiss before I found my prince. Though, come to think of it, even my prince tends to morph into a jackass on occasion."

"Not like Marcus. God, he could be a jerk. He's obsessed with that stupid paintball, like a teenager." She sighed. "Sorry about that. I can see why Alex wouldn't want anythin' to do with guns."

Hope choked on her iced tea. "Uh, that wasn't it. It was more Alex coming up with an excuse to decline the invitation. I don't think he's terribly bothered by guns." Heat crept up her neck.

Cindy crossed her arms on the table. "Marcus didn't take it

well when I called him and broke up. I just didn't feel like doin' it face-to-face."

Probably because it wasn't his idea. "He didn't make any threats, did he?"

"No, nothin' like that."

Hope relaxed, stirring her iced tea with the bamboo straw. "Well, that's a relief." Cindy watched her intently. "I've had some bad experiences in the boyfriend department. I like to make sure my friends are all right."

"I'll be fine—thanks for worryin' about me. Marcus is an idiot, but he's not abusive or anythin'."

That confirmed Hope's own instincts.

"I'm sure you're right. I'm sorry—it's a sensitive issue for me." She put her own musings on hold and did her best to be a supportive friend for Cindy.

They spent the rest of the lunch discussing how Marcus wasn't violent, just a selfish bastard, as Cindy lamented every misdeed he'd committed over the past year. Hope kept an even expression, clucking appropriately, but was left even more bewildered about why Cindy put up with Marcus at all.

By the end, Hope was desperate for escape. Certain similarities were uncomfortably clear, reminding her of an overdue phone call.

AFTER HER PAINFUL LUNCH, Hope moved on to her other reason for being in Frederiksted. The sounds of smooth jazz drifted out as she opened the door to the store. The woman behind the counter, Vera, recognized her and broke into a smile. "I've got 'em right here. Hang on a second." She spoke with a jarring New Jersey accent that made Hope's teeth hurt, especially now that she was used to musical Caribbean accents.

While she waited, Hope strolled around the shop, hands clasped behind her back as she admired the modern-art pieces hanging on the walls. She was looking at a large photograph of Frederiksted's own St. Paul's Catholic Church when Vera returned from the back room.

Hope hurried to the counter, fingers tapping her hip as Vera carefully placed several glass pictures on the counter for her inspection before gathering two more from the back room. Hope let her gaze wander over them and exhaled the breath she'd been holding in a long rush.

Alex had selected two underwater photos, and she'd picked three landscapes—a beach scene, a sunset, and one featuring the colorful stilt-wearing mocko jumbies. She'd sent the files to the store to be blown up to poster size and printed directly onto glass. They were modern and beautiful. They were also expensive, even with the discount Vera was giving her.

"Oh, these turned out beautiful!"

The shop owner nodded. "They'll make a nice addition to your resort. Each one really showcases St. Croix. I'd never heard of your photographer before, but he's really good. I might want to sell some of his pictures here in the gallery if he's interested."

"I'm sure he would be. I can't wait to see these displayed." Ideas and possibilities were colliding in Hope's head.

Vera returned to the back room to pack the photos in cardboard cases, and Hope clutched them to her like priceless treasures as she left. The shop was located on a lovely back street lined with other colorful small businesses, and Hope couldn't resist a little window-shopping after securing the pictures in her Jeep.

She ambled down the shady sidewalk, passing a talented glass artisan and an oil painter, as well as a shop that sold handmade wind chimes which bathed the street in a heavenly soft sound. She stopped to admire them, closing her eyes at the deep, relaxing tone.

After returning to the resort, she carried the pictures to one of the new bungalows and gave the contractor strict instructions on where to hang them. Satisfied but worn out, she was finally done for the day. Hope removed her sandals, and the ocean washed over her feet as she strolled down the beach toward the house. She passed Alex, teaching a pool session as the water trickled over the infinity edge. They exchanged a quick nod as she passed.

As Hope got close to the house, Cruz bounded toward her, his tail alight with happiness. They both entered, and Hope opened a beer, collapsing on the couch with a sigh as fatigue washed over her.

She picked up her phone and dialed. It had been on her mind since lunch, and Sara picked up right away. "I realized today I owe you an apology, straight from the depths of my being."

"Well, it's about time," Sara said. "There are so many things you need to apologize for, though. You're going to have to be more specific."

Hope laughed, stretching out her legs. "I've got this new friend—we get along really well. And she has been dating this complete idiot. For a year! He doesn't deserve her in any way, shape, or form. Today we had lunch, and she told me she finally broke up with him. I had to listen to her go on for two hours, complaining about everything." Hope's laughter built. "And all I could think of was, 'Oh my God, now I know how Sara has felt all these years!'"

"Trust me, you only got a small sample. I've had to put up with you my whole life."

"Oh, it wasn't fun. And of course, I had to make sure he didn't threaten her. She assured me he hadn't." Cruz circled three times in his bed, then lay down with a happy groan in the cool comfort of the house. "I didn't get into my past since we haven't been friends long enough, and I really think he's just an asshole. Of course, I'm not the best judge of that, am I?"

"Well, you're definitely improving on that front. I'm glad Alex has recovered so well. You're still happy?"

"Yes, very much. I could gush for hours, but I'll spare you." Hope closed her eyes, basking in the feeling.

"You have my thanks." Sara paused. "And you told him everything, right? Even Caleb?"

"All of it. I'm done hiding, especially from him."

"And you're confident he has told you about whatever was holding him back?"

"Yes, Sara. He has."

"Oh, don't get defensive! I'd never ask you to betray his confidence. I'm just used to being suspicious on your behalf. Though, I guess Alex has proven pretty well he's worth keeping around." Sara's laughter emanated from the phone. "You've never said. Does he have any family?"

"Yes, a younger sister who lives in Baltimore. Their parents both passed away."

"That's too bad. But at least he's lucky enough to have a little sister. Not everyone is so fortunate, you know."

"That's one word for it."

"Sticks and stones, Hope. On a more serious note, have you heard more about the trial?"

Hope closed her eyes. "It's scheduled for March. I've been advised I'll have to testify."

Sara paused. "You ok with that?"

Hope stared blankly at the dark television. "Not ok, exactly. But it needs to be done. I'm not twenty years old anymore, and I'm a lot stronger than I used to be. I'll get through it."

"I don't doubt that for a second. I'm here if you need me."

"Thanks, Sara." Cruz lifted his head and padded over to the slider, scratching on the door and drawing Hope's gaze. "I'd better go. Alex is coming up the beach now."

"Yeah, yeah. Say hello for me and make sure to let him know I'll strangle him if he steps out of line."

Hope grinned as she hung up. Sara didn't know anything about Alex's background as a SEAL, but knowing her, that wouldn't make any difference. No elite soldier stood a chance against Sara.

Alex opened the door, and still feeling warm after her phone call, Hope rushed to him and drew his head down, kissing him fiercely as she ran her hands up and down the hard muscles of his back. Eventually, she let him take a breath.

"Wow, what did I do to deserve that? I need to know, so I can do it again."

"I just got off the phone with Sara, and I was telling her how happy I am. And now, here you are in person."

"Hmmm, and this person is feeling decidedly better than he did a few minutes ago."

Hope smiled. She returned to the kitchen and opened a beer for him. "I've got some news. I'm sure you'll be crushed, but Cindy broke up with Marcus."

He snorted. "Good riddance."

"She was a little down. Maybe I can get her to go diving again. I'd love to have a real dive buddy, instead of the scattered singles."

Alex set his beer down and raised a brow. "You have a dive buddy—with benefits."

"You know what I mean!"

"She's welcome on the boat anytime. But if Marcus shows up again, I'm feeding him to Oscar."

Chapter Thirty

FEBRUARY . . .

HOPE SETTLED into the porch couch, pushing up the sleeves of one of Alex's sweatshirts as she enjoyed her morning coffee. He'd left early that morning, wanting a longer swim before work. Alex was working hard on his rehab, attacking his morning swims and his weight routine.

Hope could see the change in him—inside and out. He was more at peace and hadn't had a nightmare in months now. He was a naturally authoritative man, and she doubted that would ever change. But the cold defensiveness about him had lessened, though he still didn't speak about his past except to her.

Life was firing on all cylinders for them both.

For her, this day was all about relaxation, a day off after tirelessly preparing the photo prints for the bungalows. She liked them so much that she had several more made for the lobby and planned to add some to the restaurant. But today she'd go for a run a little later, then spend the day with a book—some quality alone time.

It was a breezy morning, and waves already pounded the shore. By afternoon, there'd be whitecaps, and the second dive could be a challenge. But at least the wind kept the oppressive heat at bay. It would be a wonderful day to hang out under the shade of a palm tree with her book. Hope was lifting the mug to her mouth when her text tone went off.

> Patti: Come to the office ASAP. 911.

Hope almost dropped her coffee, and all thoughts of relaxation fled her mind. Sprinting into the house, she changed into a staff shirt and long shorts, threw her hair into a ponytail, and hurried to the office. Relief flooded through her at seeing Martine at the front desk. *At least there's nothing wrong there.*

Martine had finally announced she was expecting a baby in the summer and was past the worst of the morning sickness. She stared at Hope and her eyes held the strangest expression— bewilderment, pride, and fear all showed on her face.

Hope rushed into the office.

"I'm here, Patti. What's going on?"

Patti gave her a sharp look and shut the door. Their daily delivery of the *St. Croix Chronicle* sat on the desk.

She bit her lip, darting a glance at Hope. "I take it you haven't seen the paper?"

Hope shook her head.

"Alex hasn't either?"

"No! What is going on?" Hope's heart was about to explode, though Patti didn't seem frightened. Instead, she shifted back and forth on her feet.

Sighing, Patti picked up a folded paper and handed it to Hope before pointing to the bottom half of the front page. Hope's breath exploded out when she read the giant headline. It was two lines, taking up the entire width of the page:

. . .

Local Dive Guide Due to Testify in Trial Is Former Navy SEAL and Decorated War Hero

A LENGTHY ARTICLE CONTINUED UNDERNEATH. In the center was a Navy photo of Alex wearing his dress blues, his left breast covered in ribbons.

"Oh no, Patti. This is the last thing he wants."

"I know. He's a very private man. I thought you should know right away." She paused, throwing Hope another uncertain glance. "I take it you knew about this?"

"Yes, but he doesn't want the whole island knowing! My God, he's only recently been able to talk about it."

Hope glanced at Patti with wide eyes. "It's the same reporter who called after the boat sank. And he called me after the shooting too. Obviously, he has been curious about Alex for a while." She swiped a hand over her forehead. "I don't get it. Why would he dig this up and write an article?"

"Child, local news here usually involves someone's dog who ran away. This is much too good of a story to pass up, I'm afraid."

"Dammit! Keep the papers here for now. The cat's out of the bag, but Alex has to hear about this from me." Hope looked down, muttering, "I wonder if I can get him to take today off." She turned back to Patti. "Ok, I'll deal with this."

Turning around, Hope dashed into the ladies room and locked herself in. She was instantly brought back to the last time she'd looked at herself in this mirror. It was the day the boat sank, and she'd realized how deep her feelings were for Alex. She snorted at her reflection. "You idiot. You were in love with him—you just couldn't admit it. Now he's really going to need you."

She lifted the newspaper and read.

By John Strickland

Local dive instructor and guide Alex Monroe has had an eventful year. Last July, he gained notoriety when Half Moon Bay Resort's dive boat sank, and he managed a rescue operation involving ten people adrift in the open ocean for four hours with no resulting injuries.

Then, in early October, he and resort owner Hope Collins were involved in an altercation with resort employee Charles Reed, which resulted in him receiving a gunshot wound as well as multiple charges against Reed, including attempted manslaughter. According to police reports, Reed allegedly attempted to rob Monroe in downtown Frederiksted and threatened him with a handgun, whereby Monroe was shot defending himself and Collins in an ensuing confrontation. Reed pled not guilty, and his trial is scheduled for next month. Monroe and Collins are expected to be primary witnesses for the prosecution.

Using publicly available military records and declassified Department of Defense documentation, it has been determined that Monroe is a highly decorated military veteran and uniquely qualified to manage both incidents listed above. He served for fifteen years as a US Navy SEAL, performing numerous overseas deployments.

Approximately six years ago, Monroe was given an honorable medical discharge from the Navy, after which he moved to St. Croix and became a dive instructor at Half Moon Bay Resort. The specifics of the particular campaign that resulted in his discharge were declassified by the DoD due to the nature of the incident and the inability to keep the details secret.

Monroe was a member of a Navy SEAL Team pursuing ISIS insurgents near Rakka, Syria, when faulty intelligence resulted in an ambush that killed eight SEAL Team members in action. Four more were injured. Monroe was critically wounded and airlifted to Germany for urgent medical attention, injuries that led to his medical discharge nearly a year later.

Monroe was granted a Purple Heart for the campaign. In addition, several members of his platoon as well as civilians present, gave testimony that resulted in Monroe being awarded the Navy Cross for exceptional heroism in combat, the US Navy's highest military honor and second only to the Medal of Honor in hierarchy. Multiple persons testified that Monroe left his Armored Personnel Carrier after their convoy was attacked, moving several of his Teammates as well as three civilians to safety before being struck by an Improvised Explosive Device himself.

Next month, Reed goes on trial, accused of attempted manslaughter. Criminal trials exist to reveal the truth and administer justice. Whatever the outcome, Monroe paid a heavy price that night. Just as clearly, he paid a much heavier price in service to his country. Monroe was contacted repeatedly for this article. His only reply was, "No comment."

HOPE READ the second-to-last paragraph again and again. She closed her eyes, picturing Alex in vivid detail as he stood in their bathroom, studying those two medals with fiery intensity. Her eyes opened to the sentence once more.

. . . Monroe being awarded the Navy Cross for exceptional bravery in combat, the US Navy's highest military honor and second only to the Medal of Honor in hierarchy.

SHE SIGHED HEAVILY at his own explanation. *"It's just another medal. I got it as a consolation prize for the same op I got the Purple Heart, the last one."*

Hope sagged against the counter. "Oh, Alex. Why can't you see it like everyone else? My God."

Her mind flashed back to that awful night. To Alex trying to negotiate with Charles—until Charles moved his gun to Hope. Then he hadn't hesitated to defend her. Taking a deep breath, Hope folded up the paper again and marched out of the bathroom toward the pier.

ALEX GLANCED at the building waves as he walked toward the gear room—they'd have some seasick divers today for sure. He grinned, glad he'd never suffered from that particular malady. Today would be a challenge, though—he looked forward to it and hummed a tune as he entered the gear room to collect some guest dive gear.

He was pulling a wetsuit off its hanger when the doorway darkened. Hope stood there, and he brightened. "Hey, what brings you to the dungeon?"

She shut the door, and his smile faded at her solemn expression. She had a newspaper in one hand and was wiping the other on her hip. She darted her eyes all over the room—everywhere except at him. Finally, she squared her shoulders and stood straight, looking him in the eye. "I just found out something you need to know. Put the wetsuit down, please, and sit at your workbench."

He turned and hung up the wetsuit, his happy mood a distant memory. "What's going on?"

"Please, just sit." She pressed her mouth into a thin gash and raised a palm against her temple.

With a knot in his stomach, Alex sat.

"There's an article in the newspaper this morning." Hope clenched her eyes shut, then snapped them open. "I don't even know how to break this to you. I'm so sorry, Alex. Here."

She handed him the paper, and the air rushed from his lungs as he read the giant headline. He clamped his mouth shut, automatically forming a neutral expression as he read, though his body tightened with every word. Hope rested a hand on his shoulder.

Alex kept the mask on his face, but his heart hammered, and he breathed like he'd just swam a mile as he fought to stay in control. He couldn't hear anything but the blood pounding in his ears as he glanced at the byline, recognizing the name.

Oh, you goddamn son of a bitch.

But the anger fled as soon as it had appeared, replaced with a creeping numbness. Finally, he sat back and rubbed his face with both hands. "Oh my God. Well, I guess it's a good thing I've been learning to cope with it better."

Hope watched him closely, as if he might explode at any moment.

"Goddamn reporter," Alex said. "He called me a few times about the trial and was fishing for information. I didn't know he'd go digging into my past, though. Son of a bitch."

She squeezed his shoulder. "I'm sorry, honey. I know this is the last thing you want to see."

He stared at the tool-covered wall, not seeing anything. The detachment spread like glacial ice all over his body. "I feel numb right now. I never thought it would come out like this. Hell, I never thought it would come out at all."

Hope took a deep breath. "Alex, would you take today off? We've got ten divers. It'd be a bigger group than we prefer, but I'm sure Robert would take them."

He turned to her, blinking. The muscles in her jaw worked as she clenched her teeth, and her concerned eyes darted over his face—waiting for his reaction. He let his gaze wander back to the scarred, well-used surface of his workbench, and he absently ran a hand over it—trying to ground himself in this new reality he'd just found himself in.

Finally, he snapped his head back and forth, trying to shake himself out of it. His voice strengthened. "I need to talk with Tommy and Robert myself. I don't want them hearing this from the damn paper."

He paused, meeting her pleading eyes. "If Robert agrees, I'll sit today out."

Hope slumped, her fists unclenching, and gave him a shaky, hopeful smile. "You know, it's actually a very complimentary article. And there's a good chance at least some of this would come out at the trial, anyway."

Alex made a derisive noise, not trusting himself to say anything more. But after a moment, he asked in a quiet voice, "Will you come out to the boat with me?"

"Of course. Let's go." She grabbed the paper, took his hand, and they walked toward the boat. He clung to her hand and walked with a halting, shuffling step. Tommy was on the bridge, and Robert was attaching a regulator to a tank when they came aboard. Alex couldn't believe how much his mood had changed since he'd stepped off the boat only a few minutes ago. Hope sat down on one of the side benches under the canopy.

"Tommy? Can you come down here? I need to talk to you both." Alex moved into the covered area, standing in the center. "Have either of you seen this morning's paper?" Both shook their heads. "There's an article in there—about me before I came here. I wanted you both to hear about it from me."

He sighed, trying to find words for the conversation he'd been avoiding for years. "I don't like to talk about my past—it's really difficult. And the whole goddamn island is finding out why as we speak." He paced from side to side, needing to be in motion. "You guys know I was in the Navy. What I don't go around saying is that I was a Navy SEAL." He stopped, waiting for their reaction.

Robert looked impressed.

Tommy just shrugged. "So what's the big revelation, man? I always suspected you were some sort of damn commando or somethin'. And after the boat sank, I was sure of it." Then Tommy grinned. "Navy SEAL, huh? Badass, man."

Alex couldn't resist a small smile, but it fell away. "It was how my career ended that's hard for me to talk about." He stopped, closing his eyes and resting both hands on his head. "The Team I was on got ambushed, and eight men were killed. I was one of four wounded. The injuries were bad enough to end my career."

"Alex," Hope said softly. "Tell them the whole truth."

He glanced at her and nodded. His head could have weighed fifty pounds, and his legs were wooden—he felt ten years older than when he'd left the house that morning. "I almost died—my hip is a mass of metal that needed a year of rehab. After I got discharged, I came here."

Alex turned to Tommy. "I don't know if you remember, Tommy—I still had a limp when I first arrived. It worked itself out over time. I've spent the last five—well, closer to six years now—trying to come to terms with it and move on with my life."

He looked to the side bench with a slight smile. "Hope has helped me a lot with that."

Alex turned to Robert. "Can you take the group today? I've been given orders to take today off." He twitched the corner of his mouth at Hope.

"Of course." Robert gave him a sad smile and shook his hand. "I'm really sorry, Alex. That's a terrible story. Thank you for what you did out there."

Alex nodded his thanks. His head was stuffed with cotton, and he was still dazed with the strange mixture of grief and numbness. His movements were slow and stumbling, like the world was in slow motion.

Tommy drew Alex into a hug, slapping his shoulders. "Take your time, brother. We got your back."

Chapter Thirty-One

HOPE TOOK his hand again as they walked back to the house. Alex was silent, his head down as they made their way across the beach. There was a muted roaring in her ears, and she was at a loss on how to help him.

Imagining Tommy and Robert scrolling through the article on their phones at that very moment, she put the paper down on the kitchen island. Alex read the article again, then started pacing in circles around the island before finally stopping, staring vacantly at the counter as he leaned on his arms.

"Can I get you anything?" Hope stumbled for something to say. "Coffee? Beer? Scotch?"

He gave her a faint smile and enfolded her in his arms. "I'm so glad you're here right now."

"Me too."

Do I dare ask him? He's calmer than I was expecting.

"Alex, why didn't you say that was the Navy Cross when we looked at it? That's the very definition of heroism."

He groaned and pulled away from her, starting to pace around the kitchen island again, faster and faster. The emotion escalated inside him now, etched upon his tightening face as his breathing deepened.

Now it's coming.

"Hope, I can't even remember it! I was traveling in the APC and heard an explosion. Then my mind is a complete blank. The next thing I remember is the hospital in Germany." He stopped, facing her with both fists clenched at his sides. "How am I supposed to be proud of actions I have no memory of? I have no idea if I actually did any of that!"

Hope's heart was breaking. She faced him, each of them on opposite sides of the island. "You can't really be questioning that, can you? I've known you less than a year, and I have no doubt you performed every single action you were awarded that medal for. How many people are alive right now because of you?"

He winced and turned away, but her voice strengthened. "My God, Alex. You are the very image of a goddamn hero. Even the reporter said as much. Why are you so hard on yourself?"

"*Because it was my fault!*" Alex roared as he whirled around. His face was shattered, and his voice anguished.

Hope took a step back, but the force of his torment only caused a terrible grief in her, no fear at all.

"I was in command of that mission! Eight of my best friends, my *brothers*, died because of decisions I made." Alex paced again, back and forth with both palms pressed against his eyes. "We shouldn't have trusted those two goddamn scouts. I *knew* they were full of shit. I even went to my CO about it. But it was the best intel we had—the only intel we had." He savagely rubbed his face, then looked at her, his eyes blazing. "*I* made the call to go ahead that night. It was my decision. This is on me. One of the guys who died was in SEAL training with me. We had been together for almost eighteen years. Maybe I did save a few lives that day, but it doesn't make up for the ones I ended."

Hope clutched his arm, which gripped the edge of the counter. The muscles rippled as if he was hanging on for dear life. "Yes. It does. I won't insult you by saying I understand what you went through out there, but even I know there's no way you could have realized eight men were dead when you ran out of that APC and started pulling people to safety."

He focused on the granite counter, refusing to look at her, while Hope searched for a way to bring him back from the brink. "You said it yourself, Alex. You did the best you could with the intel you had. That doesn't make it your fault."

Hope softened her voice. "Your friend who died. Do you think he would want you to be torturing yourself like this? For *years* now? I'm sure each of those eight men knew, just like you did, that they might not come back. What happened was *nobody's* fault—except the ISIS assholes who ambushed you."

Finally, he turned to her, his eyes enormous and vulnerable as they locked onto hers and held fast. Hope squeezed his arm— she was the one person who could get through to him. "You want to honor them, honor their sacrifice? I'm sure if you could have spoken with them, they would never have blamed you in the first place. So, *stop blaming yourself.*"

Hope rested her forehead against his shoulder, but he turned and pulled her into an embrace, holding her tight. "I don't know what I'd do without you right now."

She pulled back, cupping his face in both hands as she pierced him with her gaze, hopefully straight into his soul. "A year ago, you saved me from drowning. Now it's my turn. You're not alone anymore—we'll get through it together, I promise. You don't have to face this by yourself."

LATER, he told her to set out the newspapers for the guests like they usually did. "No point in hiding anything now."

She texted Patti.

Hope: Alex says put the newspapers out.

Patti: Is he ok?

Hope: Coping.

Patti: I'm so sorry. He doesn't deserve this. But I'm so proud of him.

Hope: We all are.

SHE SIGHED. *I just wish I could get him to see it.*

Alex went for a long swim directly off the beach in front of their house. The waves continued to build as the day went on—he dove through them like they weren't there.

She went down to the kitchen to load up on food. Gerold and Pauline were both full of worry, and Hope did her best to reassure them as Gerold prepared a feast for their dinner, seasoning two T-bone steaks and prepping potatoes for her to roast. Hope had to smile. *Steak and potatoes—Gerold knows him well.* He added two slices of cheesecake, and she made her way back.

It was over two hours before he returned. Hope refused to let herself worry—where water was concerned, she was convinced Alex was invincible. Still, the unacknowledged knot in her stomach relaxed at last as she glimpsed his assured stroke heading toward her. Meeting him at the waterline with a towel, Hope wrapped it around his waist as she gave him a long kiss, then held him as the waves washed over their feet. He clung to her tightly.

As they returned to the house, Alex sat on the porch couch and Cruz approached, laying his head on Alex's knee and offering what comfort he could. Alex bent over and gave the dog a thorough belly rub, bringing a smile to Hope's face as she went inside.

As the sun descended to the horizon, she grilled the steaks while the potatoes roasted in the oven, a salad completing the meal. Hope set the outside table, wanting Alex to be near the ocean. Of course, he was quiet during the meal, but more relaxed now. The combination of a long, hard swim and a good meal set his mind and heart a little more at ease.

Hope's nervousness manifested in mindless chitchat, talking about the new prints she had chosen for the office and ideas she had to sell Robert's photos and split the profits with him. Then she moved on to towel designs for the bathrooms and paint chips for the lobby.

Alex stared at her with a genuine smile on his face.

"Oh dear. I've been babbling, haven't I?"

He leaned forward and kissed her deeply. "I cannot even begin to tell you how much I love you right now. I actually feel content."

"Good. You deserve to."

He tipped his head back and finished his beer. "Content, but also very tired. I'm going to turn in. I know it's early, but I think I'm about to crash hard."

"Of course. I'll clean up."

She settled on the sofa in their great room with a book. Cruz occasionally padded to the closed door of their bedroom, whining, before returning to Hope. Finally, her eyelids softened, and she went to bed herself, listening to Alex's steady, deep breathing as she fell asleep.

LATER THAT NIGHT, Hope awoke to Alex exploding up in bed and roaring out an agonized, tormented scream. He took great, heaving gasps, his hands pressed against his eyes. She reached out a hand to him, letting it hover above his shoulder as she hesitated.

No. No more avoiding—for either of us.

She rested her hand on his rock-hard shoulder. He was covered in a fine sheen of sweat and didn't react to her, just sat frozen except for his gasps. Eventually, he removed his hands from his eyes, resting them on his bent knees while still breathing heavily. He sat there for several moments before he turned and melted down to her, his head on her bare breast. She wrapped him up tightly and stroked his hair. Gradually, his breathing calmed.

Neither of them spoke.

Hope let her hands and body express her love, and he began to settle. As time passed, the occasional blink of his eyelashes against her skin let her know he was awake. She continued to stroke his head, offering the comfort he desperately needed, even if he wouldn't ask for it. Hope was prepared to stay like that all night, just holding him. She wanted to ask what he was thinking, but didn't want to intrude now that his body had calmed.

Alex answered her unspoken question by turning his head and kissing her breast. In no rush, he moved his tongue slowly in ever decreasing circles until he hit the center. Then he moved to the other breast as their deepening breaths filled the still night air.

He moved on top of her, and she pulled him in for a deep kiss, putting every ounce of emotion she possessed into it. Alex met her, his need even greater. She deepened the kiss as she brushed her hands over his hair and shoulders.

She opened wider, and he slid inside her. Then he collapsed onto her with a deep sigh, his head cradled in her shoulder and not moving. He breathed deeply, inhaling her scent as she tightened her arms around him.

He wrapped his arms under her back and rolled them over, relaxing to stillness underneath her as he returned his face to her neck, his hands on her hips. He whispered into her ear, "Please."

Alex was anything but a passive lover, but tonight he needed her to take the lead.

Hope slowly moved above him as the cool sheet caressed her back, and he took a deep breath beneath her. She established a deliberate rhythm, both of them totally silent.

Moving her head to his, she kissed each closed eye and traced her mouth slowly across his forehead. Then Alex lightly stroked both hands up her back, his fingers spread, while keeping his head buried in her neck and remaining still beneath her.

As Hope continued moving above him, her only indication of his response was his steadily deepening breath on her neck. His breathing became her universe—her sole focus. She kept the same slow rhythm for the longest time until he ripped down the sheet covering her and returned his arms tightly around her waist, which she took as a signal to move faster.

His breath continued to quicken, hot against her neck, eventually becoming ragged and irregular, no longer echoing her movements. She moved forcefully against him. Now he was gasping but still making no other sound and remaining unmoving.

Finally, Alex filled his lungs, holding his breath as he slid his feet up the bed and pinned her in place with his thighs. He crushed his arms around her as his entire body convulsed.

It went on and on, the release he so badly needed. His single, held breath became deep, panting inhalations as Hope softly kissed his brow.

His breathing eventually slowed, but he stayed in the same position, his head tight against her neck and his thighs locking her to him as he held her tightly. Her breath also calmed. She remained still and silent, just letting him exist in this safe place with her and concentrating on him.

His head moved slightly. Her neck was wet from his tears.

Oh, my love. You have so much grieving left to do, but this is a start.

Eventually, Alex moved his lips to her ear. "I love you."

"I love you too."

Nothing else needed to be said.

Chapter Thirty-Two

ALEX STOOD under the canopy of the dive boat as Tommy descended the ladder from the wheelhouse. They had just returned from the morning trip, and Robert had already left for an appointment. Several days had passed since the article came out, and Alex was trying to get back to a regular routine. He had insisted on working the day following the article's release.

He'd been quiet and done his job with less than his usual enthusiasm. Alex strongly suspected either Tommy or Robert had talked to the guests and told them not to talk to him about the article, because only one guy had—and Robert had steered him away to show him an imaginary fish before Alex could respond.

He found a pair of sunglasses on the side bench and was straightening to add them to the lost and found when Patti boarded. She nodded to Tommy. "Good trip today?"

"Yeah, pretty routine. The weather's cooperatin', so that helps."

Alex hadn't seen Patti since the article and doubted she was here to ask about the dive trip.

"How are you, Alex?" She spoke softly, and Tommy joined her side, both facing Alex.

"Handling it." He bounced his gaze between the pair and gave a deep sigh. "Actually, I'm glad you're both here. I wanted to apologize to you."

Patti opened her eyes wide. "What on earth for?"

"I should have told you both about my past a long time ago. I just . . . couldn't." He turned to Tommy. "I can tell you and Robert have been giving me my space the last couple of days. Thanks for that."

Tommy nodded, his face grave. "Whatever you need, consider it done."

Alex motioned to the side bench, and Tommy and Patti sat side by side while he sat across from them. "It's really important to me that you two realize I didn't come here as a last resort. Or that I looked down on it." He took in the palapa and the structures halfway down the pier. "This place helped save me. You two are a big part of that. And even Steve."

He looked at his clasped hands. "I was broken when I first arrived here. And you guys accepted me, even with my bad moods and silences."

"Oh Alex," Patti said. "We could all see how much you were hurtin' back then. But it was also clear what kind of man you are. What happened to you in Syria was an awful thing, and you're the kind of man who needs to wear the world on his shoulders. I just hope you finally find some peace."

Alex gave her a ghost of a smile. "Maybe someday I will. If this had happened a couple of years ago, I'm not sure what I would have done. I might have bolted like Steve did." He shook his head. "I was so pissed at him for leaving. But he might have done me the biggest favor of my life. He brought me Hope. In every sense of the word."

"I'd forgotten about your limp until you mentioned it," Tommy said. "Seems like you've fully recovered."

"Physically, yes, for the most part. Though that water rescue after *Deep Diver* sank wasn't exactly fun. That's really the only flare I've had in my hip, and it went away." Alex stared steadily at Tommy. "The one thing I couldn't stand the thought of, if it all came out, was people pitying me. I dealt with that for a solid year when I was rehabbing at Walter Reed Hospital. Thank you, Tommy. I've never felt even a hint of it from you these past few days."

"Hell, man. You don't need anyone's pity. You're too damn stubborn to die."

Alex grinned.

"I wondered how on earth you were able to knock Charles out," Patti said. "Now I guess I know."

"I was a bit slower than I used to be, but all my skills were still there when I needed them. That was a good feeling. Well, up until I got shot." All three of them laughed at that, and Alex shook his head. "I'm sorry I kept it from you, though. I wish I'd told you after I got shot—that was when it made the most sense. You both deserved better."

"Well, maybe I do," Patti said, with a gleam in her eye. "Except for the minor matter that my cousin tried to kill you. But Tommy doesn't."

"Hey!" Tommy turned to her, one hand on his hip. "You get to work in the air conditionin' with Hope. I'm the one who has to put up with his lame-ass jokes all day. Workin' with this guy is *rough*."

A warmth spread through Alex's chest as his smile grew. "I take it back. Neither of you deserves me." They had a good laugh, and then he stood. "Let's go get a beer. It's been way too long since we've done that. We can rinse the boat off later."

They stepped back onto the pier and headed toward the

pool bar with Alex in the middle. He put an arm around each of their shoulders, and soon Tommy had them all laughing again.

Maybe things were going to be ok after all.

TWO WEEKS LATER, Hope opened the slider and sat at the outdoor table. There was a slight breeze, and fast-moving clouds raced across the night sky as the moon peeked through them.

Completely relaxed, she stared at the scene—so different from last year.

There was always a tranquil peace to the resort, and now Alex was able to feel it once again. The first few days after the article came out, he'd been tense—only going between the pier and the house to avoid unnecessary contact with anyone. He told her he'd had a good conversation with Patti and Tommy that helped.

But after that first group of divers left, the issue faded away on the resort, and things returned to normal. Well, a new normal —Alex was quieter, still coming to terms with it. But at least his goofy sense of humor was back, and he hadn't had any further nightmares.

A soft pop nudged Hope out of her reverie as Alex came outside with two wine glasses and began pouring rich, deep-red liquid into them. The soft breeze rustled her yellow and black sundress, one of his favorites. Setting his phone on the edge of the table, Alex queued up a soft instrumental island music playlist and sat down as marimba and steel drums filled the air.

He handed her a glass and raised his with a very sultry smile. "Happy Birthday, baby."

Hope returned his smile—thirty-seven today. She touched her glass to his, then drank, the taste of the wine exploding in her mouth. Chocolate, berries, and pure velvet. "Oh my God! What are we drinking?"

Alex laughed. "No idea. Gerold picked it out."

"Oh, wow. We'll have to thank him when we go down to dinner."

He smiled. "Well, did you have a good day today? Since you insisted on working."

She took another sip of the amazing wine. "Yes, it was great. And I don't need a big fuss made over me. I'm not eight, you know. A nice glass of wine, followed by dinner with you down at the restaurant, is the perfect celebration."

His eyes smoldered. "Oh, I have no intention of ending the celebration that early."

Returning his look, she brushed a lock of hair from her face as a wispy breeze traveled through the porch. "What a beautiful night. It's just—"

Footsteps came from the stairs behind, so she turned around. Gerold climbed onto the porch, carrying a tray covered by a silver cloche in one hand and a folding stand in the other.

"Good evenin', you two. I'd like to present your first course, lobster bisque." He set the stand in the corner of the porch and removed the cloche, revealing two soup bowls and a covered decanter. After pouring the soup, Gerold brought the bowls over to their table, carrying a pepper grinder under one arm. "Pepper? I highly recommend it. Really brings out the flavors."

Hope stared openmouthed at Alex, who wore a secret smile and looked very pleased with himself.

Gerold laughed. "Hope? You look a little surprised. Pepper?"

"Yes!" She snapped to. "Thank you. I thought we were eating in the dining room."

He ground the pepper over her bowl and then did the same

with Alex's. "Well, someone else had a different idea and made all kinds of dire threats if I didn't comply."

Alex laughed and mock-punched him. "Oh, shut up. You thought it was a great idea."

Grinning, Gerold said, "We'll be back with your main courses after a bit." He bowed and disappeared down the beach.

Picking up a spoon, Hope turned back to Alex. "You started with my favorite."

"I wanted a little more privacy tonight."

"I can't wait to see what the main course is."

"Well, don't look at me. I told Gerold to surprise us." He looked up at her. "Really."

She put her spoon down. "You are the sweetest man."

"Don't tell anyone!" Then he sobered. "I know I haven't been very good company for the last couple of weeks. I wanted to make up for that tonight."

"You're always my favorite company."

"I can't begin to tell you how much you helped me that day. Or that night."

"You've been there when I needed you. Now I'm just returning the favor."

Alex reached out and held her hand. "It's a lot more than that."

She shook her head, looking around her again. "A year ago, I started my day in such a good mood, positive I was going to get that promotion. Oh, I was furious when I didn't! I still can't believe I quit on the spot and stormed out of my boss's office."

He brushed his thumb over the back of her hand before letting go. "I can picture you doing that, right down to the expression on your face."

"Well, it was totally unlike me. I've always craved safety and stability, and I was wrecked by the time I got home. That was the night Sara entered me in the lottery, and you know the rest." She pushed away her empty soup bowl.

"I do." He scraped his chair back and stood. "I'll be right back."

A few minutes later, he returned with a wrapped blue box about fifteen inches long in his hands. He handed it to her with a kiss. "Happy Birthday."

"Oh, Alex! You really didn't have to." Hope unwrapped it to reveal a handmade wind chime with butterflies hanging from the long metal tubes. She swallowed the lump in her throat. "How did you know I wanted this?"

"Maybe because both times I went with you to pick up photos for the bungalows, you had your face glued to the window of that shop next door?" He leaned down to kiss her again. "I went in one day and thought the butterflies were a good choice for you. Let me know where you want it and I'll hang it for you."

"It's perfect. Thank you."

"No, thank you. Now I can finally touch your butterfly whenever I want to." He ran a finger over her tattoo with a blazing smile. "You have no idea how worked up I got over this before we got together. It was becoming an obsession."

"Really?"

"Oh, yeah." He returned to his seat. "I used to fantasize about touching it. And that night on my deck, I finally got to. Right before I almost fell over the rail into the damn ocean."

"I could tell how much pain you were in that day. But in the end, I think Horseshoe Key was a better setting, anyway." She paused. "You're the first person I've told the real story behind my tattoo to in . . . probably over fifteen years. At this point in my life, you and Sara are the only ones who know the whole truth."

Hope swirled the beautiful ruby-red wine before taking a

sip. "Sometimes, I can't help but think what a waste it was—all those years building a fortress around myself so I wouldn't get hurt again. But everything that happened led me here to this very moment. We're very well matched, you know."

"*Very* well matched, especially in some areas."

She let her eyes become smoky as she stroked his leg with hers. "I didn't realize you had carnal thoughts about my tattoo."

He couldn't hide a smile. "You can't even begin to imagine."

Their gazes met, and the moment held until footsteps came from behind her. This time it was Charlotte, setting her tray on the folding table before clearing away their soup bowls. She set two covered plates before them, then removed the cloches simultaneously to reveal filet mignon and grilled shrimp.

"Oh, yeah!" Alex lit up.

"Enjoy." Charlotte collected her things with a grin and withdrew.

Hope enjoyed watching Alex eat, obviously relishing every bite. "You are such a carnivore!" She laughed as Alex shrugged, unrepentant, and they returned to their meals. The soft music, wine, and wonderful dinner were further elevating her good mood. "I never asked how your day was."

"Pretty normal. The usual for these days—meaning busy. I had to bring April on to give Robert a day off." He poured the rest of the wine. "You really know what you're doing, Boss Lady."

"I'm sure there are more speed bumps coming in the future because that's just how life is. But I am so happy with how the resort is doing. And yes, I'm going to say it—I'm proud of myself." She put her fork down, finished.

"You should be." He leaned forward and kissed her hand. "I'm incredibly proud of you." He stood up and carried their finished plates to the corner table. "I'll be back in a sec." He threw a smile over his shoulder as he went back inside.

Cruz had been hanging out on the porch with them, retreating to the far end when their food was delivered, and returning when the coast was clear. "What's he up to now, Cruz?" Hearing his name, he approached her with a doggy smile, looking for a pat on the head. "You didn't run away when Gerold and Charlotte appeared. Maybe you're finally trusting people a little more?"

The dog turned and cocked his head as Alex elbowed the slider back open, candlelight glowing on his face as he carried a small cake toward her. It was the perfect size for two—a circular white frosted layer cake with *Happy Birthday Hope!* written on it and a candle of a palm tree alight.

Alex set it in front of her and leaned in for a long kiss. "You're going to have to settle for me telling you happy birthday. The evening has been much too wonderful to subject you to my singing. No one needs to hear that. Go on, make a wish."

"How can I? All my wishes have come true."

He leaned casually in his chair, one elbow on the table and looking incredibly sexy. "I'm sure you can think of something."

She blew out the candle. "I kind of wanted to hear you sing."

He laughed—the full, exuberant laugh that took years off him. "Trust me, you don't. I can't carry a tune to save my life. Cruz would run away and never come back."

Hope cut two pieces. It was a white cake with raspberry filling between the layers—her favorite. Knowing Gerold had made it, her expectations were high, but she was still blown away. Light and creamy, with strong vanilla flavors and maybe a hint of cinnamon? It was the perfect accompaniment to the rest of the red wine.

She refrained from licking her plate when she finished it as she firmly set the fork down. "Thank you, love. This has been just wonderful."

"It's not over yet. Dance with me?"

He pulled her close, holding her left hand in his right as they danced to the slow beat of the island music.

"I was remembering the last time we slow danced." Her voice became huskier.

"Oh? I don't recall that."

She pressed against him, feeling the evidence. "Liar."

"That was my line."

He brushed his lips over hers, then opened his mouth and deepened the kiss. The sensation traveled all the way to her toes before rising up again. Finally, he let go of her hand, wrapping her tightly in his arms as they moved together. They danced together for several songs, guitar and steel drums set to the lapping of the waves just in front and the moon reflecting on the ocean.

Hope breathed out an easy sigh, feeling like melted butter as he stroked her hair. "How is it possible, Alex?"

"What's that?"

"One year ago, I was at one of the lowest points in my life, completely lost and alone. I didn't even know you existed. And now I'm here, and I can't imagine my life without you."

He leaned his cheek against her forehead. "I feel the same way. I couldn't have gotten through the past two weeks without you."

"I'm only trying to help you the way you helped me. I can't describe it, what it means to me that I can always count on you. I don't have to be afraid anymore."

He pulled back, watching her closely. "I will *always* be there for you."

"Believe me, I know."

"Let's go inside. We've still got lots of celebrating left to do, baby."

Chapter Thirty-Three

AT FIRST, Hope wanted to deny the warm light radiating through her chest. She sat in her home office, scanning the profit-and-loss sheets and making sure the figures were correct. They were. Most of the bungalows had been remodeled, and the others were booked solid.

The resort was thriving.

In January, she'd reviewed Steve's previous employee raise amounts for the last several years. There wasn't any consistency, which wasn't unusual since the resort could have large swings in revenue based on the economy, weather, or guests' whims. Still, the largest raise he'd given base workers was two percent, which she considered stingy.

Hope had given every employee a five-hundred-dollar Christmas bonus, with double going to Patti and Gerold. Alex had flatly refused his. But given how well the resort was doing, she'd recently given everyone a five percent raise, with Patti and Gerold receiving ten percent.

Alex's increase had been more difficult to determine. Previously, he'd had a unique arrangement where part of his salary included his apartment as well as all meals. But his apartment was now the spa, so she couldn't justify holding back that portion of his salary. Talking about this with him would get her nowhere—only ending with him insisting he didn't need any more money.

"That's not the point, you stubborn man," she said to the empty room.

Alex clearly had no issues with the fact she was technically his boss and paid him, but his male pride rose to the surface now and again.

So Hope had simply increased his salary by twenty-five percent and not said anything to him. He'd notice eventually, but hadn't said anything yet.

Now, she was pleased to see the financial results of the raises hadn't impacted the overall profit much. She drew a small salary herself, but poured most of the profits back into the resort, especially with renovations occurring. The insurance settlement after the hurricane had only covered a portion of them.

She and Patti were interviewing several candidates to be the resort's first massage therapist. They had several promising choices, and Hope couldn't wait to get it going.

Rising, she took a few minutes for a stretching session. As she increased her running mileage, it was a constant struggle to keep her legs and hips loose. With the triathlon approaching next month, she'd nearly stopped her morning swims to concentrate on running. She missed them, but didn't have the energy to do both. Hope had no idea how triathletes did it all. She was pondering her next project when her phone rang.

"Hello, Hope. This is Danae Robertson, the prosecutor. Can I talk to you for a few minutes?"

Hope's stomach sank to her knees. "Sure. Now's a good time."

"I wanted to let you know Charles's trial date has been set. It's going to start March eighth."

Well, at least Alex will celebrate his birthday before it starts. "Ok. Well, I'll certainly do what I can to put him away."

"I know. I don't think you'll run into too much trouble. The defense attorney will question you, but I wouldn't expect any curveballs for you."

What are you trying to say?

"Well, that's a relief, I guess."

"I talked to Alex earlier today. And I wanted to reinforce the point with you too. The article that came out was really great for our side. Alex is pretty much the best witness I could hope for."

Yeah, I'll bet.

"But I imagine the defense is going to go after Alex hard. I told him to prepare himself. I'm wondering if the attorney is going to try to argue Charles was only defending himself, and the gun went off accidentally. I just wanted to let you both know Alex could come under some tough questioning." She paused. "He just said he'd be ready and hung up on me."

Hope sighed and shut her laptop. "Alex is a private man. He doesn't like airing his dirty laundry for public consumption, and he has had to deal with that a lot lately."

"Yeah, I got it. That's why I'm calling you. His testimony is really important, Hope. He could make the difference between Charles going to jail or walking free."

"You want me to make sure he's on board."

"Look, I don't think the defense attorney wants to dig into his past and bring up that last mission any more than he has to. It's counter-productive to his case. But Alex needs to be prepared, and it seems like you're the best person to help with that."

"Yeah, I probably am."

After ending the call, Hope called it a day. She glanced out the windows of the office, but *Surface Interval* hadn't returned yet. Alex had a very dedicated group of divers this week, and she'd hardly seen him. Grabbing a paperback from her nightstand, she settled on the porch couch to wait.

Cruz came over and rested his head on her knee. She scratched behind his ears. "You're always here to say hello, aren't you?" She gave him a few more scratches to his evident delight. "Where did you come from? Did someone dump you beside the road? I can't believe someone would do that to you." She smiled, and he thumped his tail in response. "Well, you know you're loved now and that's what matters." She settled in to read as Cruz settled on the floor beneath her.

HOPE ALTERNATED her attention between her book and the beautiful scene before her. The sun had just set, casting the soft, puffy clouds in a soft-pink hue as the palm trees spoke softly in the breeze. Alex had hung her wind chimes, and the long metal tubes hummed a beautiful deep tone.

She drifted her gaze up the beach and broke into a wide smile as Alex walked up the beach toward the house, but it fell at his weariness. She checked her watch—it was nearly seven. His feet dragged as he walked.

The current dive group was taking a toll on him. They had booked three dives per day, plus several night dives. A backup captain had worked to give Tommy two days off, but the group had made it clear they only wanted Alex as their guide. Today was their final day of diving, needing to take tomorrow off to clear all excess nitrogen from their bodies prior to flying home.

Alex climbed the stairs, and Hope sat up on the couch, patting the spot next to her. He sat down, slumping onto her shoulder with an enormous sigh.

"That bad, huh?" She asked, kissing his head.

"The group was ok, except for one guy. There is *always* one guy. I seriously thought about shutting off his air on the last dive. He questioned and challenged me on everything. I'm a pretty patient man, Hope, but I finally got in his face this morning. He'll probably lodge a formal complaint to get me fired—sorry about that. Well, not really."

She laughed as she leaned her cheek against him. "Little does he know you're sleeping with the boss." She kissed his head again. "You've really been working hard. You haven't put in less than a twelve-hour day all week."

He closed his eyes and snuggled closer to her. "Yeah, I even took them on two night dives. And that guy got lost on both of them. How do you even get lost on a night dive? All you can see are people's lights! I'm not sure he even knew which way was up." He sat up and rubbed his eyes. "God, I'll be glad when he's gone. He clearly has not learned the asshole-boat statute."

She thought about that statement for a moment. "Ok, I'll bite. What is the asshole-boat statute?"

"I didn't teach you this? It's very important information you need to know." His forehead creased as he frowned. "Maybe you do need to fire me. This is a serious transgression of my instructional duties."

"Would you shut up and tell me?"

"What you just said makes no sense."

She glared back at him.

The frown instantly transformed into laughter as he held up his hands. "Ok. Ok. Here it is."

He sat up and faced her, making sure he had her full attention. "This is a universal diving maxim. It's true the world over. And it is this, Ms. Collins. On every boat, there is an asshole. Any time you board a boat, your first duty is to identify the asshole, so you can avoid them. If, after close inspection, you cannot determine said asshole—" He paused. "It's you."

At first, Hope only stared at him. Until the laughter came bubbling up. She held her hands over her mouth, her shoulders shaking.

"I swear it's true. The statute has never failed me. Though I will admit, there's been a couple of times when I've been the asshole."

"Well, maybe you never taught me this important maxim because it would never apply to me."

He softened his eyes. "You'll never be the asshole." Alex leaned back with his arm over his eyes. "But believe me, it's a very good idea to find out who it is and prepare yourself. I've learned that in spades this last week."

She kissed his cheek before standing. "Hang on. I'll be right back." Returning with two bottles of beer, she handed him one, saying, "You look like a man who needs a drink."

"Only one?" He rolled the cold bottle over his forehead, then drank half of it in one shot.

"Hmmm. I guess you didn't have to search too hard for the asshole when Marcus was on board."

Alex shook his head and exhaled through his teeth. "You'll never know how hard I had to hold myself back from punching that guy. I just don't get it. You're with the woman you supposedly love and she's scared to death, but you want to take pictures of it? There's nothing worse than a terrible diver with a camera. When he's an asshole on top of it, it's the perfect storm."

"I could tell you weren't happy about his camera. I had no idea why. Well, until he shoved it in my face as a six-foot moray swam in between my legs."

"Well, don't blame me." Alex moved in and nuzzled her neck. "That eel was doing my job, after all. I had to get him out of there."

"Oh, I do love you." She let him rest on her shoulder for few minutes then sat up. "Come on, sailor. Change into your formal-wear, and let's head down for dinner."

While she waited, Hope's thoughts returned to her phone call with Danae, but her musings were interrupted when Alex returned, his hair still damp. He wore a Cuban shirt and cargo shorts and was actually matching.

He held an elbow out to her. "Your chariot awaits."

They settled in at the restaurant and ordered. "How's your training for the race coming along?" Alex asked.

"All right. The race isn't until after the trial, so I've still got time. It's so much harder running in the heat compared to Chicago, so I'm still getting acclimated to it. I heard from a triathlete in my running group that Gerold is fast. Compared to you two, I'm pretty sure I'm going to get my ass handed to me."

"Don't talk like that. All you can ever do is your best. Then the time doesn't matter."

"Uh-huh." Hope smirked. "Says the guy with the 2:44 marathon PR. You doing any special training for the swim?"

"I'm working on my speed more. I'm not worried about the endurance, but I haven't worked at holding a fast pace for a while. I'm enjoying it, and I really threw myself into it after that goddamn article came out. Those long, hard swims helped me deal with it."

After they finished their entrees, Hope studied Alex care-fully. Figuring he was probably recovered from the day's ordeal with his group, she broached the subject. "I had an unsettling phone conversation today."

"Let me guess. It involved a prosecuting attorney."

"She told me she spoke to you earlier."

"Yeah. Can't say I'm looking forward to it."

"Me either." A molten ball formed in her gut at the thought.

He took her hand. "You ok with this? I know it could bring back some bad memories for you."

She smiled. "I guess that makes two of us, huh? I've got your back if you've got mine."

"Always."

"You feel like you can talk about things a little easier now?"

Alex shrugged. "Yeah, but it will never be easy. I'm trying to view it as a mission. I've got a job to do, so when the time comes, I'll just focus and get it done."

"You know, this is actually similar to what you did in the Navy."

His face went blank. "How's that?"

"Well, you spent many years defending us against bad people. Testifying is a little like that, isn't it?"

"I hadn't thought of it like that, but I guess you're right."

"Just think about that when you're on the stand. Your testimony could make a big difference."

"At least I don't need to worry about scorpions in my boots." He studied her closely. "I'm here if you need me during this, ok?"

"Right back at you, sailor."

Chapter Thirty-Four

MARCH . . .

Hope tucked a crisp white blouse into her blue skirt as she stretched her calf, still tight from her ten-mile run yesterday. Taking a deep, calming breath, she finished the outfit with a suit jacket and buttoned it, nervously fussing with her hair in the mirror. She glanced into the closet at Alex, who was tucking a long-sleeved white shirt into a pair of khakis. He moved to a garment bag tucked into the corner of his side, unzipping it to reveal a gray jacket, which he pulled off the hanger.

Forgetting her nerves, Hope moved into the closet with a smile. "Ha! You do own a suit. I've been wanting to know what was in that garment bag but didn't want to snoop. Do I spy camo behind it?"

Alex turned to her with a smug grin as he waved an index finger at her. "Don't let it go to your head. I only wear a suit under the greatest duress. And yes, I kept a few uniforms. That's an old daily-service uniform." He made sure he had her full attention. "And I absolutely refuse to wear a tie, even to court."

She peeked around his shoulder at the open garment bag, discovering several shirts and coats inside it. Easily visible was a long-sleeved desert camouflage-patterned shirt with a patch reading Monroe on the right breast. Right behind it hung a dark-blue jacket with gold embellishments on the shoulder, and a white one behind that. She swept her gaze back to Alex as he pulled on the gray jacket, looking very respectable and even more handsome than usual.

His gaze changed as he broadened his smile. "You know, with your fancy business outfit there, all you need is your hair in a tight bun and a pair of eyeglasses, and you could make one of my biggest fantasies come true."

"Oh, stop it. You need to keep your head in the game, Mr. Monroe."

"Maybe after we get home, then."

Her smile faded. "If we're still in the mood." She left the closet to brush her hair. "And I feel terrible your birthday pretty much got canceled because the trial was moved up. First they delay it, and then they move it up at the last minute. You were so wonderful to me, and I feel like I let you down." She ran the flat iron over a section of hair as Alex came up behind and wrapped his arms around her waist.

"I hope you know better than that by now. Besides, I love my octopus. I put him on the shelf above my workbench."

"I saw the glass artist displaying a similar one and knew it was perfect for you."

He squeezed her tighter. "It's something I think about, you know. You arrived in mid-March, and my birthday is March fourth. I had no idea how much my life was about to change in less than two weeks. I actually thought I was content. Not happy, mind you—I wasn't that deluded. But I could have kept on like that. Boy, did that change after you arrived." He kissed her neck. "Every day I spend with you is a gift." Their eyes met in the mirror, both reluctant to break the contact. Finally, he nuzzled her hair. "Come on. Let's get some breakfast. If there's one thing I've learned, you never go to battle on an empty stomach."

A DULL GRAY rain fell as Alex drove them to the courthouse in Christiansted, which was a cheery lavender and white plantation-style building that almost mocked the seriousness of what took place inside. The trial had started yesterday, but Danae had told them they didn't need to appear until day two. Yesterday, the police officers and forensics people gave their testimony.

Danae stopped them in the lobby. She was a forty-year-old woman wearing a tailored suit, her dark hair up in a stylish French roll. She explained that the police were finishing up this morning, then Hope would be called, and they would finish with Alex's testimony.

Hope sat on the hard wooden chair in the front row next to Alex, butterflies fluttering through her abdomen. The courtroom was windowless and paneled in medium wood. It was a standard layout with the judge facing two tables where the attorneys and accused sat, and the jury off to one side. A smattering of people sat in the large gallery of chairs located behind the tables and a short wooden railing.

Judge Cosgrove, a white-haired Black man with a lined face, passed papers back and forth between Danae and another man Hope assumed was Charles's attorney. Alex pressed his leg against hers, offering his solid support.

They sat directly behind Danae's table, and Charles sat at

the defendant's table a short distance away. Hope was closer to him than she had been that night in Frederiksted. He faced the front of the courtroom, dressed in an orange jumpsuit, his hands cuffed as he clasped them together on the table. His dreadlocks were tied back neatly and hung down his back. Danae had already informed them Charles wasn't expected to testify.

A few minutes before they were scheduled to begin, Hope was surprised as Cindy sat down on her other side. She squeezed Hope's hand. "You were there to hold my hand and support me when I needed it. Now I'm here for you."

"Thanks, Cindy. It means a lot."

She had read the newspaper article, so she knew Alex's full background now.

The trial resumed. The police officer named Perkins took the stand and explained they had found the bullet which passed through Alex's shoulder and were able to determine it had been fired from Charles's gun. He also testified the bullet had been fired from very close range. He referred to a drawing of the crime scene showing the distances between the regulator bags, Hope, and where Charles and Alex had fought.

Eventually, both attorneys ran out of questions for him, and Hope was called to the stand. She stood and walked through the swinging wooden gate at the front of the gallery near the jury, on the other side from where Charles sat. Her butterflies increased to small, fluttery birds, and her pulse raced as she sat down and was sworn in. A flood of memories from Caleb's trial threatened, but she closed her mind, concentrating on the present. Turning to Alex, the birds calmed back to butterflies at his comforting nod.

She turned her gaze to Charles, and iron determination spread in her gut as she met his eyes head-on. Sitting at the table, he wasn't nearly as intimidating. His expression was neutral, with none of the leering menace he'd exuded that night.

Then he narrowed his eyes and glared at her before dropping his gaze to her breasts. When they returned to her face, a tiny but suggestive smile crossed his face, and Hope repressed a shudder. But that made her feel like a victim.

No way in hell am I giving you the satisfaction of seeing me react, you son of a bitch.

Her dread settled as red hot anger kindled, and she straightened.

We gave you a second chance!

Danae asked standard questions of Hope, establishing her position as owner of the resort and the hurricane necessitating the new regulators, as well as hiring Charles in an effort to help him. Soon Danae was done, and the defense attorney stood.

Bruce Camarino was a pale, average-looking white man with short brown hair and wearing a tan suit too big for him. As he stepped in front of the table he shared with Charles, his scuffed dark-brown shoes were visible.

He gave her a professional smile. "Good morning, Ms. Collins. I just have a few questions for you."

She nodded, clasping her hands in her lap.

"Why exactly were you there that evening? Couldn't Mr. Monroe have picked up the regulators without you?"

"I had to submit the claim for insurance reimbursement. My signature needed to be on the receipt."

Hope had calmed during her questioning by Danae, and she answered with a clear, strong voice. Her previous trial against Caleb was a distant memory.

She wasn't that broken girl anymore.

"Were you aware that the dive shop Mr. Monroe purchased the regulators from was located in a less-desirable portion of Frederiksted?"

"Yes. Before we left, Alex mentioned he didn't like the idea of me coming with him, but I explained why I had to be there and we drove down."

"Were you concerned at all, walking in the area?"

"Yes, it was a bit unsettling. Several streetlights were out, and there was very little traffic on the street."

"Did you feel relieved knowing you were walking with Mr. Monroe?"

"Yes, of course." She darted a glance at Alex, who gave her a small smile.

"Especially knowing the extent of his military career?"

Hope hesitated, choosing her words. "I knew he had been a SEAL, but I didn't understand the extent of his training at that point—how skilled he was at fighting."

"Oh? Did you feel Mr. Monroe overreacted to the situation?"

Hope glared at Camarino. "He got shot."

"Perhaps Mr. Monroe was trying to impress you with his expertise. Is that possible?"

"Of course not!" she snapped before calming herself. The attorney was trying to get a reaction out of her. "My God. How else was he going to react when a giant hulk of a man loomed out of an alley at us?"

Camarino affected an innocent expression. "By greeting his co-worker politely, perhaps?"

"Charles never gave him the chance."

"Objection!" Danae called. "This is irrelevant. Mr. Monroe isn't on trial here."

Judge Cosgrove stared intently over his black reading glasses, then spoke with a smooth Caribbean accent. "Sustained. You're wanderin' into the weeds here, Mr. Camarino. Do you have any further questions for this witness?"

"Yes, Your Honor." Camarino paced with his hands clasped behind his back, then stopped, turning to her. "Ms. Collins, do you believe Mr. Monroe would do anything necessary to defend you?"

Great, how do I answer this? I know damn well he would.

"Alex's Navy career ended in tragedy. It's a difficult subject for him, as it would be for any of us. But he spent a large portion of his life defending what he believed in—what he loved—and risking his life when necessary. So the answer to your question is yes. I also know Alex isn't a violent man and has the skills to defuse any situation with the smallest amount of risk."

"Did Mr. Reed ever behave inappropriately toward you during his employment at your resort?"

Hope resisted the urge to look at Charles. "No. He's very intimidating physically, but he never spoke to me in a threatening way prior to the night of the robbery."

"No further questions." Camarino went back to his table.

The judge glanced at the wall clock. "Let's break for lunch. We'll reconvene at 1 p.m."

Hope stood from the witness box with a relieved sigh. Charles's eyes tracked her progress to the wooden gate, but he faced forward when she made her way down the front row.

Alex was giving the back of his head a hard stare when she returned, but stood and gave her a quick kiss on the cheek. "You doing ok?"

"Yes, I'm glad it's over. It went fine." She met his concerned eyes, the message passing between them.

Hope, Alex, and Cindy ventured across the street to a deli for lunch. As usual, Alex was hungry and dove into his sandwich, while Hope picked at hers, lifting it up only to put it down again.

"Why are you acting all nervous?" Alex asked. "You're in the clear now."

"But you're not. I can't stand the idea of that defense attorney grilling you. You don't even look concerned!"

Alex pointed at Cindy. "Keep her calm, ok?" Cindy gave him a thumbs-up as he turned back to Hope. "It takes more than a lawyer on a tropical island to scare me. Now that it's finally here, it's time to go to work. I've had time to prepare myself, so I'll answer his questions and do everything I can to put Charles away. I'm as ready as I'll ever be."

Chapter Thirty-Five

SHORTLY BEFORE ONE O'CLOCK, the trio returned to their seats behind Danae. Surprised, Hope examined the gallery around her. The courtroom was packed, and a low hum resonated through the room as people talked quietly.

Guess they're here for the main attraction.

Soon the judge banged his gavel and called the trial back in session. Alex approached the stand and was asked to state his name. "Alexander Monroe."

Hope's butterflies were back and had multiplied. Alex had a long history of doing what needed to be done, whether he wanted to or not. But that didn't stop her from being nervous for him. He settled into the witness chair, serious and unruffled, giving no hint he was going to testify under oath about the worst experience of his life. She took several long, calming breaths, and Cindy clutched her hand. Hope shot her a tight smile.

There was a rustling in Alex's empty seat, and Hope turned as Patti sat down. She leaned to Hope and whispered, "Sorry I wasn't here this mornin'. We had a little issue with a guest that needed my attention, but it's all settled now. I'm here for you, child." Patti took the hand Cindy wasn't holding and squeezed it, giving her a solemn nod. Hope's nerves settled further, and they all turned to the proceedings in front of them.

After Alex was sworn in, Danae stood and walked around her table. She established Alex's history on the island as a dive guide for the last six years.

"And what was your employment before that?"

"I was a Navy SEAL for the previous fifteen years."

"And how did your Navy career come to an end?"

His jaw tensed, and he breathed out a long sigh. "Sixteen of us were hunting ISIS terrorists in Syria when we were ambushed. I was injured and received a medical discharge."

"Objection! How is any of this relevant?" Camarino stood with both hands on his hips, glaring at Danae.

"Relevant!" Danae answered. "I don't see how Mr. Monroe's background as a highly-skilled Special Forces operative could be any *more* relevant to these proceedings."

"Overruled. You may continue, Ms. Robertson."

Danae nodded at the judge before turning back to Alex. "This is the tragedy Ms. Collins referred to earlier?"

"Yes."

"Thank you for being willing to speak of it. I know it isn't easy for you. Is it true that you were critically injured in this battle, and later awarded the Navy Cross for exceptional heroism?"

"Yes."

"So, it sounds like you're a man who is trained to recognize a dangerous situation and possesses the skills to deal with it effectively."

"Again, objection! Is she going to question this witness or marry him?" The gallery broke into nervous laughter as Camarino sat back down.

The judge banged his gavel, scowling ferociously. "Quiet! Enough of that. Consider yourself warned, Mr. Camarino." He turned to Danae. "I think you've established that your witness has served his country in exemplary fashion. Move on, Ms. Robertson."

"Yes, Your Honor. When Mr. Reed stepped out onto the sidewalk in front of you, did you perceive him as a threat right away?"

Alex leaned back and crossed an ankle over the other knee. "Yes."

"But he was your co-worker. That didn't put you at ease?"

"No. I hardly interacted with him, and the conversations we'd had weren't friendly. We worked in different areas of the resort. And it was obvious he was a threat as soon as he stepped out of the alley."

"Did he say something specific that made you regard him as dangerous?"

Alex raised a brow. "Yes, he said he wanted the four regulators I carried, then pulled a gun and threatened Hope and me."

"Did you try to talk your way out of the situation?"

"Of course. I was trained to always attempt de-escalation of any threatening situation before resorting to force. I tried twice to talk him out of it and complied with one of his demands by setting the regulators on the ground."

"And what happened at that point?"

"He turned the gun on Hope, so I had to rush him."

"Please elaborate."

"I ran toward him and grabbed his gun hand. We started fighting, and right before I knocked him out, he shot me in the shoulder."

Danae nodded and stopped near the jury panel. "Why did you choose that moment to rush him?"

Alex's face went blank. "Because he moved the gun toward Hope."

"So you were ok with him pointing a gun at you, but not at Ms. Collins?"

"I wasn't thrilled about it, no. But I wasn't about to stand there and let him shoot her." Alex glanced at Hope, and she sent him a faint smile, a soft warmth spreading through her.

"So your testimony is that you had no choice but to attempt to disarm Mr. Reed?"

"Yes, that's correct."

"No further questions, Your Honor." She returned to the table.

"Your witness, Mr. Camarino," the judge said.

The courtroom was completely silent. No one shuffled in their seats or even coughed. The jury leaned forward, paying rapt attention.

Camarino paced back and forth in front of the witness stand. "You had no choice, so you ran toward Mr. Reed to disarm him. That is correct?"

"Yes."

"Mr. Monroe, are you familiar with the principle of Occam's Razor?"

"Yes."

"Please enlighten us."

Alex pressed his lips tight, then answered, "When faced with two alternate explanations, the simplest one is usually correct."

Pride surged in Hope's gut.

Nope, definitely not a dumb sailor!

Camarino couldn't hide his surprise at Alex's answer but recovered quickly. "We've heard your explanation for the events of that night. Let me present Mr. Reed's. You are a former elite soldier, trained to respond instantly to threats. Ms. Collins has already testified that it was a dark, ominous area and she felt uneasy. And it has been established that you are a man who will do whatever is necessary to defend what you love. You and Ms. Collins have a romantic relationship, do you not?"

"Yes."

"And do you love her?"

"Yes."

"Isn't it possible that Mr. Reed was simply walking out of that alley to cross the street that night? And that you saw him, immediately perceived a threat, and overreacted to protect Ms. Collins? And he simply defended himself against you?" He lifted both arms away from his sides, staring at Alex. "Isn't that a simpler explanation for all this, Mr. Monroe?"

"No, I would not say that. And he pulled—"

"Oh, come on! You *attacked* my client! You hit him several times in the face, breaking his nose, then knocked him completely unconscious. Do those sound like the actions of someone merely defending his girlfriend?"

"Yes, they do."

"Mr. Monroe, you could have killed Mr. Reed!"

Alex uncrossed his legs, straightening. "No. My only intent was to disarm him."

"I see. You applied *only* enough force to knock him out. Four punches to the face would have been too many, but three was just right? You expect us to believe that in the heat of attacking, you knew exactly how much force to apply?"

"Yes."

"And we're supposed to believe you?" Camarino's voice rose as he stood in front of the witness stand, his hands on his hips and his eyes hard. "Look, I'm sure you had a lot of training on how to fight, Mr. Monroe, but I imagine you had a lot *more* training on how to kill. More than fifteen years of it. So why should we believe you only meant to disarm Mr. Reed and weren't trying to kill him?"

Without moving a muscle, Alex changed his entire demeanor.

His eyes became hard and full of deadly ice as he glared at Camarino. The blood drained from Hope's face as she stared at a man she'd never seen before. There were indrawn breaths around her as others noticed the change too. Her thoughtful, loving partner was nowhere to be seen—Hope was staring at the cold, deadly professional soldier Alex had once been. Cindy and Patti both clamped their hands on hers.

As Camarino stumbled backward, Alex leaned forward in his chair and said in a soft, deliberate voice, *"Because he's still sitting there."*

Camarino and Alex stared at each other for a long moment in the silent courtroom before the defense attorney blinked several times, stepping back further. Alex relaxed, leaning back in the chair. He was just the witness again, his eyes focused and intent but no longer deadly. Hope exhaled a shaky sigh.

Ok, I guess Alex wins that round.

Camarino resumed his pacing to regroup. "You run a dive operation. Why didn't you buy the regulators yourself, instead of using a dive shop located in a dangerous area?"

"Gordon at Emerald Isle Scuba does a lot more volume, and I could get better prices by having him order them."

Camarino stopped and raised both brows. "Oh. So you were willing to risk Ms. Collins's safety to save a few dollars?"

"Of course not."

"But you knew the dive shop was located in a dangerous part of Frederiksted, didn't you?"

"Frederiksted isn't exactly Fallujah or Kabul."

Several titters of laughter reverberated around the courtroom as the judge banged his gavel. Another glow radiated through Hope's body. She squeezed Patti's hand, and they exchanged smiles.

Camarino continued. "But wasn't this a very poor decision on your part?"

"Objection!" Danae called. "The witness has answered this multiple times already."

"Sustained. Do you have anything else, Mr. Camarino?"

"Yes." He turned back, a tiny smile crossing his face. "Mr. Monroe, have you ever been under the care of a psychiatrist?"

"Objection!" Danae slammed her hand down on the table, her eyes blazing.

Camarino barked laughter. "You're the one who opened up his past for questioning."

"I'll allow it," the judge said. "Please answer, Mr. Monroe."

"Not since I was discharged, no."

"But you were previously?" Camarino asked, his tone smug.

"Yes, it's the standard of care for persons wounded in combat."

"Have you ever been diagnosed with Post-Traumatic Stress Disorder?"

Alex hesitated. "Yes. While I was recovering at Walter Reed."

"It would be perfectly normal for a man who suffered a terrible tragedy such as yours to have lasting effects. For it to make a person much quicker to perceive a threat—even one that isn't there. Isn't it possible your experience in Syria clouded your ability to judge how dangerous the situation was with Mr. Reed?"

Alex straightened, narrowing his eyes as they pierced into Camarino's. His posture stiffened. Not the deadly operative like before, but he was genuinely angry now, though his voice was tightly controlled. "Absolutely not. The *only* way my past affected that night was my ability to call on the skills and experience gained from nearly eighteen years of serving my country. Years I spent trying to ensure people just like you didn't have to walk around thinking about another plane flying into a building."

Alex leaned forward, tapping his index finger on the front of the witness stand railing. "I'm *highly* acquainted with the difference between an enemy combatant and a common criminal. I applied enough force to subdue him—nothing more."

"No further questions, Your Honor." The defense lawyer returned to his table as Hope swallowed the lump in her throat. She exchanged a quick smile with Patti and Cindy.

"Any rebuttal, Ms. Robertson?"

"Yes, Your Honor." Danae returned to the floor as Alex settled back in his seat. "Mr. Monroe, is it possible you might have mistaken Mr. Reed's intentions that night? That he was simply out for a . . . walk?"

"No. He admitted to us he'd been watching since we went into the dive shop. He knew exactly what he was doing." He tightened his jaw and flicked his gaze to Hope before returning his attention to Danae. "And he said he'd been watching Hope a lot longer than that."

"And is it your testimony you have the skills necessary to disarm someone without causing them permanent damage?"

"Yes. I've had years of extensive training on the application of non-lethal force. In hand-to-hand combat."

"No further questions."

"You're excused, Mr. Monroe," Judge Cosgrove said.

Chapter Thirty-Six

THERE WAS a collective hum throughout the courtroom as Alex left the witness stand. Hope watched his confident, quiet stride, and the entire jury followed his movement. Charles tracked Alex as he walked to the gallery, as if sizing him up. Alex stopped as a spectator at the end of their aisle stood, and they shook hands.

The judge banged his gavel and checked the time. "Let's call it a day. We'll start again at 9 a.m. tomorrow."

The crowd rose as the judge exited. Cindy had to work and said a quick goodbye to Hope. The spectator at the end of the aisle got Alex's attention again as Patti wrapped an arm around Hope's shoulders. "You ok?"

"Yes. Very relieved to have it over. For both of us."

Patti shot a dark look at Charles, but he was focused on the bailiff. "I'm sorry Alex had to go through that—all of it. I talked to him yesterday. But he's a strong man. And he has a strong woman helpin' him." They embraced, Hope leaning into the contact.

There was a murmur and shuffling throughout the gallery as spectators gathered their things. The bailiff wore a bored expression as he approached the defendant's table to escort Charles out of the courtroom.

Without warning, Charles lunged for the bailiff's gun as screams echoed through the courtroom.

The bailiff spun away, protecting his weapon, and Charles growled, shoving the man to the ground. He whipped his eyes around frantically before settling on Hope, who had broken apart from Patti. With a furious roar, he leaped the wooden railing and pushed Patti aside. As she toppled into a chair, Charles plowed into Hope, who reacted instinctively. She balled up both fists and hit him on the chest and abdomen as hard as she could. It was like punching a tree trunk.

"Get off me, dammit! What's wrong with you?" She only half heard what she screamed as his momentum tumbled her backward. Shock and anger surged through her.

Off-balance, both fell to the tile floor between the wooden fence and row of seats.

Hope landed on her back with a loud *oomph!*

She was dimly aware of screaming around her, but Charles was crawling up her legs. That occupied her full attention as adrenaline thrummed through her veins. She kicked him in the face repeatedly, snapping his head backward. But her barrage didn't stop him—it only made him angrier.

His face contorted into a terrifying visage of rage.

Sneering, Charles was stretching a hand toward her throat when two hands grabbed the back collar of his orange jumpsuit and hauled him several feet away, throwing him onto his back. Charles coughed and gasped as a hand chopped into his larynx.

Alex kneeled over him and pressed his knee into the center of Charles's chest as he placed his forearm against Charles's neck. Not pushing, but the threat was implicit as he leaned in. "You're a really slow learner, aren't you?" He snarled the words, his face inches from Charles's.

Pandemonium raged as people dove away from the two men. Hope lay on the floor, stunned and gasping, just watching as her mind tried to sort out what was happening.

The two men stared at each other, and Alex flexed his forearm as he began to press down on Charles's throat. Alex's face was expressionless, but his eyes were deadly.

The landscaper wheezed and raised both arms above his head. Charles stared at Alex with terrified eyes, and Alex relaxed his arm slightly.

Glancing around at the chaos, Charles shouted, "I'm sorry! I lost it. I won't cause any more problems, I promise. I'm sorry."

Alex spoke without moving, his eyes still blazing into Charles's. "Hope, are you all right?"

"Yes, he didn't hurt me." She tried to keep her voice steady. Alex was on a razor's edge right now, and she didn't want to push him over.

The two men were nearly nose to nose. In a whisper-soft voice and all the more deadly for it, Alex spoke to Charles. "This is the second time you've gone after Hope. If you and I get into it a third time, it's going to end very differently for you. Understand?"

Charles lay on the floor, wide-eyed and blinking. He jerked his head in a nod.

Hope looked around, but no one else had heard Alex's words.

Alex darted a glance to the bailiff, who stood there opening and closing his mouth like a fish, and spoke much more loudly. "Any time you feel like jumping in would be good, pal."

His words spurred the man into motion. With shaking hands, he unholstered his weapon, pointing it at Charles. "Get up. Slowly."

Alex removed his forearm from Charles's throat, rising with

both arms away from his body. Charles did likewise, his hands straight up in the air.

"Move to the center of the room, away from everyone," the bailiff directed, speaking with more confidence now. Charles followed directions with exaggerated slowness, his face blank.

Relief surged through Hope, followed by white-hot anger. She bit down on that—Alex probably had enough for both of them.

They stood in front of Patti, who sat stunned in her chair with her hand against her chest. Alex flicked his eyes around the room before focusing on Charles again. He wrapped an arm around Hope and drew her in, so he stayed between Charles and the two women. The bailiff stood balanced on the balls of his feet, both hands on his pistol firmly aimed at Charles, who stood alone in the middle of the room with his hands up.

The door at the front of the courtroom burst open, and Judge Cosgrove stormed into the room, his black robe swirling around him. "What on earth is goin' on in my courtroom?"

Danae cleared her throat before speaking in a wavering voice. "Mr. Reed attacked the bailiff and Ms. Collins. Then Mr. Monroe subdued him. Again."

The bailiff gave him a quick rundown of events.

Judge Cosgrove turned toward Charles, his eyes wide and incredulous. "You attacked two people? Durin' your *trial?*"

Camarino had stood frozen at his table throughout the whole episode. Now he closed his eyes and slumped, both hands on top of his head. Charles apologized again, this time to the judge, his eyes bulging as sweat dripped down both temples. His dreadlocks had broken free, cascading over his shoulders.

The judge whirled to face the bailiff, his voice tight with fury. "Get him out of here. Take him to the holdin' cell here in the courthouse."

Still aiming his gun at him, the bailiff followed Charles as he shambled out of the room, both hands reaching for the sky. As the door closed, the courtroom erupted into a deafening roar of voices.

Deprived of his gavel, the judge put two fingers in his mouth and blew a shrill whistle. "Quiet! All of you! Court will reconvene in one hour. We'll decide where to go from here." He turned to the defense attorney. "Mr. Camarino, I suggest you use the time to have a long heart-to-heart with your client."

"Yes, Your Honor."

The judge panned his stony gaze around the courtroom. "The session in one hour will be closed to the public. I don't want anyone in this courtroom except necessary personnel." He evaluated Hope and Alex. "You two both come back."

They nodded.

Judge Cosgrove waved his arms, his black robe swishing around him. "All right! Everyone out of my courtroom. This isn't a circus, despite today's events."

After the judge exited, the jury left their box through another door as the crowd shuffled out of the gallery. Camarino rushed through the same door Charles had. Alex had wound his free arm tightly around Patti and held both women close.

Danae raised a shaking hand to her brow as a coil of hair tumbled free from her French roll. "Well, that's something you don't see every day. You're both all right?"

"Yes, we're ok." Hope was numb all over but not terrified, which surprised her.

You really *aren't that broken girl anymore.*

Danae turned to Patti. "I'm sorry, but you're going to have to leave. Alex and Hope, you can take off for a bit if you need a walk or anything."

Alex looked at Hope, who straightened and said, "I'm fine. We'll stay here."

The pair turned to Patti. As Alex's arms enfolded her, she broke into sobs.

"It's ok, Patti. We're both fine."

Her glassy eyes met his. "How can you say that? He just attacked you two. Again. In a courtroom."

"It was a dumb, half-assed move on his part. If that didn't prove he belongs in prison, I don't know what does."

Hope shook her head and pressed a palm to Patti's cheek. "What did he think would happen? I was more shocked than scared. With Alex and an armed bailiff nearby, I have no idea what Charles thought he was going to accomplish."

Patti watched her closely, placing both hands on Hope's shoulders. "Are you sure you're all right, child? He didn't hurt you?"

Hope drew her close, wanting to reassure her. "My knuckles are a little sore. It was like hitting cement."

Patti pulled back, and the two women stared at each other for several moments. Then Patti nodded. "All right, then. I'll be off now." Gripping her purse with both hands, she marched from the room. Hope and Alex returned to their seats behind Danae.

"What happens now?" Alex asked, keeping a protective arm around Hope.

"It's up to the judge," Danae said. "It's not like the jury can just forget what happened. I imagine Bruce is trying to talk him into pleading guilty." Danae shot Hope a crooked grin. "Nice moves, by the way. Did Alex give you some pointers?"

Hope gave a shaky laugh, a strange wave of pride rolling through her. "No, that was mostly reaction. I took some self-defense courses years ago, but that's the first time I've used any of it."

Alex looked like he was trying to hide a smile, but gave up

and let one rise. "I jumped Charles mostly because I was afraid of what you'd do to him. Now I know not to step out of line."

Hope leaned into him, relaxing in his embrace as Danae turned back to her papers.

Despite his teasing words, Alex's eyes were deadly serious as he whispered to her, "As long as I'm around, no man will ever hurt you. I promise."

Hope raised a hand to his face and quietly kissed him. Then she settled into the hollow of his shoulder to wait.

LESS THAN AN HOUR LATER, the jury filed back in. Camarino came out of the door in the front of the courtroom, followed by Charles, who now sported full wrist and ankle shackles, a length of chain joining them. The bailiff followed him, a hand on his weapon and his eyes never leaving the defendant.

Charles kept his eyes glued to the floor as he walked to the table and sat. Alex had taken the seat on the other side of Hope this time and was closer to Charles. He leaned forward, resting his elbows on his knees as he stared laser beams into the large man's back.

They rose as Judge Cosgrove entered again and called the court back into session. "I've spent the last hour lookin' over court cases where a defendant acted in a similar manner. Every case concluded that actions such as Mr. Reed exhibited do *not* constitute the basis for a mistrial. In short, it is up to me to decide whether to proceed or start over with a new jury."

The judge straightened and scowled at Charles, glaring over his glasses. "Given your constitutional right to a speedy trial and that your hearing was already delayed once, I see no justification to declare a mistrial. I also don't want to reward your actions in any way, shape, or form, Mr. Reed."

Judge Cosgrove turned his gaze to Camarino. "Did you have

an opportunity to discuss matters with your client? How do you wish to proceed?" He bent his head and wrote on the document before him.

Camarino stood. "Yes, Your Honor. My client wishes to proceed with the trial and the not-guilty plea."

The judge snapped his head up. "Mr. Reed? Do I understand this correctly? You do realize I cannot and will not tell the jury to disregard your actions. They will become part of the public record of these proceedings. You still wish to continue with a not-guilty plea?"

Charles stood. "Yes, Your Honor." He spoke quietly, but his deep voice reached the far corners of the nearly empty courtroom. Camarino sat stone-faced beside him.

"Very well. We will reconvene tomorrow mornin' as originally planned for closin' arguments. Court is adjourned. Bailiff, please escort the defendant out now. Before anyone else leaves." He gave the bailiff a long, hard look.

All eyes followed Charles as he shuffled out, his shackles clanking in the silent room.

Once the bailiff returned, the assemblage rose as the judge, still glowering, stalked out of the courtroom.

Danae turned around, her face calmer now and her hair once again in order. "You guys are ok? Hope?"

Alex gripped her shoulders, and she smiled at the prosecutor. "Yes, thank you. I just can't believe he did that."

Danae shook her head. "Me either. Are you two planning on returning tomorrow for closing arguments?"

"No. We've had enough of Charles," Alex said. "We both work tomorrow, but please keep us updated. Hope's easier to reach by phone since I'm out on the water most mornings."

"Of course," Danae said. "I'll let you know as soon as I have any news."

Hope said goodbye to Danae before moving forward to

wrap Alex in an embrace. They held tightly as the relief washed over her in wave after wave. Relief and fierce pride at how well they had both handled being on the stand.

And everything that had followed.

Hands entwined, Hope and Alex made their way out of the courthouse. They got into the car, and Alex turned on the air conditioning full-blast, closing his eyes and breathing deeply.

Hope's stomach clenched. Everyone had been concerned about her. No one had asked Alex if he was doing all right. Or how testifying had affected him. She reached for his hand. "You doing ok?"

He turned toward her, his smile indicating he understood what she was asking. "Yeah, I'll be all right." He tightened his hold on her hand. "Both of us went through the wringer today."

"We did. And we're both still here. Together."

He lifted her hand to his mouth. "Always."

Time to cheer him up a little. Both of us. "Besides, you didn't need my help today—you were fantastic on the stand. I'm so proud of you, and I almost feel sorry for Charles. He didn't stand a chance against you. That night or today."

Alex's smile got bigger. "Hey, I'm the one who got shot, you know. Where's the sympathy for me?"

"Oh, I have something else in mind for you."

Later that night, they lay in bed, facing each other as they cooled down. Hope ran her hand over Alex's shoulder, his skin still sweaty beneath her fingers. "Oh, we are good together."

His only response was a deep, satisfied rumble.

"Too bad we have an early morning." She sighed. "Plus, I have my long run first thing. Now with the trial over, I can finally concentrate on the race. I've been trying to juggle every-thing this last week—fitting it all in."

"Running is one activity that doesn't go well when you don't put in the work."

"At least that and my busy morning will keep my mind off Charles." She paused, tapping her fingers on his warm back. "You know, if the trial goes to the jury, it's possible there might be a verdict by the end of the day tomorrow."

"I don't care anymore. I'm really sick of that guy." He pulled her tighter.

A thought occurred to her. "You know what I'd like to do? You don't have anything going on tomorrow afternoon, do you?" Alex shook his head. "Let's go for a dive, just you and me."

"You don't want to wait for the verdict?"

"No. The jury could decide in an hour or a week. We're not putting our lives on hold for that. It's time to move on."

"Well, you don't have to ask me twice. You want to take the boat?"

"Yes, I would. You pick the site. Someplace that's fun and easy—I just want to enjoy myself tomorrow."

A slow smile crossed his face. "I can deliver on your request."

She ran a finger down the center of his slick chest. "Besides, you and I have a history of very good experiences on that boat when we're alone."

Chapter Thirty-Seven

THE GEAR ROOM was hot and stuffy in the tropical afternoon. Alex finished filling the last of the tanks, his mind a jumble of thoughts as he tried to make sense of the whirlwind that had been the past month. Starting with yesterday. His stomach clenched as anger rolled through him. "I can't believe that idiot went on the attack. In a courtroom." Alex had damn near pushed the guy he'd been talking to into his seat in order to get past him. Hope had done a pretty good job on her own until he got there and threw Charles off her.

Alex had kept a close eye on her this morning before work and insisted they have lunch together, but she showed no signs of being severely traumatized by the encounter. He understood firsthand what post-traumatic stress was like, but Hope acted fine. His anger turned into a snort as he pictured her kicking Charles in the face. "She's a tough woman—you already know that."

And after yesterday, anyone on the island who had been in the dark about his history knew all about it now. But his past being uncovered hadn't been the disaster he'd feared. In fact, his friends here at the resort didn't really treat him differently, except sometimes he caught a glint in their eye as if they were proud to know him.

Because they don't know it was my fault.

He shut off the air compressor, his ears ringing in the sudden silence. On the surface, he understood Hope's reasoning that he wasn't to blame for the Syria debacle, but deep down, it was another story and not something he could just let go of.

On the other hand, Alex was downright proud of how he'd handled testifying. The damn defense attorney hadn't been able to trap him, and he'd had no trouble keeping his cool. On the stand anyway. "I thought Charles had more brains than that." Maybe he *had* just snapped.

Talking to himself in the stifling room wouldn't look good to anyone who came upon him, so Alex turned his attention to far more pleasant things. He slung his BCD over a shoulder and headed toward the boat as the steady breeze ruffled his hair. He was screwing his regulator onto the tank when he looked up.

Hope walked his way, dressed in a form-fitting rash guard with the resort logo and tight board shorts. Her legs went on forever. The wind whipped her hair around as their eyes met, and his mouth went dry at the sight of her.

Warmth spread through him as he remembered her testimony, how her eyes had flashed when Camarino kept trying to get her to implicate Alex, and how quickly she'd regained her composure. Seeing Hope in front of him made his own troubles disappear, and he greeted her with a smile. "Good timing, baby. I'm about ready here."

She stopped on the dock and parked a hand on one hip. "I specifically came down here fifteen minutes early so I could help you. I'm not incapable, you know."

That only made him smile wider. "I'm well acquainted with your capabilities. But I'm still faster than you."

She stuck her tongue out at him as they made their way to

the entry area. As he held his hand out to help her aboard, Alex drew her toward him for a long, feverish kiss. "I've never seen you wear that shirt. It shows all your curves, you know."

"At least I'm wearing a shirt. How am I supposed to concentrate on diving with you parading around like that?"

"I've got a shirt. You want me to put it on?"

"Don't you dare." She breezed past him and set her beach bag in the dry area before turning around. "Where are we going this afternoon, Captain?"

He frowned at the whitecaps outside Half Moon Bay. "I'd thought about the Frederiksted pier again. But with the wind this high, the surge would knock us around like pinballs. So I've got another site picked out that's a little more protected. Boat ride's gonna be a little rough today." He faced her again. "Might be a good day to have you drive back. You could get some experience driving in the waves."

"Fine by me." She climbed the ladder to the wheelhouse as he watched her every motion, then turned around at the top. "The lines, Mr. Monroe. You're becoming distracted."

"Yes, ma'am." Grinning, he saluted her and threw the lines before climbing up to the wheelhouse to move the boat from the dock. It was a twenty-minute trip north to the dive site, and driving in the rough water kept him occupied.

After mooring the boat, a dripping-wet Alex made his way to their tanks to turn them on, only to find Hope had already done it. "Very nice," he said with a smile, patting the side bench in front of her tank.

It was hot out of the wind, so he pulled his wetsuit down to his waist and sat next to her. "Let me go over the site. This is a great dive—exactly what you ordered, and on a windy day like today, it's perfect for one of the main features of the site." He paused. Her eyes were glued to his chest, and she wasn't listening to a word he said.

He tried to keep a straight face. "Ms. Collins, you're not attending. I present important information at these briefings, and I expect your full consideration."

She whipped her eyes to his, sending him an absolutely smoldering look. "I may be a bit hot for teacher."

He pursed his lips together and tried to concentrate. "Hey, you're the one who wanted to do this. I would have been perfectly happy to spend the afternoon in bed. Pay attention."

"My apologies. I'm riveted now."

"Thank you. This site is called Chapel. There's a nice reef we can explore, but the main feature is a limestone cavern that's similar to, you guessed it, a chapel. It's big, and in the middle is a rock that sticks up from the ground, like an altar. There are some holes in the top of the cavern that let a lot of light shine in. It can be really beautiful in there."

"An altar—oh dear. You're not going to sacrifice me, are you?"

"Depends on how you behave. We're not off to a promising start."

"I told you, I'm riveted now, hanging on your every word. Please proceed."

God, I love this woman.

"Thank you. The other awesome feature of this site is how you get out of the cavern. It's a feature called The Cannon. One of the big holes in the ceiling is near it. The Cannon is a large hole in the sidewall, and when it's windy like today, there is a strong surge pulling water back and forth between the hole in the ceiling and the hole in the sidewall. So if you time it right, it's like getting shot out of a cannon."

Hope's face exploded into a giant smile. "That sounds like fun."

"It is. I'll show you how to do it once we get there and wait for you outside. After that we can explore the reef." He started pulling his wetsuit back up. "Best of all, this late in the day, we've got the site to ourselves."

After they jumped in, Alex only removed a portion of the air from his BCD to slow his descent and stay close to Hope—she had a sticky ear and couldn't sink as quickly. A school of sergeant majors followed them, four-inch yellowish fish with thick vertical black bars, curiously darting around them. This was a relaxing, fun dive, and Alex took his time leading them down to fifty feet before guiding them to the hollow gray seamount.

After Hope returned his ok signal, he proceeded through the large entrance into the expansive domed cavern. Plenty of light entered, so flashlights weren't necessary. He smiled as the late-afternoon sun was at a perfect angle to shine into the holes in the ceiling.

The altar was lit in sunbeams.

Several more shined down through other holes, casting the room in a prism. He moved aside so he could watch Hope's expression. Her eyes widened and became soft as she stopped, hovering while she looked around the room.

As the ocean surface far above them rippled in the wind, the sunbeams moved, throwing rainbows of light around the room. It was a beautiful sight, and it was rare to experience it with no one else present since this was a popular dive with many operators on the island.

Alex took Hope's hand and led her forward, tracing his thumb over the back of her hand as he shined his light into a large crevice packed with orange squirrelfish, their black eyes enormous as they rested in the darkness and waited for night.

Hope squeezed his hand and moved closer to him, resting her head on his shoulder for a moment. They looked at each other, and deep emotion welled up in him. There was nowhere on earth he'd rather be at this moment. Their gazes held for a long moment, and then Hope squeezed his hand and let go, moving toward the altar as he searched the wall next to it. There was a resident frogfish that lived here, but he couldn't find it.

When Alex turned around, Hope was sitting on the rock altar—enough divers had contact with it that no life grew there, and it was only a rock. She sat with her fins crossed at the ankles and her hands clasped in her lap, watching him with her head tilted to the side and a small smile. Sunbeams danced around her, bathing her in fractal sunlight.

Her pose was clearly meant as playful, but his need for her nearly overwhelmed him. He rushed over, back kicking at the last moment to stop his forward momentum and stopping right in front of her face. Her expression changed to match the strong emotion in his. He clasped both her hands in his and held tightly, riveted to the sight of her beautiful face awash in rainbows.

Finally, Alex shook himself and led her toward the back of the cavern. The push and pull of the water was easy to spot.

The Cannon was going to be something today.

Turning to her, he signaled her to stay put and watch him. The gray limestone wall of the cavern was a thin shell here, only an inch or two thick, and the opening was roughly circular, about four feet across.

He timed it to approach The Cannon during the slack between in and out movements of the water, then gripped the sides of the opening with his hands, remaining horizontal and looking at Hope. He held on, moving back and forth with the water's movement so she could see what was happening as a flutter in his stomach steadily built with an accompanying grin. Finally, the powerful surge of water moved toward his face as his regulator hose vibrated madly.

Then the water became slack.

The surge reversed as Alex held himself in place against the powerful motion, then he turned to Hope and raised his eyebrows, letting go of the sidewall. The water propelled him forward, and he couldn't help the whoop that came out as he was shot ten feet out of the Chapel.

This is awesome!

Chapter Thirty-Eight

WITH ELATION BARRELING THROUGH HIM, Alex spun around and returned to The Cannon, keeping to the side of the opening as Hope moved into position. She stayed in place through several cycles of the surge, getting used to the movement. With a wide-eyed glance at him, Hope let go and was pushed out even further than he was, screeching the whole way.

She turned to him, her eyes sparkling, and grabbed his hand, tugging him back toward the entrance of the Chapel to repeat the experience. The second time, she went through first and waited for him, then insisted on doing it a third time. Alex couldn't remember the last time he'd had so much fun on a dive.

After their third round, Hope had less than half a tank left, so he moved them onto the reef, finding plenty to explore there. Before long, they were at seventy minutes and it was time for their safety stop.

They moved up to fifteen feet, both vertical in the water. He grasped her arms and pulled her to him as he rested his mask against hers. With both of them relaxed and content, it was a completely different experience from the last time they had been in this position after her accident.

Alex removed his regulator and began slowly kissing her neck and then her cheek. Hope removed hers, and their lips met. As the kiss deepened, their heads moved, trying without success to find an angle that didn't bang their masks together. Finally, both laughed and pulled away, replacing the air supply in their mouths.

He drew Hope in again, resting his hands against the tank behind her after adjusting his buoyancy to keep them neutral. She stilled as she lay her head against his shoulder, melting into him.

Alex rested his head against hers and closed his eyes, utterly content.

Once back on board, they went through the awkward process of removing their tanks. Alex stood—he still felt the strong emotion and an even stronger need. As she passed by, he grasped her arm, pulling her to him as he kissed her deeply, swiping his tongue over hers and heating up with each passing second. "Did you bring that towel, by any chance?"

She gave a low throaty laugh that sent his pulse skyrocketing. "As a matter of fact, I did. I think we're both a little over-dressed."

"Oh, I can take care of that. In fact, I plan on tasting every inch of you."

He pulled down the zipper of her wetsuit.

"Oᴋ, throttle down as we crest the wave. That's it," Alex said as Hope drove the boat back through the large waves. He steadied her with his hands on her shoulders, both of them fully clothed now. Hope stood in front of the wheel with him just behind, ready to help if needed. The bench seat was designed so the driver could sit or stand comfortably, but it was a very tight fit with the two of them standing. Alex found himself wedged between Hope's backside and the bench.

Not at all an unpleasant sensation.

He ran his hands across her shoulders and down her arms, then back up again. He couldn't stop touching her.

Hope didn't throttle down in time, and they slammed down into the trough, throwing him against her again.

"Dammit," she said.

He felt stirrings again, though he wasn't sure how that was possible, given what had just transpired between them. He looked down at the deck as he slowly ran his tongue over his lower lip, visualizing the side bench they'd broken in twice now. Another wave pressed him against her, and he bent down to nuzzle the side of her neck.

"Stop it, Alex. I'm trying to concentrate here."

He smiled behind her but stopped the kissing.

Oh, this woman . . .

"Don't blame me—you're the one driving."

She laughed at that, and he settled for wrapping his arms around her waist, giving her pointers on driving over the rollers.

A much bigger wave approached and Alex grabbed the throttle from her, powering all the way down and grabbing the wheel as the wave slid under the boat.

"That's it. I've had enough. You take over. This is stressing me out, honey." She slid under his arm and sat on the bench.

Alex took the wheel with a smile. But as he drove south, the stirrings developed into a painful ache, and he tightened his jaw more with every minute. He'd thought concentrating on driving the boat would help, but it didn't.

Eventually, Hope slid over on the bench and stood behind him. She put her hands under the front of his shirt before dancing her fingers from his stomach up his chest.

He inhaled sharply.

"Looks like you've got a situation going on there. Would you like some help with that?" One hand headed south now.

Please don't stop.

She didn't, and he couldn't concentrate anymore as she took a firm grasp of him.

They were heading down the west coast of the island, and he looked to the left, seeing a shallow bay that offered some calm water. He spun the wheel to port and headed in, Hope holding tightly to avoid being thrown off-balance.

Then she resumed her stroking, and he couldn't get the engine shut off fast enough.

In the sudden silence, Alex spun around and smashed his mouth to hers with a groan, pushing her down onto the bench in a sitting position. He lifted a knee onto the padded surface, ready to climb on and press her onto her back.

"Stop," she commanded.

He lifted away from her mouth, shocked.

She patted the bench next to her. "You sit here. Right now." Hope raised a brow at him. "It's my turn. You do tend to get bossy, you know."

"Ok." He sat, throbbing now.

She pulled his shirt off before removing her shorts and bikini bottoms. Alex reached to remove his own shorts, and she ordered, "No. Leave them."

He moaned as Hope climbed onto his lap, one knee on each side of him. She stroked a finger down the side of his face. "You have no idea what you do to me. How much you turn me on. But I'm going to show you."

As her mouth moved to his, he expected frantic passion, but she was controlled and slow, kissing him with a hot, open mouth. He was so hard it was almost painful.

She opened his shorts, climbing down to kneel on the fiber-glass deck. "Oh, you *do* have a situation going on, don't you?"

Then she couldn't speak, and he threw his head back and raised his arms to grip the back of the bench as her hot mouth encircled him. Eventually, he tipped his head forward and watched her.

Until he realized he was about to have a big problem.

"Baby, I need the rest of you. You can do whatever you want, but please come up here."

Hope laughed and rose to kneel on his lap, once again with one knee on either side of his legs. Completely still, her eyes were half-lidded as she slowly stroked his chest with both hands. She reached lower and took him in her hand, a slow smile rising across her face.

"Oh my. I didn't think your situation could get any bigger, but apparently I was wrong." She spoke with the throaty voice she only used when highly aroused, and he was about to lose it.

Her smile fell as she grabbed a handful of his short hair with the other hand, yanking his head back and holding it still as she impaled herself extremely slowly, her golden eyes boring into his.

He was panting now.

She began to move achingly slow.

Their eyes were still locked together, and he started to lift her shirt, but she firmly pressed his hands down to his sides. "Oh no. You're going to sit there like a good boy, Mr. Monroe."

She cocked her head to the side. "Hmmm, I think we might be beyond that at the moment. You're going to sit there and not move, *Commander* Monroe."

He wanted to make a witty comeback but was beyond words at this point. She resumed her deliberate pace, her eyes still riveted to his. Alex was completely helpless, trying to keep it going as long as possible as he held totally still.

Without warning, she closed her eyes and kissed him savagely, crushing his mouth with hers, their teeth scraping as she clenched his hair with both her hands. At that, he couldn't take any more as he finally embraced her and pulled her toward him. He buried his face in her shoulder.

He had no idea what sounds came out of his mouth, except they hurt his throat.

AFTER, he had to work to get his breathing under control. He was utterly empty, yet so full of emotion he couldn't speak. Eventually, he lifted his head and stared at her, drinking in her every feature. The sun was near setting and bathed her face in golden light. Her eyes were on fire.

She wore a small, secret smile that widened into an unmistakable look of triumph.

He smiled in return and drew her close, murmuring into her ear, "Was I that loud?"

She laughed, the sound like gently falling water, and said, "Oh, Alex. That made me feel like a goddess."

"That's because you are."

Chapter Thirty-Nine

THERE WAS an extra spring in Hope's step as she strolled hand in hand with Alex down the brick promenade of Frederiksted the next afternoon. Even a ten-mile run this morning couldn't dampen her stride. Both had the afternoon free after a vendor canceled an appointment with Hope, so they were en route to a lunch date. Hope squeezed his hand, biting her lip to hide a grin as she remembered yesterday's private dive trip.

Alex turned to her, a broad smile lighting up his face. "Someone's having naughty thoughts."

"What? How can you tell?"

He laughed. "You have very expressive eyes. And I was thinking about it too."

Alex made her feel safe to her deepest core, and that brought out sides of her she didn't know existed. And thoughts about him making her feel safe naturally brought back memories of the trial. She wasn't looking forward to seeing Charles again whenever the jury decided on their verdict, but she was confident he wouldn't try attacking anyone again. A slight chill ran through her as she recalled Alex's whispered threat to Charles. This man she'd made a life with might be charming and funny, but there were aspects of his personality that were anything but.

She shook off her foreboding. The sun warmed her shoulders, and it was far too beautiful a day to spend brooding.

The hostess showed them to their table, and they ordered drinks.

Closing her eyes, Hope heaved a sigh. The weight of the trial was *over*!

"Wow. That was a big sigh. Maybe yesterday wasn't as good as I thought?"

She narrowed her eyes, knowing it would bring a grin to his face. "I think you know better. That sigh was sheer happiness that the trial is mostly over—no more testifying! And hopefully, no more brawls. Of course, there's still the mystery of the verdict."

Alex shrugged. "Nothing we can do about it but wait. If the jury finds Charles not guilty, we'll deal with it then. Besides, if you're looking to uncover a secret, maybe you can solve the mystery of the extra money that has been appearing in my bank account."

Hope couldn't hide her smug smile. "I wondered when you'd say something about that. Everyone got bigger raises this year, Alex. Since your apartment isn't part of your salary anymore, you got a little more."

"More than a little." He took a drink, then stared at her. "I'm doing fine financially, you know. When I was discharged, they awarded me a disability benefit as well as a full pension, even though I was a little short of my twenty years. I've mostly banked it for the last six years. I'd like to start paying more of our household bills anyway—it's only fair."

"The utilities and taxes are rolled into the resort, so honestly, there aren't a lot of extra bills to pay." She let her gaze become sultry. "I'm sure we can find other methods if you feel like you want to contribute more."

Alex traced a finger down her arm, bringing a shiver. "Be careful what you wish for. You might get it."

Hope opened her mouth to respond when her phone rang. Her stomach dropped at the caller ID.

It was Danae.

Hope swiped to answer, rushing the phone to her ear.

"We've just received notice the jury has reached a verdict. They're breaking for an hour to eat lunch, and then we're reconvening at 2 p.m. Does that give you and Alex enough time to get here?"

Hope's watch indicated they had plenty of time. "Yes. Alex and I are in Frederiksted now, so we've got enough time to get there."

SHORTLY BEFORE TWO, Hope and Alex were back in the lavender building. Clasping hands tightly, they took their seats behind Danae, who gave them a tight smile before facing forward. Once again, Alex sat on Hope's other side, closer to Charles. Now that the culmination of the whole ordeal was finally here, Hope couldn't stop fidgeting. She took several deep breaths, but when Alex pressed his leg against hers, she calmed.

Flanked by two bailiffs, Charles shuffled through the door at the front of the courtroom, his legs and wrists shackled once again. Alex leaned forward and gave him an intense stare as he proceeded across the floor, but Charles never raised his gaze from the floor. One bailiff returned to the front of the courtroom, while the other stood near Charles. Hope's shoulders eased as a little of the tension drained out.

The gallery was nearly full as the jury moved to their seats. The trial had been big news, so that wasn't unexpected, though

Alex wished otherwise. The judge called the proceedings back into session and thanked the jury for their service. "Mr. Foreman, has the jury reached a verdict?"

An older white man with a wispy white comb-over stood in his rumpled blue suit, his hands shaking slightly as he studied the piece of paper he held in both hands. "Yes, Your Honor, we have."

"What say you?"

"On the count of attempted robbery, we find the defendant guilty."

The foreman paused but didn't lift his gaze from the paper before him. "On the count of assault with a deadly weapon, we find the defendant guilty."

A murmur went through the crowd at this, and the judge banged his gavel for quiet, then glared until the gallery was silent. "Please continue, Mr. Foreman."

"Thank you, Your Honor." The foreman took a deep breath. "On the count of attempted manslaughter, we find the defendant . . . guilty."

Hope clamped her eyes shut briefly before exchanging a smile with Alex as she slipped her arm through his. Shackles clanking, Charles rested his face in both palms, his shoulders heaving with deep breaths.

Once again, the judge thanked the jury before excusing them. He scheduled the sentencing for one week, then adjourned the trial. The other bailiff returned to the defendant's table, and Charles stood as both men watched him closely.

He ignored Alex but met Hope's steady gaze. To her surprise, he mouthed, "I'm sorry," before turning away and trudging off. Charles disappeared into a door in the back wall of the courtroom without a backward glance.

Danae turned around with a relieved smile. "Guilty on all counts." She made eye contact with Hope and then held Alex's gaze. "You two should be proud. You made a real difference here. And Charles didn't help himself much, either."

"Thanks," Hope said. "How long do you think he will serve?"

"With his long prior record and the fact that he used a gun this time, a pretty long time, I'm sure. Judge Cosgrove isn't known for being lenient, and after Charles's meltdown, I doubt he's feeling warm and fuzzy. The sentencing range would be ten to twenty years, and I expect the judge to come down toward the longer end of that." She glanced back and forth between them. "Do you want to be present for the sentencing?"

Alex shook his head. "No. He's going to prison, and that's all I care about. How about you?" he asked, turning to Hope.

"Same. You can call me with the sentence, Danae. And I'll let Alex know. We're both ready to put this behind us."

ALEX WRAPPED his arm around Hope's shoulders as they walked out of the courtroom. The late afternoon sun warmed the cobblestone street beneath them. Now the cheery paint scheme of the building complemented Hope's mood, and she leaned closer to Alex.

"Ok, I was wrong when we were at lunch. About being happy the trial was over," Hope said as Alex raised a brow at her. "*Now* I'm happy about it. It's done and we can move on."

They were walking along the sidewalk toward Alex's car when a dark-haired man with a pen tucked over one ear and carrying a notepad approached them. "Alex and Hope. Congratulations on helping to put Charles away. Thought I'd officially introduce myself. I'm John Strickland, from *The Chronicle*."

Alex's relaxed, easy countenance disappeared, and he stormed up to the man, his face thunderous and clenching both hands at his sides. "Who the *hell* do you think you are? You had no right to dig up my past and print it, you son of a bitch." Hope gripped his arm, trying to pull him back.

"I had every right—it's my job. I tried to talk to both of you, and the more you evaded my questions, the more curious I got."

Strickland stared steadily at Alex. "Look. All the information in that article was available in DoD documents. I didn't even need to file a Freedom of Information request. Well, I used a source in the Navy to get your photo, but that was it. I don't understand why you're so tight-lipped about it. You're a war hero, for God's sake."

"Because it's nobody's goddamn business!"

Hope stepped between the two men, forcing Alex back a step. "That's enough, Mr. Strickland. You did write a positive article about Alex, but what happened in Syria is intensely personal for him. Don't expect him to thank you for it. Now, we need to get home."

She tightened her hold and steered Alex to the car.

"Thanks." Alex shot a dark look at Strickland's retreating back. "If you hadn't broken that up, I would have probably punched the guy, and that wouldn't have been good."

"Definitely not."

Alex generally ran cold when upset, not hot. But Strickland's article was a completely different situation, and she didn't want to find out what he might do. Hope had saved several copies of the paper and was extremely proud of how Alex had been portrayed. But he had a long way to go before seeing the positive side of the article.

As they drove home, Hope distracted him by recounting a mysterious fish she had seen while walking on the pier. Alex perked up his ears and pinpointing the fish consumed the rest of the ride, ending with him breathing a satisfied, happy sigh when he finally identified it.

Mission accomplished.

THAT EVENING, they took their dinner to go and spread out a blanket on the beach in front of their house. Cruz lay nearby but wasn't inclined to crash their party. Alex opened a bottle of champagne and filled two flutes before they toasted.

"To the end of a very long ordeal," Hope said. "With a satisfying end, no less."

"And I got to see some of your badass fighting moves."

Hope laughed, opening and closing her fist. "I'm happy to let you do the fighting. My hand is still a little sore."

"I'd prefer to keep the fighting to a minimum. Besides, I've got you to fight for me. I'm in the clear now."

"Not my style. If I come across any trouble, my running is going well enough now that I can just sprint away."

Alex laughed as he leaned back on an elbow. "You look like you could tackle that half-marathon right now."

"The rest of the field wouldn't stand a chance."

"Too bad it's not until next week."

Hope faced him with a big smile as she held up her flute. "You, Gerold, and me. Look out world, because here comes Team Half Moon Bay!"

Chapter Forty

THE WAVES CRASHED in a rolling curl along the seawall, sending a fine mist into the dark early morning. Hope watched, mesmerized. Alex stood on one side of her and Gerold on the other. It was 5:30 a.m., and they stood in the bayfront park of Christiansted next to Fort Christiansvaern, its yellow stone ramparts muted in the darkness.

"Man, I'm glad you're swimmin' in that and not me," Gerold said to Alex.

Hope had to agree. A strong storm had swept through the previous day. The sky was still and clear now and the roads were dry, but the ocean still exhibited the storm's effects as whitecaps were visible all along the bay. Another roller boomed along the seawall.

"It's an advantage for me. It's not bad enough to cancel the swim, but it'll slow a lot of people down. I'm used to swimming in rough water." Alex windmilled his arms, warming up. All three wore sweatshirts to ward off the early-morning chill.

"I need to go check my bike again. Good luck." Gerold fist-bumped Alex, then went to inspect his bike for the five hundredth time. Alex drew Hope to him.

"How long do you think it's going to take you to swim 1.2 miles?"

"Twenty-five to thirty minutes. Might be closer to thirty with this water. Might be more if somebody clobbers me in the head. There are only a few hundred people doing the long course, so we're doing a mass start. I'll just try to get toward the front."

A short distance offshore to the north lay Protestant Cay, home to The Hotel on the Cay and the starting line of the triathlon. "I need to swim across to the cay before six, so I'd better get going."

Several swimmers were already in the water. Alex peeled off his sweatshirt and handed it to her, standing before her bare-chested. He wore only a pair of tight, thin competition swim shorts that covered him to mid-thigh.

Hope admired the effects of his weight training. He'd been working hard since the gunshot wound, and the results were apparent as her gaze meandered from his broad shoulders down his chiseled chest to his six-pack.

At her sharp intake of breath, Alex looked up from inspecting his swim goggles. "Do *not* look at me like that. These shorts don't exactly hide my thoughts, ok?"

She laughed, fanning herself with a hand. "Sorry, I can't help myself. How you're dressed is precisely the problem. But I'll find something less stimulating to watch."

They made their way over to the ramp. There was an aura of nervous anticipation in the air as athletes bounced up and down. "Have fun out there—I think you're one of the few swim-mers who will actually enjoy the rough water."

He broke into a sunny smile. "I think it's fun."

They came together for a final kiss, then he was off, swim-ming toward the small island. The crowd continued to build, and the sky was now a dusky blue as she walked behind the seawall. Spotting Cindy, who was competing in the half-marathon, she exchanged a quick good-luck hug.

Eventually, Hope found Gerold standing in his sweatshirt and cycling shorts, arms crossed as he shifted from foot to foot. "Nervous?"

"Yes. Very." He breathed out a big sigh. "You?"

"Not yet, but I'm sure I will be by the time you get back from your ride."

"How's Alex doing?"

"I don't think he gets nervous."

Gerold snorted. "Figures. He told me he expects to swim this in under a half hour. That sound right to you?"

"It's really fast, but he wouldn't say it if he didn't think it was possible. How long will it take you to bike fifty-six miles? We need to know when to expect you."

"Three hours and a quarter or thereabouts. Bein' a local, I've got the advantage of knowin' the course."

Hope brought her hands to her mouth as a laugh escaped. "Oh my God! Alex drove me up that hill you're climbing, The Beast. I can't believe you're riding up that thing."

He grinned, relaxing a bit. "That's the signature of the race! Six hundred feet and an average grade of fourteen percent with a max of twenty-one. I've always wanted to do this race, and now I am."

She shuddered. "Your idea of fun and mine are very different, Gerold. I only hope I don't let you down. I'm not the caliber of athlete you two are. I'd dearly love to break my half-marathon record of 2:04, but I don't think this is the year for it."

Gerold put an arm around her shoulders and gave her a squeeze before letting go. "Don't worry about it. We wouldn't even be doin' this if it weren't for you."

Hope peered at the sandy beach on the cay, where a large group of swimmers milled around. Most of the men wore similar shorts as Alex, so she couldn't pick him out. The race announcer kept up a steady stream of chatter over the loudspeakers as the start time approached.

Hope glanced at her watch. It was 6:25 a.m.. "Only five minutes away now."

ANXIOUS EXPECTANCY and random cheering swirled in waves around the crowd. The sun had risen and cast golden ripples on the turbulent bay.

"Does Alex breathe to the left or right? That sun could be right in his eyes. Man, I'm glad I'm not doin' that part."

"You already said that. Relax, you'll do fine. So will Alex." Hope turned to him with a raised brow. "You do realize he was a SEAL, right? I don't think a little sunlight is going to bother him much."

Gerold shook out his hands. "I know. I'm ramblin'."

The announcer started counting down from ten, and Hope rushed to queue up her sport watch. Several cannons from nearby Fort Christiansvaern boomed, startling her into hitting start on her watch by reflex. The swimmers started in a frothy pack from the shore of the small island to loud cheering from the assembled crowd. The course was an irregular triangle, with the swimmers heading north, then east, followed by a long leg south back to the bayside park to transition to the bike leg.

"Well, I'd better get ready." Gerold hugged her and departed as she stayed to watch the race. Several swimmers were already distancing themselves. The crowd settled down once the race got going.

By the time the swimmers had rounded the second buoy and headed south, the leaders had formed a pack of four, though they were indistinguishable at that point. There were several pro triathletes in the field, but Hope had her fingers crossed Alex might squeeze out a top-ten finish.

They were twenty minutes into it now, so Hope left her post to find a better vantage point for the swim finish. Being a competitor, she was able to enter the transition area and stand near Gerold as he waited to tag off from Alex and begin the bike leg. A long wooden ramp had been built to help the swimmers run from the water up to the bike area.

As the lead pack got closer, the crowd noise swelled, and the announcer became more animated, describing which pros the swimmers might be. As they neared the finish, Hope stood on her tiptoes, craning her head to see better. One swimmer had a clear lead, and three others were in line slightly behind, the hands of the swimmers behind nearly striking the feet of the one in front. Then the first swimmer stood on the ramp, running up as he ripped off his swim cap and goggles.

"And first out of the water is pro Michael Jameson, here all the way from Australia!" the announcer boomed. "His swim time was a hair over twenty-six minutes."

Hope stared at the rough water. It was an amazing time—she couldn't fathom being that fast.

Jameson was quickly followed by the trio of swimmers. "We have three finishers coming out in a tight bunch. They're going to have almost identical times." The announcer kept a keen edge of excitement in his voice while speaking clearly. "Ok—number two has a time of 26:10 . . . and it's . . . another pro—James Lathim, from Boulder, Colorado. And right on his heels is our first local finisher, with a blazing time—a member of Team Half Moon Bay, Alex Monroe! And just behind him is another pro . . ."

Hope and Gerold gaped at each other.

Third out of the water!

Fortunately, Gerold was all ready to go—his helmet clipped

and cycling shoes on. Hope jumped up and down as Alex ran up and slapped hands with her star chef, who ran his bike down the chute out of the transition area to the mounting line. Then Gerold pedaled away. Alex stood bent over, both hands on his knees and breathing heavily, but grinning at her.

Hope ran over, crushing him to her. "Great job! You were third out of the water. You even beat some pros." She gave him a quick kiss and pulled off her backpack, handing him a towel.

His breath had calmed a little. "Thanks. I gave it everything I had. That was a lot of fun."

"Well, according to Gerold, we have about three hours to kill before my run starts." She pulled out an insulated water bottle from the side pocket of the backpack and handed it to him. "You feeling ok? Need anything?"

He straightened after drinking the entire bottle. "I feel great!"

There were water bottles in plastic garbage tubs filled with ice, and she refilled Alex's before sliding close to him. "You look pretty great too."

"I think you're a little biased." He looked around the transition area. "There's a changing tent over there. Hand me my stuff?" She gave him the backpack, and he was back shortly, dressed in shorts and sport sandals.

Alex also wore the team tank top she had designed. She and Gerold already wore theirs. It was made from technical fabric to wick sweat away and custom printed with the resort logo and Team Half Moon Bay. Their first names were printed on the back.

"I'd like to stay off my feet while we wait. Let's look for a shady spot before they all get taken," Hope said as they walked around the park, finally deciding on a spot under a broadleaf tree near the yellow wall of the fort. "I've never toured that fort before. Too bad I have to run, or I'd drag you through that. It would be interesting."

"More the other way around. I've been through it a bunch of times, but I'd do it again in a heartbeat." Her surprise must have shown because he smiled. "I told you military history is one of my interests, you know."

"That's right, you did. Maybe you can take me through it sometime."

She surveyed the yellow fort for some time before turning back to Alex. He stared at her, his eyes broadcasting concern. Hope repressed a sigh. That look had been on his face often enough in the past week that she didn't need to ask about it. "I'm fine. I really am."

His gaze softened. "If that changes, I'm here for you, ok?"

"Of course." She reached a hand to his face and gave him a soft kiss.

His words brought back the whispered threat he'd made to Charles, and a small shiver slid down her back. Charles wasn't the man she had to come to terms with. There was a lot more to Alex than he let on, and she was still trying to process it all. It would take some time to reconcile these two sides to him. But that was an issue for the future.

Loud cheering erupted from the swim exit as the crowd supported the final swimmers leaving the water, and Hope turned her mind back to the race.

Alex stretched out his long legs, leaning back on his elbows and looking completely recovered from swimming over a mile. "You ready for your run?"

"I hope so. I ran several ten-milers, but nothing longer—it should be enough, but I'm kinda feeling the pressure."

"There's no pressure. Only what you're putting on yourself. Just relax and enjoy it. From the map, it looks like a great course

—you run on the grounds of The Buccaneer Resort and their golf course. Put your watch away and have a good run."

"Funny you say that, because that's exactly what I plan on doing. I'm going to start my watch, then put it in my pocket until the finish." She gave him a smile. "I can't wait to see you there. Like I told you, I'm done running from you."

Alex's eyes softened, and he studied her face. "Doesn't matter—I won't let you go this time. No matter how fast you run, I'll still end up catching you."

She laughed, relaxing on the grass. "I'd say you already caught me."

"Good. Because I'm strictly a sprinter these days." A spark was back in his eye. "Not built for endurance anymore."

"Oh, I beg to differ, Mr. Monroe." She leaned forward and grazed her lips over his.

Soon it was time for Hope's pre-race meal, and she opened the backpack, pulling out two bananas and bagels with peanut butter. "You still ok eating this? Or would you rather go to a restaurant and have a real breakfast?"

"This is a real breakfast—hand mine over. I'm starving."

"You're always starving."

He drilled her with his eyes, moving them down and then back up her body.

"Oh, sure. Now that you're out of your skimpy shorts, we're back to normal, are we?"

"Eat your breakfast, Boss Lady. You need your carbs."

Chapter Forty-One

HOPE KEPT a close eye on the time and began her warmup shortly before 10 a.m. It was heating up quickly, and she had removed her sweatshirt hours ago. Now she took off her loose shorts and stood in her race attire of a form-fitting tank top plus a pair of tight compression shorts that went to mid-thigh.

Alex didn't even bother hiding his stare.

"Do *not* look at me like that. I need to concentrate now."

"I am one lucky man." He didn't soften his gaze much. "Let's head back to the transition area. From the cheering, I think the first cyclist is coming back."

He placed his hand on the small of her back to usher her through the crowd, softly brushing her ass.

"Alex . . ."

"Purely an innocent slip."

She glared at him, and he lowered his sunglasses to wink at her with a gorgeous smile.

Oh, this man.

Several pro athletes rolled in, quickly changing shoes before taking off on the run. Hope bounced on the balls of her feet, nervously touching the white cap on her head and craning her neck as she watched for Gerold. He was a very good cyclist, but not a professional—fifty-six miles was a good equalizer. She kept looking at her watch and swore time was slowing down.

Hope was fidgeting with her shirt the next time she looked up. Gerold's dark skin and light-blue tank top were flying toward her. She peeked at her watch—3:08. *Wow!*

Gerold's sweaty fingers brushed hers and Hope was off, running out of the park and onto Hospital Street. She slid her watch into her tight pocket and enjoyed the view. Colorful multistory buildings in shades of turquoise, yellow, green, and many other colors surrounded her as she ran through downtown Christiansted.

After five miles, she hugged the left shoulder of the highway, skirting the northern coast of the island. She felt great—13.1 miles was long enough for that to change drastically, but she was very pleased with her pace that was difficult but maintainable.

After leaving town, the jungle aspects of St. Croix reasserted themselves, and she was flanked by towering trees on either side of the road. Thick vines wound around them, exploding with colorful yellow flowers.

At mile eight, Hope turned down the long entry drive to The Buccaneer Resort. She dumped a cup of ice water over her head as she ran through an aid station. The heat was intense—she was surprised her skin wasn't sizzling.

Climbing the hill, her pace dropped a bit, and she smiled at the expansive view. In the distance, but getting closer, was the storied pink building with white trim where Clark's cocktail contest had been held.

Next up was the golf course. Hope ran along an improvised trail of grass delineated by orange cones. It wove around the bluffs next to the ocean, and the breeze provided a welcome respite as the turquoise water pounded the jagged rocks below. Palm trees dotted the landscape, waving lazily.

She made a point to absorb the beauty of her surroundings—to be grateful for what her body could accomplish.

Soon she was running back down the entry road, passing the same aid station and drinking two cups of water as she ran through. Still going strong, Hope grinned as she rejoined the highway, headed back toward Christiansted and the finish.

Only three miles left!

The strong, invincible feeling lasted until mile eleven when it came crashing down. The heat pounded down on her, each breath became a struggle, and her feet were like daggers of hot glass.

Her body protested with every step.

Hope pictured Alex and Gerold waiting for her at the finish line and gritted her teeth, slowing her breathing and denying the pain. At the final aid station, she drank again and poured a cup of ice inside her hat before wrenching it back on her head. The hot sun which had been bombarding her immediately softened to a comforting warmth as the ice cooled her scalp.

At mile twelve, the course turned away from the ocean and headed back into downtown Christiansted. The long street was a solid mass of spectators—the sound was all-encompassing. Emotion swelled inside her, and she found more speed. Turning right onto King Street, the course made its final stretch toward the bayside park.

So close now!

A tremendous smile split her face as she passed the thirteen-mile mark and spotted the finish arch just ahead.

Alex and Gerold could probably see her now.

That gave her an extra gear, and she sprinted toward the finish line as the announcer said, "And crossing the line now is the leader of Team Half Moon Bay, Hope Collins—and she broke the two-hour mark, with a time of one hour, fifty-eight minutes!"

Hope lifted her hands on top of her head, stunned at what she'd just heard. As she slowed to walk, she spotted Alex and Gerold standing to one side, both cheering for her.

She locked eyes with Alex, and tears threatened at the pride in his eyes. Hope sprang at him, wrapping her arms around his neck and her legs around his waist as he spun her around.

"You beat the two-hour mark! I'm so proud of you."

"Oh God, I'm really tired now."

Alex had stopped spinning to give her a kiss.

"Uh, I'm not sure I can get down without every muscle in my body cramping. This wasn't my smartest move—I got a little carried away."

He laughed and gently eased her down, one leg at a time. She managed it without cramping, but it was a near thing. Then she embraced Gerold, lighting up at his warm smile.

"Come on, guys. I need to keep walking—I can't just stop."

She shuffled slowly around the grass of the park for several minutes, one man on each side of her. Eventually, her heart rate returned to normal and her blood got back to its usual business. She was drenched from head to toe.

Alex held up the backpack. "You want to get changed?"

"Oh, yeah."

Hope headed toward the changing tent, pleased they had a few freshwater showers available. They were in the open, only to rinse off the salt and sweat, but it was wonderful. Inside the changing tent she dressed in dry clothing, including a fresh custom tank top and pair of cargo shorts.

And most wonderful of all, flip-flops.

She breathed an ecstatic sigh as she wiggled her toes, finally freed from her running shoes. After finger-combing her hair into some sort of order, she put on a resort baseball hat and returned to her team.

"They've got free hamburgers for athletes. You hungry?" Gerold asked her.

"Yes. Ten minutes ago I was sick to my stomach, but now I'm starving. You willing to lower your standards to eat mass-produced hamburgers?"

"After a three-hour bike ride, my standards are nonexistent. If it's hot, I'm eatin' it."

She turned to Alex. "I don't even need to ask if you're ready for lunch."

"Yeah, but I probably don't deserve it. I only worked for thirty minutes today—you two are the heroes."

Their race entry also included a free draft Leatherback beer, so they took their plates filled with hamburgers, potato chips, and watermelon to the beer garden. Hope raised her plastic glass. "To Team Half Moon Bay!"

"Well, you didn't have any trouble runnin' today, did you?" Gerold asked.

"I didn't pay any attention to my pace, and I think that helped. I felt great out there. Well, except for a low point at mile eleven, but it went away." Hope held her beer to Gerold's. "You did great! That was a really tough bike course, and you conquered The Beast!"

"It was great to get to the top of that." Gerold took a swig of beer, looking back and forth between Alex and Hope. "I bet you two are *very* glad to have the whole Charles ordeal done with."

"Definitely," Alex said. "I'm fully recovered, and the judge pronounced the sentence last week—pretty much threw the book at Charles. He's serving twenty years. The prosecutor told us he's being transferred to a prison in Florida."

Gerold gave him an appraising glance. "So how did you manage to drop him? Twice?"

"Training. We trained a lot, Gerold. Most of it is technique and using momentum correctly. And SEALs outfitted in full combat gear aren't light either, so I could handle the extra weight. I think it's safe to say he's out of our lives now—and Patti's too, which is good." Alex laughed. "And we're also out of hurricane season."

Hope grinned. "So, if there aren't any hurricanes or co-worker thugs around, how are you going to keep busy without needing to defend everything around you?"

"Maybe Patti will keep hirin' her criminal relatives," Gerold said with a teasing smile.

Alex's smile slipped away as he watched her. "Make fun of me all you want. I don't need to protect everything, but I'll never stop defending Hope."

He held his glass up to hers. She swallowed the lump in her throat as she touched hers to it, and Gerold added his.

A man standing in the middle of the lawn tapped a microphone and announced they were starting the award ceremony. "Come on," Alex said. "Let's go sit on the grass over there." He pointed to a large, shady area, where a crowd was clustered around a podium with three places on it.

"You think it's worth staying?" Hope said. "There were a lot of teams."

Alex leveled a stare at her. "Ms. Collins, it's good form to cheer on your competitors, even if you don't place."

"Thank you for the sportsmanship lesson, Mr. Monroe. Please, lead on." They settled on the cool grass under a large flame tree, Hope easing herself to the ground.

I only hope I can get up again.

The announcer started with the individual competitors. She enjoyed it thoroughly as people of all ages and sizes walked up to stand on the podium and accept their awards—it was a wonderful spectacle of accomplishment and inclusiveness.

As they started the relay-team awards, Hope settled back on her hands, gently stretching each leg.

"In third place is Team Wilson Adventure Tours." Wild applause sounded from a cluster across the lawn as the three people climbed to their spot on the podium.

Hope wasn't expecting her team to win an award, but it was lovely sitting under the tree, and her attention started to wander. She studied the ocean in front of the park, noticeably calmer than that morning.

"And second place goes to Team Beastmode." Louder applause came from a section of people right in front of the podium.

Alex would have been even faster in these conditions.

"And our winner, with a combined time of five hours and thirty-two minutes, is Team Half Moon Bay!"

Gerold erupted to his feet and Alex also rose, but Hope didn't understand at first. There was wild screaming to one side, and she looked to see Cindy applauding excitedly.

We won?

Hope started to get to her feet, but both calves threatened to cramp. "Gonna need a little help here." She looked at Alex, who took her hand, gently helping her to her very stiff feet. Hope began hobbling toward the podium when her hamstring twitched dangerously, and she had to stop and stretch. Sympathetic laughter rippled through the crowd.

Alex was slightly ahead and turned around. He returned to her and promptly picked her up, one arm under her shoulders and the other under her knees as he carried her to the podium to the crowd's wild applause. Most were on their feet now.

Hope narrowed her eyes, even as she laughed. "Dammit, Alex. Put me down *now!*"

"You sure? Not sure you can climb those stairs to the top spot." He wore an enormous smile, clearly enjoying himself.

"I will if it kills me."

He set her down before bowing to her with a flourish, and the crowd went even wilder. Gerold was laughing too. He came back and took one elbow as Alex took the other, and they helped her shuffle to the top of the podium.

The race organizers placed medals around their necks before presenting a large trophy crowned with a swimmer, biker, and runner to Hope. She raised it over her head, Alex and Gerold holding on as well from both sides of her as the crowd applauded.

Cindy jumped up and down, wearing her own medal for the half-marathon race, and Hope beamed in return. She was proud of her accomplishments.

All of them.

Even more, she looked forward to the adventures still to come. With Alex in her life, there were bound to be plenty. And she wouldn't have to face them alone.

Hope and Alex exchanged a smile, their eyes lingering. At the same time, they moved toward each other, ending in a kiss that sent the audience into paroxysms of cheering.

Then several cannons at the fort exploded, wrenching Hope away with a yelp. Puffs of white smoke curled over the clipped lawn.

She leaned into Alex as she watched the scene in front of her. He pressed back, and she soaked in the moment, enjoying the men on either side of her, the cheering crowd, the yellow Danish fort in the background, and the beautiful, tropical water behind it all.

THANK you for continuing with Hope and Alex's love story! The excitement—and their romance—continues in *Rising Hope*.

Discover the adventures to come that Hope was speculating about. Are their lives about to change forever?

RISING HOPE: HALF MOON BAY BOOK 3

**Balmy days, sultry nights.
And a discovery that changes *everything*.**

Half Moon Bay Resort owner Hope Collins makes an exciting, yet dangerous, discovery. Dive guide and former Navy SEAL Alex Monroe recognizes its potential, and understands better than most the associated peril.

As a couple, both must learn to confront the unknown and explore new territory. Hope must learn to trust her own strength. Alex struggles to reconcile the man he used to be with the one he is now. They must overcome their pasts if they are to look toward any future together.

Together, they embark on a high-stakes adventure that could end in an unbelievable reward. It could also be fatal.

And when Hope faces the ultimate danger, can she help Alex face his greatest fear?

Can they rise together?

Rising Hope is the third installment in the enthralling Half Moon Bay series of steamy beach romance novels. It continues Hope and Alex's story, showcasing the strong, relatable characters and sizzling chemistry readers have come to love.

Order Rising Hope: Half Moon Bay Book 3 now!

WANT MORE of Hope and Alex? How would you like a free short story featuring them? Sign up now for my Beach Read Update , and I'll send you an electronic version of my short story *Tropical Hope*.

This is a quick, fun read that is set between books 1 and 2 of the Half Moon Bay series. Hope and Alex are trying to reunite after she has been off the island for several days, but obstacles keep getting in the way!

My Beach Read Update subscribers hear about all my free content, plus exclusive offers and sales. I'd love to have you along!

Sign up to download this exclusive bonus today.
(www.erinbrockus.com/vip)

If you're already on my list, I've got you covered! At the bottom of each newsletter is a link to all my free content for subscribers. Just find your last email from me to read this bonus, as well as any others you might have missed. Or you can simply sign up again—you'll have your bonus in a flash.

KEEP READING for my Author's Note as well as an excerpt of *Rising Hope*, Book 3 of the Half Moon Bay series . . .

Author's Note

Thanks for staying with me to the end! *Defending Hope* was a fun book to write, though I'm not sure Alex would be very happy with me.

Watching these characters develop and their relationship deepen is as much an adventure for me as it is for you. Sometimes, they do very unexpected things—like the spicy swim scene. I had no idea that was going to happen! I blame Alex.

It was nice to see Hope get settled in her new life and make a friend. Alas, poor Cindy has terrible taste in men (where have we heard that before?) but she was smart enough to realize it and dumped the idiot!

I've taken some liberties with Frederiksted to help the flow of the book. The Frederiksted Pier is a very popular dive though. And if you're setting a series in the Caribbean, a hurricane has to make an appearance at some point. At least it didn't destroy the resort!

If you have ever dived off the coast of Lanai, in Hawaii, the dive site I named Chapel will no doubt be familiar. The real version is called Cathedrals—specifically, it's Cathedrals II. And what I called The Cannon is actually known as the shotgun.

And yes, it's as much fun as I made it out to be. Sadly, I've never been able to go through it multiple times on a dive.

The triathlon is based off a Half-Ironman race my husband did there. The Ironman-sanctioned race isn't held any longer, but it lives on under another name. The race is very similar to what I describe, except I've taken some liberties with the run course. I made the distance between Christiansted and The Buccaneer Resort further than it actually is (the real race was two loops on the run). Fort Christiansvaern is fascinating and highly recommended for a tour.

And now the Half Moon Bay series is moving on. What's next for Hope and Alex?

Trust me—you want to know!

Erin Brockus
October, 2021

Turn the page for a sneak peek at *Rising Hope*, Book 3 in the Half Moon Bay series . . .

Rising Hope Excerpt

GENTLE MORNING LIGHT shined through the double windows of Hope's home office as she sat at her desk, sorting a pile of business mail. The first envelope was from the St. Croix County Treasurer, and Hope was highly suspicious it was her property-tax bill. She immediately moved it to the bottom of the stack.

Next was an envelope from her insurance agent, so she opened that one and was rewarded for her courage. It was a final, delayed settlement check for the hurricane damage. Smiling, she set that on a desk tray to be deposited later. Eventually, she worked through the whole pile except for the ominous treasurer envelope. With a deep sigh, she opened it.

Hope read the letter three times, her pulse pounding louder in her ears with each read through.

"This can't be right."

Patti had paid the taxes for the previous year, so Hope hadn't seen them until now. The amount was outrageous. She ran her finger down the letter once again, pausing at the property-size listing and narrowing her eyes. She'd never investigated how much land she owned but had always guessed it was ten to fifteen acres. This letter described it as more than fifty.

She stood up, turning to the tall filing cabinet behind her as she tapped her fingers on her crossed arms. "I know that plat map was in here somewhere when I went through everything after I first arrived."

With a shudder, a vivid scene came to mind of the mess the former owner, Steve Jackson, had left when he'd exited the island unannounced the night before her arrival. Pulling open the top drawer, she flipped through one file after another, then went to the next drawer. She skipped right past the document before some part of her mind started ringing alarm bells.

Hope's heart leapt as she froze, then thumbed back a few files until she found it. With a loud whoop that sent Cruz into a tizzy of barking, she pulled the plat map out of the drawer and returned to her desk. She inspected the oversized piece of paper for the next ten minutes. Finally, she sat back in her chair, stunned.

The tax assessment was correct.

Her property was fifty acres. The oceanfront parcel was roughly twenty, but the majority of the property was on the eastern side of the highway—over thirty acres. The mountains rose steeply on that side of the road, but there had to be some good, flat land there.

"Huh, how about that? Not all oceanfront, but still a very nice bonus I didn't know about."

Cruz cocked his head, and she returned his look. "What do you say? You up for a little adventure?"

He woofed and wagged his tail, which she took as enthusiastic support.

Fifteen minutes later, Hope walked out the front door dressed in hiking shoes and long pants and covered in a cloud of insect repellant. She walked down the resort road to the highway with Cruz trotting at her side. As they approached the busy road, Hope scooped him into her arms and marched across the highway during a break in traffic.

"I'm glad you're not a big dog. At least I can carry you. You stay away from the road, ok?"

She put him down on the other side and walked along the edge of the jungle, parallel to the road. Cruz loped ahead of her, then turned into the foliage and disappeared. Hope followed and discovered a faint path, really just bent grass and a thinning of the foliage, leading into the jungle.

As good a place as any, I guess.

She turned to follow him. Once out of the sunlight, the temperature dropped and the humidity increased. Cool beads of sweat ran down Hope's back. She tried not to think what animal might have made the trail, or if she was about to come face-to-face with a wild boar or something else equally terrifying.

Then she relaxed, confident Cruz would alert her to any danger. He was having a wonderful time, confidently bounding ahead over the vines and fallen trees covering the path, and she was enjoying the adventure too. He scrambled up a sizeable fallen tree blocking the path and stood on top, surveying his domain. He glanced at her, then hopped to the far side. She followed, climbing over the fallen tree herself.

They continued for nearly half a mile as the jungle closed in around them. Hope brushed vines out of the way, petrified of stepping on a snake. She was far from the highway now, and unease prickled down her spine.

No one knew she was here.

She'd watched local-news reports about the drug activity in the Caribbean and had experienced an attempted armed robbery firsthand. With effort, she pushed the thought away.

I'm safe on my own property, for heaven's sake.

She was thinking about turning around when the tree line ahead thinned out. The path opened into a large clearing, and as she took a long drink of water from the bottle she carried, her misgivings were forgotten.

They were replaced by sheer wonder.

In front of her was an enormous natural pool of water, Cruz lapping at its edge. The pool was surrounded by large boulders for most of its perimeter, but the area directly ahead had a gentle, sandy entry. "Well, I guess that explains the animal track. This is a great source of water, and it must be fresh."

Hope approached and inspected the water, which was a vivid blue and extremely clear. The rock formations continued underwater, and the pool looked deep. The side opposite her was around fifty feet away, and the pool was nearly two hundred feet long. The area was silent except for the occasional birdsong and exuded a peaceful aura. Ample sunlight drifted in, creating a perfect temperature.

To her left, the rock formations rose into a sheer, dark-gray wall that was part of a bigger hillside, but there was no waterfall or other source of water for the pool. She started toward the rock wall, trying to keep to the edge of the clearing so she didn't need to scramble over the boulders. She only got halfway before the jungle butted right up against the rocks.

Hope inspected the gray wall. Moss grew abundantly, and rivulets of water ran down it, turning it nearly black. Then she saw something else.

It wasn't solid.

There was a considerable black opening in the middle of the rock face that plummeted straight into the pool. She studied it but couldn't find any way to access the cave except through the water.

Taking in the scene in front of her, a smile spread across her face. "This is amazing! What an incredible spot."

Hope picked her way back to the sandy beach entry and removed her socks and shoes. She took a few steps into the water, surprised how cool it was, but it had a wonderful effect on her hot feet as she wiggled her toes in the sand. Her eyes were drawn back to the black cave and clear water around her. What wonders could that water be hiding?

Still smiling, another thought occurred to her. "Alex would *love* this!"

Cruz had curled up on the sand and closed his eyes. Hope left the water, sitting on one of the big flat rocks and swiping the sand off her feet before replacing her footwear. "Sorry, Cruz. It's not naptime yet. Back we go."

He popped his head up at his name, and as she started toward the trail, he jumped up to take his place in front of her. From the way the dog acted on their little trek, he had likely already discovered the pool. She didn't like the idea of him crossing the highway.

But who knows where you lived before you found me?

It was already 3 p.m. when she opened the front door, greeted with a welcome blast of air-conditioning. Sweat saturated her clothes, and she peeled the collar of her shirt away, curling her lip. "Yuck. Shower first, for sure." Cruz hurried to his water bowl as she headed into the master suite to get cleaned up.

After dressing in a floral sundress, she took a glass of iced tea onto the back porch as Cruz trotted down the stairs to the sand. She was standing at the open windows when a voice came from the beach. Alex bent to rub Cruz's belly as the dog lay at his feet, tail thumping. "Hey there, buddy. How are you doing?" Alex had a big smile on his face. Hope laughed quietly, enjoying the sight. She leaned against the window frame as Alex approached.

I'll never tire of looking at him.

He moved with a strong, graceful confidence, and she responded just to the sight of him. Smile lingering, he climbed the stairs onto the porch and saw her. As their eyes locked, his smile faded, and without a word, they crossed to each other for a long, delicious kiss.

Eventually, he moved his mouth to her hair and inhaled deeply. "You smell incredible. How do you do that?"

"It's no mystery. I just got out of the shower." She rested the side of her head against his chest, taking a breath of her own. "You smell pretty good yourself."

"I had a refresher this afternoon, and they wanted to do it in the ocean, not the pool, so I showered after." He broke their embrace and led her over to the patio couch. "Think my days of that are numbered, though, with the spa open. I was lucky it was empty this late—no way I'm showering with other people around."

"Sorry to disrupt your routine. I just love Selena. She gave me a massage yesterday. The guests are going to love her!"

Alex breathed out an easy sigh. "Tomorrow's my day off, and I'm really looking forward to it. You know, I never cared about days off before you came into my life—the more I worked, the better. Maybe we can do something fun."

He widened his eyes as she started laughing, both hands over her mouth. "What?"

"Funny you should say that. I think I can deliver on your request." Hope pursed her lips to keep from spilling the beans. "I have a surprise for you, but you're going to have to wait until tomorrow morning. I'll tell you this, though. You and I are going on a little adventure."

Order Rising Hope today!

CALYPSO KEY SERIES:

Main Novels:

Visions of You: A Small Town Single Dad Romance

Because of You: A Small Town Fake Relationship Romance

Memories of You: A Small Town Second Chance Romance

Shades of You: A Small Town Forbidden Romance (Coming Oct, 2024)

Associated Short Stories and Novellas:

Traces of You: A Small Town Rivals to Lovers Romance*

* Subscriber exclusive

Standalone Books:

In Too Deep: A Second Chance Romance

Beached in Bali: A Friends to Lovers Romance

Dive into steamy small-town romance, where passion meets paradise!

Erin Brockus writes steamy small town romances that transport readers to exotic, tropical destinations, and provide a perfect beachy getaway from everyday life. Her mature, relatable characters are impossible not to root for, and she weaves breezy romantic adventure into her stories, emphasizing scuba diving and the ocean.

Drawing on her twin passions for diving and travel, Erin infuses her characters and narratives with a sense of excitement and passion. Her idea of the perfect day involves sipping a cocktail on the beach after exploring the ocean depths.

Erin lives in Washington wine country with her husband, who is also a scuba instructor. She is currently hard at work on her next island adventure. When she's not writing, you might find her out for a run or cycling through the countryside on the next quest for adventure.

www.ingramcontent.com/pod-product-compliance
Lightning Source LLC
Chambersburg PA
CBHW031629200726
48288CB00019B/456